FIREFIGHT

IN

Darkness

SECOND OF THE DRYAD QUARTET

KATIE JENNINGS

Sapphire Royale
publishing

Published by
Sapphire Royale Publishing

ISBN-13: 978-0615718910
ISBN-10: 0615718914

Visit the author at:
www.katieajennings.com
www.facebook.com/katieajennings
www.twitter.com/dryadquartet
www.katieajennings.wordpress.com

Praise for "Firefight in Darkness"

"Not sure it can get better than a fiery redhead serving up demon on a platter! Katie Jennings has out done herself again on the second installment of The Dryad Quartet, *Firefight in Darkness*! Once again we are brought back to the world of Euphora, but only for a short while. Blythe's journey will take her on a dangerous adventure to earth, where she literally hunts down the demons of her past."

– Cassie Deaton with Shadow Kisses Reviews –

"Second in the series and so much better. I liked *Breath of Air*, the first in the Dryad Quartet, but I loved *Firefight in Darkness*. The book had a good pace and the storyline was action packed. The powers of the two girls formed the whole feel for the stories, not just their personalities. I enjoyed that this felt more grown up than the first. There was adult subject matter (bad parenting, infidelity, family betrayal), even cursing when appropriate. The author let it be what it was and didn't pull any punches to make it fit into a particular genre. It is YA and very appropriate for all audiences, but I didn't feel like I was reading a children's book."

– Natalie Gibson, author –

"After reading *Breath of Air*, I couldn't wait to read this second book in the Dryad Quartet. *Firefight in Darkness* is a story that is as fiery and feisty as the main character, Blythe. Jennings has once again managed to create a merging of both fantasy and modern day worlds that both sweep you away while engulfing you in her passionate characters. Get ready for an action-packed fantasy that has it all!"

– J.L. Firestone, author –

"This is clearly an example of a tale so strong and compelling, so well-conceived, that one wonders whether it might've written itself. Kudos to Jennings for making it look so easy. ...This is as much a coming-of-age story as it is one of redemption and repudiation...

– Saul Tanpepper, bestselling author –

For my mom, because she loves cowboys.

Thea & Sebastian
Mother Earth & Father Sky

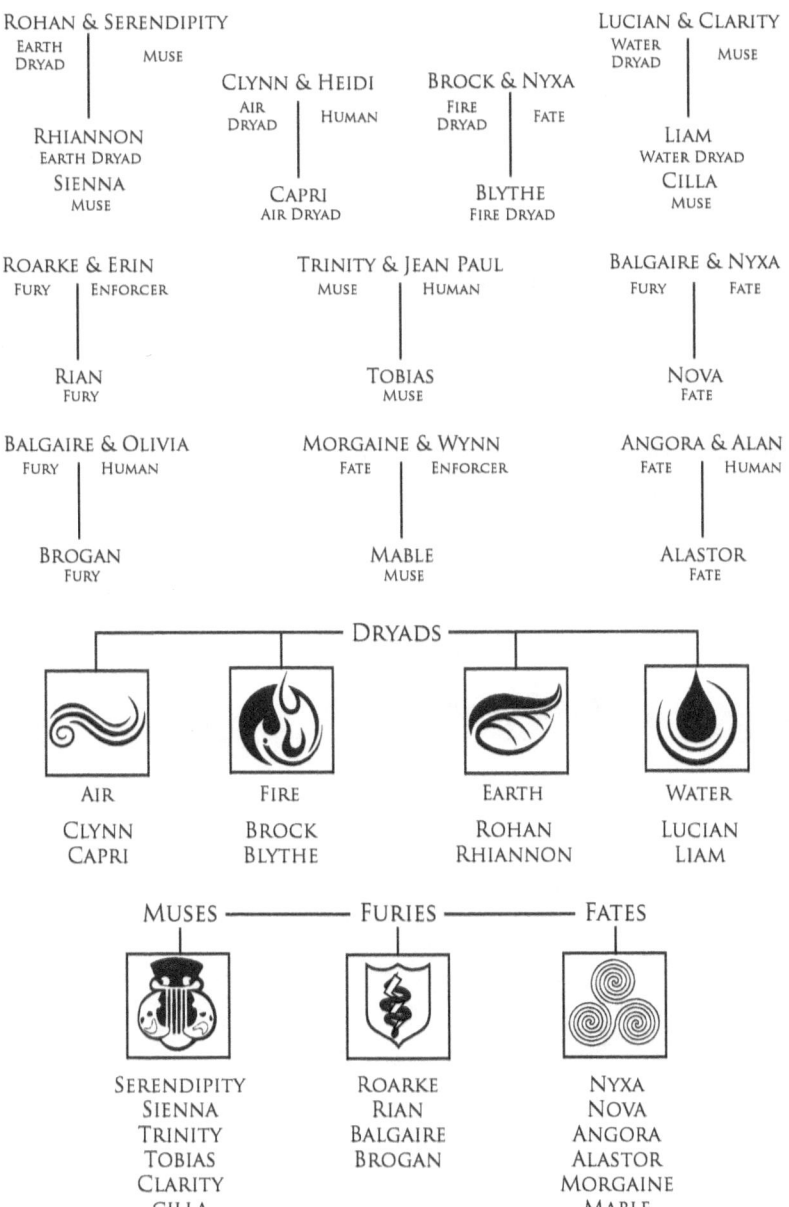

Rohan & Serendipity
Earth Dryad | Muse

Rhiannon
Earth Dryad

Sienna
Muse

Clynn & Heidi
Air Dryad | Human

Capri
Air Dryad

Brock & Nyxa
Fire Dryad | Fate

Blythe
Fire Dryad

Lucian & Clarity
Water Dryad | Muse

Liam
Water Dryad

Cilla
Muse

Roarke & Erin
Fury | Enforcer

Rian
Fury

Trinity & Jean Paul
Muse | Human

Tobias
Muse

Balgaire & Nyxa
Fury | Fate

Nova
Fate

Balgaire & Olivia
Fury | Human

Brogan
Fury

Morgaine & Wynn
Fate | Enforcer

Mable
Muse

Angora & Alan
Fate | Human

Alastor
Fate

— Dryads —

Air	Fire	Earth	Water
Clynn	Brock	Rohan	Lucian
Capri	Blythe	Rhiannon	Liam

Muses — Furies — Fates

Muses	Furies	Fates
Serendipity	Roarke	Nyxa
Sienna	Rian	Nova
Trinity	Balgaire	Angora
Tobias	Brogan	Alastor
Clarity		Morgaine
Cilla		Mable

Prologue

I hear his footfall's music,
I feel his presence near,
All my soul responsive answers,
And tells me he is here.

Her name was Blythe, and she was Fire.

She was a protector of those she loved, a quick talker with a sharp tongue, and most of all, she was a relentless fighter for any cause worth fighting for.

And as far as she was concerned, if anybody had a problem with it they could go straight to Hell.

The club was bursting to capacity, the surrounding streets of Los Angeles writhing with life and sound and empty promises. It was hot, spontaneous and anonymous, and it suited her mood perfectly.

She sauntered through the crowd, her head held high and her eyes glittering with arrogance and anticipation. This was her time; not her father's, not anyone else's, and she couldn't give a damn if no one even missed her. She wasn't living for them anyway. It was time to let go and live for herself.

Music thundered around her, pumping its beat into her veins, shuddering and pounding until her entire body felt like it was a livewire ready to electrify the whole room. Men eyed her, their attention diverted from nearly every other woman in the club. She knew her appeal and she knew how to use it.

Within minutes she was downing top shelf tequila in the presence of people vying for her company, eager to be seen with her, as if she was some hot and famous celebrity. She supposed she looked like one, working her confidence like she really was famous. Well, hell, she was more than just famous. She was a damn Fire Dryad.

Not that any of these poor saps had a clue.

Despite her thrill at seeing her current companion's eyes widen with shock as she lit his cigarette with the tip of her thumb, she knew she didn't really belong here with these people. She had responsibilities; she had a duty to the world that none of these hopeless and vain humans could ever understand. But she wasn't here to worry about that, or about her godforsaken bastard of a father. No, she was here for her. And no one was going to hold her back, not anymore.

Chapter One

May 21st, 2010
Santa Monica, California

It amazed Blythe to still remember his words, even if the sound of his voice was lost somewhere in the gritty memories of time. The last thing he'd said before he left, his final goodbye.

You're the best thing that ever has and ever will come from me.

Maybe the man himself was nothing more than a distant memory to her now, but those words had been all her young mind could hold on to at the time, despite the fact that they were more than she had wanted from him in the first place.

Because to her, he was a murderer. To her, he was nothing. But as abruptly as he had been convicted and taken away from her, he was now being thrown back in her face like a consolation prize. Hey Blythe, sorry we messed up, here's good ol' dad back for you to cherish and love. Just pretend the last fifteen years didn't happen and nothing has changed, okay?

Well screw them and their excuses. She and her father had both gotten the raw end of the deal in this scenario, as had poor Capri. And if they thought they could justify their actions they were wrong. It only made her blood boil. The Council allowing him to return home didn't make up for what they did. The only thing that would was ultimate justice.

She wanted that bastard half-demon's head on a platter and she wasn't going to rest until it was done.

But until that happy day, they expected her to just welcome back with open arms the man who had been the bane of her existence since she was four years old. She should just forget that her mother had disowned her because her resemblance to him was so great that the damn woman couldn't bear to even look at her. And she should also forget the way the others had shunned her, convinced she would inevitably run the same course as her father and grandmother before her. Fire was bad blood, they said—like a sickness, a disease. She'd succumb to it in time and she'd be the worst of them all.

Well damn them all to Hell because she wasn't succumbing to any such thing. She was perfectly fine, thank you very much. Her work ethic was on par, her outlook positive (most of the time) and her penchant for trouble fairly normal for a girl just shy of twenty. What more could she have shown any of them to prove she wasn't like those before her? And yet they still judged; all of them.

She wondered how much would change now that he was coming back. How much would *she* change?

Her life hadn't been a cake walk since her father had been banished, but it certainly hadn't been terrible either. No, she had been lucky enough to have a good man with a good son to take her under his wing. He filled her father's shoes despite what everyone thought, and it was to that man she owed her very life. She was the person she was today because of him.

Clad in her favorite lime green bikini, she lay facing the Pacific, the sand fitted to her body beneath her oversized bright orange beach towel. Her shoulder length vivid red curls splayed casually around her sharp featured face, sunglasses perched on her freckled nose to hide her eyes. Eyes that at first glance looked light brown, but in the sunlight transformed to gilded amber.

Above, a flock of seagulls called into the wind, hovering mid-flight as they scanned the sand for a shot at a free lunch. Children screamed in shock and exhilaration as they stood at the brunt of chilly waves that crashed ashore, sending creamy white foam coasting up the sand. Salt hung heavy in the air, moist against her sun-kissed skin even as the sun glowed brightly down upon her and dried it. It was warm enough to tingle her skin, to ease her cares away if she let it. Hadn't heat always soothed her? After all, it was a part of her heritage, her bloodline of Fire.

Of every place in the world she had ever been, she had never felt more at peace than she did here. Maybe it was because Southern California was almost always guaranteed to have nice weather. Or maybe it was because the people who walked around her were so tanned and beautiful; the men athletic and fit, the women slender and infectiously happy. But no, she didn't think it was either of those two things. What brought her to this place time and time again was the sea. The sea drew her. Water, in its most real and brutal form, drew her. And it was all because of Lucian.

Thinking of him ached somewhere deep in her heart, causing her to rub her chest in an attempt to soothe the pain. How often had he chased away the last lingering dregs of one of her nightmares, rocking her back to sleep, his voice as comforting as his arms as they held her close. And how often had he thrilled her with fairytales and stories of pirates and barbarians, always knowing how to enrich her mind and make her laugh. He'd always smelled like fresh soap and peppermint, a combination that seemed silly but even now still offered comfort when she hugged him and caught that scent.

He would be worried about her; he always was. But he wouldn't say it out of fear of making her feel closed in. He never wanted her to feel like he was restricting her or holding her back in any way. She was free to come and go as she pleased, and he always made it clear that the moment she wanted nothing more to do with him, he would understand.

But even if she left it was never for long. He was the only person who had ever given a damn about her. She could never abandon him, or his son.

Liam. All of the stars she had wished upon so arrogantly as a child must have miraculously decided to join together and give her Liam for a friend. For a brother. God knew she hardly deserved him.

He was her rock; the sturdy lighthouse she could always find in the stormy sea of her reckless heart.

Where she was wild and carefree, he was steady and kind. Where she was impatient and temperamental, he was grounded and reasonable. And though sometimes she saw the moodiness he kept brutally in check boil over and consume him, he was always back on his feet in no time, smiling and laughing. No wonder she adored him—he was everything she wished she could be.

He understood her in a way that went deeper than most, as if he could see her so much clearer than anyone else. To him she wasn't bad; to him she wasn't a goner. He believed in her and he stuck by her. Something had to be said for a guy like that.

But even he couldn't save her from dealing with the issue at hand. What was she going to do about her real father coming back to Euphora? She was desperately running out of time to figure it out.

He was coming home tonight.

Would she know him the instant their eyes met? Would she recognize herself in his eyes, his nose, his chin? What would he say to her? Would he apologize for not being there all these years, for letting himself be banished over something he hadn't even done?

She couldn't help but be irritated that he had let this happen. If it had been her, she would have fought tooth and nail to prove her innocence and to name the one who was truly guilty. Why hadn't Brock done that? Why had he given up and gone away if he didn't need to?

At least now she knew she wasn't destined to screw up. Yes, her dead grandmother had issues but her father was an innocent man...

Had they been so quick to assume he was responsible for the raid that had led to Capri's kidnapping and her mother's death because of *his* mother's actions? She could certainly relate to that feeling; but she knew first hand that the crimes of the parent did not always translate into the child. Her grandmother's decision to have a baby with demon blood had been her own, and had nothing to do with Brock. It was despicable that they judged and assumed the son and the granddaughter were bound to make similar mistakes.

It was a load of crap in her opinion.

But was any of that going to change now? She had a pretty good feeling that Rohan wasn't about to let go of his prejudices any time soon, but Blythe knew that there was more to his bitterness than the crime Brock had been banished over. Her father's history with Rohan's wife, Serendipity, was a story she was well familiar with. If anyone should be upset about the outcome of that love triangle it should be Brock, not Rohan. Brock had lost the girl, hadn't he? And then he had married Nyxa.

Giving birth had been the only good thing Nyxa had ever done for her. After that it was nothing but a lifetime of anger and bitterness.

That was another angle she had yet to consider. Would her father and mother get back together now that he was home? Would Nyxa try and mend the tattered relationship she had with her daughter? Hah...as if. The woman was a walking grudge, she didn't forgive anybody. Not like Blythe wanted anything to do with her anyway; that ship had sailed long ago. As far as she was concerned, she didn't have a mother.

Feeling anxious, she checked the time on her watch. She had three hours until Thea and Sebastian would be arriving on Euphora, Brock at their side. Until then, all she could do was wait.

With a sigh, she shifted until she was sitting up on her elbows, her lightly tanned legs crossed in front of her. She watched the ocean for a moment, calmed by the sight of it, deep blue velvet with scattered diamonds glittering on its surface. She glanced at the humans around her, wishing her life was as simple. Sure, they may think their lives were complicated, but dealing with kids, a mortgage, planning dinner parties, going to work…none of that remotely compared to what she had to deal with everyday.

One mistake from her and lava could seep from the ground, destroying everything in its path. One mistake and the Earth's core temperature could skyrocket, causing worldwide damage that was irreparable. One mistake and a brushfire could consume countless miles of land, until there was nothing left but dust.

So while they worried over petty problems, they couldn't possibly understand what it was like to have *real* problems. But she couldn't fault them, they were human after all and she enjoyed their way of life too much to give up on them for good. But the fact remained that she could never stay with them, could never live amongst them for long.

At some point, she had to go home.

"This one is pretty."

Blythe's eyes flicked up in the mirror as she looked at the pale blue dress Capri was holding. It was knee-length and strapless, and made of shimmering silk.

"You're kidding, right?" She snorted, whirling around, her lips curved into a smirk. "Honey, if you don't stop picking dresses that you really want to wear, you're never going to find one for me to wear. You did say you wanted to help, right?"

Capri blushed, but tilted her head up indignantly anyway. "I wasn't looking for myself. I happen to think that this dress would look lovely on you."

"That may be, but I can tell by the way you're looking at it that you see yourself in it a lot more than you see me in it. Pale blue isn't really my color, anyway." Taking the dress from Capri's hands, she held it up in front of Capri so she could see it against her coloring. "See, it's perfect for you. Now find something for me."

Knowing she was caught, Capri gently set the blue dress aside before rummaging through the closet once again. When she resurfaced, she had another knee-length dress in hand, this time a leaf green number with a heart shaped bodice and skinny shoulder straps.

"This one is eye-catching," Capri concluded, eyeing the dress speculatively. "And unlike the other dress, it would look horrible on me."

With a wink, she tossed the dress at Blythe, who held it up against her body as she examined herself in the mirror.

"Hmm…yup, this one will do." Blythe quickly put on the dress and did a quick 360 so she could see it from all sides. "What do you think?"

"It looks gorgeous with your hair…but you know what I really think?" Capri walked over and wrapped her arm around Blythe's shoulders, meeting her eyes in the mirror. "I think he could care less if you were wearing a dress made of diamonds or a trash bag. He's going to be looking at you, Blythe, not your outfit."

Sighing, Blythe turned and hugged her friend, holding her close. "I know. God, I've never been so nervous before. And it's starting to piss me off because I never get nervous over anything…"

"Nothing has ever been this important." Pulling away, smoky eyes soft, Capri smiled.

"Exactly." Blowing out a breath to chase her bangs out of her eyes, Blythe grinned. "Which means that I should at the very least take the time to put on some makeup."

As she turned to head into the adjoining bathroom, there was a brisk knock on the door.

"Come in!" Blythe shouted, continuing into the bathroom, setting up what little makeup she owned on the vanity.

When the bedroom door opened, Rian poked his head in.

"I just wanted to let you girls know that we've got about twenty minutes until showtime."

"Thanks." Capri smiled as she walked over and kissed him, lingering for a moment. Blythe rolled her eyes and continued applying blusher to her cheeks, chuckling to herself over the lovebirds.

Who knew that the deeply serious and quiet Rian could actually smile? She could remember him before Capri came back to Euphora, but seeing him now…it was like he was a whole different person. He actually seemed like a pretty nice guy, and she had to congratulate Capri for unlocking whatever it was that he had held inside of him all these years.

"I'll see you down there in a few minutes." Capri pulled away, only to kiss him again a second later, a bright smile on her face. He backed away, looking a bit flustered as he glanced at Blythe, who was eyeing him from the bathroom, amusement clear on her face.

"Okay, baby," he murmured as he kissed the knuckles of Capri's hand delicately. Then he was gone.

Blythe watched as Capri gently shut the door and then stood, unmoving.

"You okay?" she called out to her friend, even though she knew the answer. God, lovesick people were embarrassing sometimes. She hoped she never acted that ridiculous over some guy.

"What?" Capri blinked, whirling around, seeming to forget where she was. "Oh, the dress, yes, I should put it on."

"You know, I get that you're all gaga over your new boyfriend, but you shouldn't forget that you came in here to help me get ready."

"Right, I'm sorry." Standing at attention, Capri parked herself in front of the bathroom door. "What would you like me to do?"

"Nothing." Blythe couldn't help but laugh. God, Capri was so cute. "Just put your damn dress on."

"Yes, ma'am." Capri grinned, grabbing the pale blue dress from the chair before slipping behind the changing panel. When she emerged, Blythe glanced over and nearly gushed.

"I swear, honey, you look like an angel. No wonder that boy is crazy over you."

"Oh, well…" Capri brushed at the silk skirt, feeling exposed. "It's just a dress."

"Just take the compliment." Applying one last stroke of mascara, Blythe turned around to hunt for her shoes.

Pouting, Capri watched Blythe sit down on the bed and tug on a pair of strappy gold stilettos.

"Just wait, Blythe. The day you fall for some guy and start making lovey dovey faces I'm going to give you a taste of your own medicine."

"Hmmph, please." With a grunt, Blythe got to her feet and strutted over to slip on simple gold strand earrings and a necklace. "I'm immune to the advances of men. They can't woo me and I will never go gaga over one. Besides, I have ridiculously high standards that no man could possibly ever meet, so therefore I will live life as a spinster. Your kids will call me Crazy Auntie Blythe and I'll have twenty cats living in my room and life will be amazing."

"How are your standards impossible to meet? I'm sure there's someone–"

"Hey, if you can tell me where I can find a guy who's mysterious but honest, clever but not a complete nerd, tough but not a macho-man, and passionate without being obsessive, then I think you'll have the man for me."

"Well, even if he doesn't exist, I'm sure you'll stumble upon someone who meets most of your criteria sooner or later."

"Maybe, but I'm in no hurry." Taking one last look in the mirror, Blythe turned to face Capri. "It's time, isn't it?"

Biting back an excited grin, Capri nodded. "Yes, it is."

If she hadn't known better, she would have thought that the courtyard was on fire.

Bright red, flashy yellow, and vivid orange flowers rioted throughout, filling nearly every nook and cranny of the gardens with their fiery personality. Someone had even put flowers in the trees and in the ponds.

Tables and chairs were set up around the dance floor on the patio, each with several tall tapered candles already alight with flame as centerpieces. Circling the tapers were tea lights so every table appeared to be filled with beacons of light.

Above her head and over the entire courtyard, fireflies danced. And against the night sky the brilliance of their glow illuminated everything in a warm, golden light.

Strung across the cobblestone pathway was a large sign with the words "Welcome Home Brock!" in bold cursive letters on both sides. She had a feeling it was the Muses' doing, as the sign with all its gilded designs and patterns was obviously painted by a magnificent artist, most likely their latest protégé.

Beneath the sign stood Lucian and Liam, their arms crossed and their eyes fixated on the artwork above them. Both were tall and lanky, with long faces and brilliant blue eyes. The only difference between them other than age was hair. Liam's was jet black, framed around his face, while Lucian's was bright white, long and pulled back at the nape of his neck.

When they noticed Blythe and Capri approaching, their faces lit up with identical goofy grins.

Blythe's eyes filled at the sight of it.

Annoyed with herself, she brushed away the tears before they could fall, forcing herself to smile. After all, she was supposed to be happy tonight. Her long lost father was returning to her an innocent man. Everything that had been wrong in her life was suddenly about to be righted. She had no reason to feel that while something wonderful was about to begin, something even more special was coming to an end.

"You're crying already? He's not even here yet," Liam joked, pulling her into a one armed hug and messing up her hair.

"Oh, shut up and hug me, idiot." She laughed and held on to him, fighting back the tears but letting her emotions run their course. She pulled away and turned to Lucian, who pouted at her for good measure.

"Do I get a hug too?" he asked, amusement glittering in his eyes.

"You get an even bigger hug," Blythe announced as she threw herself on his tall, slim frame, hoping he didn't notice the single tear that slid down her cheek. Holding herself against him, she breathed in the scent of peppermint and sighed. "You know that this won't change anything, right? Not between us."

She felt him stiffen, knew it had been on his mind.

"I know, honeypot." He held her at arm's length, his all-knowing sapphire eyes inspecting her with his trickster's grin. "But you were his first and I have to respect that. Even though, in a way, you will always be mine."

"Of course I will. Nothing can change that."

She saw relief flash in his eyes and seeing it made her throat tighten. She never wanted him to believe for one second that she would abandon him or forget about him. She may have a one track mind when it came to a lot of things, but not when it came to her own heart. And in her heart, Lucian was her father, bloodlines be damned.

"The Muses certainly outdid themselves on the decorations, don't you think?" Capri's father, Clynn, asked cheerfully as he approached, Rian at his side. Rian went immediately to Capri, his arm protectively wrapping around her.

That was something Blythe had noticed about her friend's relationship with the Fury. He was extremely protective of her, as though vicious monsters were waiting for a chance to jump out of the bushes and eat her. It was something that she knew would personally irritate the hell out of her, as she was entirely confident she could slay her own dragons. But judging from the way Capri leaned against him, clearly content in his arms, the arrangement suited her just fine.

"Yes, Clarity has been going on and on about their plans for the welcome home party all week. I suppose this is their way of trying to assuage their guilt," Lucian replied with a smirk.

"I suppose we all feel a bit responsible," Clynn mused, though there was sadness in his tone. "Maybe we were just too quick to judge him."

"Dear friend, no one expected you to be of sound mind at that time, what with losing a wife and daughter in the same evening." Patting the other man's back compassionately, Lucian eyed his own children warily. What would he have done if it had been his child who had been taken instead? He would have believed anything as truth just to have justice…

"At least we know the truth now," Capri put in, laying a hand on her father's arm in comfort.

"And once this demon hunter guy catches Dante, we will have justice once and for all," Blythe added, fire in her eyes. "None of this will have been for nothing."

"My little warrior," Lucian said fondly, wrapping his arm around Blythe. "If there's a battle to be won, she's there."

"Injustice pisses me off," she insisted seriously, though she had to bite back a smile. "Besides, if this guy can't find Dante fast enough for my taste, I'll just have to go find him myself."

She felt Lucian tense beside her, and knew she had crossed one of his invisible lines. In fact, everyone around her seemed apprehensive at her words, as though none of them agreed with her. Only Liam exuded nonchalance.

"You won't get the chance. I bet that bounty hunter brings us Dante within a week. I hear he's good…very good."

"Well, we'll just have to see, won't we?" Blythe shifted away, glancing around the courtyard where everyone had begun to gather.

The Muses, dressed in flowing gowns of soft pastels, were perusing the gardens and making the final changes to the décor. Their kids, including Tobias, were hovering nearby, attempting to look indifferent but it was clear they were anything but. Anxiety and nerves practically crackled in the air from them and their mothers.

Rohan and Rhiannon stood quietly side by side near the cobblestone walkway, their eyes and faces blank. Blythe figured that both of them could care less about being there, but had only shown up because Thea expected it.

The Fates lined the opposite side of the walkway with their children beside them, looking dark and broody. Nyxa was at the front, pretending to look coolly unconcerned, but Blythe could see the truth on her mother's face. They may not know much about each other, but Blythe knew the woman enough to know she was edgy and very, very eager. She could see it in the twitch of her mouth, aching to smile, and the way she kept pushing back her dark curls with agitated movements, as if the moment Brock arrived couldn't come fast enough.

She spotted her half sister, Nova, and her stepbrother, Brogan, standing on either side of Nyxa as a show of support. Both looked tense, as though painfully aware nothing good was going to come out of the event to come.

She supposed she should be bitter that while she had been disowned, Nova and Brogan had been cherished. For all of Balgaire's faults–namely framing Brock for the raid he had orchestrated all those years ago—he had loved his son. And Nyxa loved Nova in a way that she would never, ever love Blythe, even though Blythe was her first child.

While Blythe was the spitting image of Brock, Nova was the spitting image of Nyxa. So if for no reason other than narcissism, Nyxa adored Nova and kept her close, showing her the motherly devotion she had never wanted to share with her other daughter.

Annoyed that it bothered her, Blythe tried to shrug it off. Screw them if they wanted nothing to do with her. She hadn't needed them then and she certainly didn't need them now.

When she felt Lucian's hand touch her shoulder, she whirled around to face him, trying to replace the anger and resentment blasted on her face with a cheerful smile.

Behind her there was a sudden flash of gold light that bounced off the walls of the castle and lit up the courtyard. Her stomach clenched as she simply watched Lucian's face.

The look in his eyes, that mixture of contentment and grief, staggered her.

"He's here," he murmured, smiling. "Are you ready to welcome him home?"

Chapter Two

That was really the million dollar question, wasn't it, she thought unsteadily. Was she ready? Well, she was as ready as she was going to be.

But when she turned to face the entrance gates and saw Thea and Sebastian emerge from the meadow, her worries and cares fell to the wayside. A thrumming excitement replaced it, pumping through her veins at lightning speed, racing her heart to the finish line.

Everyone around her lined up along the cobblestone pathway, leaning over each other to catch a glimpse of Brock as he came through the gates. Blythe stayed where she was, Lucian and Liam holding her hands while Capri placed a supportive hand on her shoulder.

Thea and Sebastian paused just inside the courtyard, then parted and made way for the man of the hour.

When he walked through the gates and the golden light from the fireflies lit his face, Blythe felt her breath catch in her throat.

Good God, he looked like her.

Even though she was several yards away, she could see it. And it certainly wasn't just physical.

There was an electricity to him that seemed to spark and ignite the air, giving him a magnetism that was impossible to ignore. He walked like a king surveying his kingdom and gifted his people with a smile as radiant as sunlight.

He was a large man, tall and built, but beneath the tailored, gunmetal gray suit Sebastian must have given him, Blythe could see the weight age had added to his midsection. But this did nothing to detract from the power and charisma he exuded. Even from this distance she could feel the shock of it to her system.

Applause erupted from those crowded around the walkway as he approached. To Blythe's surprise, the first thing he did was go to Nyxa.

Though she couldn't hear what was said over the applause and cheers, she watched him pull Nyxa against him and kiss her, a move that had Blythe rolling her eyes. And when he pulled away from Nyxa, crossed the aisle, and took Serendipity's hand in his and kissed her knuckles in a gallant gesture, Blythe saw Rohan's face redden with rage.

Annoyed, she waited for him to make it through the rest of the crowd, wondering if he even cared enough to notice she was there. She'd been told he was a ladies' man and that he could be self-centered, but those were not really things she considered to be faults so much as basic nature. But it bothered her that he hadn't run to her first, seeing as she was his blood and all.

Thea and Sebastian followed Brock as he walked through the crowd, shaking hands and exchanging words with the others, and as he neared the end, Blythe caught Thea carefully watching her.

Realizing her frustration was clearly projected on her face, Blythe readjusted her lips into a bright smile and beamed in Thea's direction. Even though the smile was forced, the moment Brock approached and shook Clynn's hand, she felt a real smile itch to take its place.

He was so close, and she could hear his words to Clynn even though she couldn't quite process them. When he reached over to shake Lucian's hand, then Liam's, she felt jittery nerves spark in her system, combating with the irritation she was determined to hold on to so she could give him a piece of her mind.

She barely noticed the moment both Lucian and Liam let go of her hands and left her to stand on her own. Even Capri backed off, joining Rian as they all watched the two Fire Dryads greet each other for the first time in fifteen years.

When his eyes met hers…damnit, the same color and shape and everything…she forgot all about being annoyed with him.

"Took you long enough," she managed, cocking her head and grinning at him, hoping he didn't notice the tears she knew were hiding just behind her eyes.

"Jesus, Blythe…look at you." Brock stopped and just stared at her for a moment, taking her in. His voice was deep and husky, with a hint of suave to smooth it all out. It was a voice that could command others, a voice people turned heads to listen to, one that you wanted to hang on every word and drink in every syllable.

She'd wondered before if she would notice the family resemblance. Now it hit her as though she had discovered her male twin.

Not only did they have the same eyes, they had the same wide mouth with the slightly fuller upper lip, the same delicate cleft chin and strong jawline. Even the same high and sharp cheekbones and slender nose. And, she imagined in his youth, his now cropped white hair had been fiery red.

He was handsome…very handsome. But she could see the lines age and abuse had carved over his face.

"I always knew you were the best thing to ever come from me," he announced, the initial shock he'd felt replaced by excessive pride. "Look at how gorgeous my daughter is! Takes after her old man."

With that, he pulled her into a hug and held her close. Her face was pressed against his chest, her arms around him as her eyes closed.

This is…weird, she decided. He felt so different than what she was used to…and he smelled different too. Like stale whiskey and barroom smoke. It wasn't an altogether terrible scent, but when she pulled away and looked at him, she felt she understood him better than before.

The past fifteen years had been hard on him. And, like many men, he'd turned to alcohol to heal the pain. Could she really blame him?

"Why don't we give you two a moment alone while we all go inside and get seated for dinner," Thea suggested, resting her hand on Brock's shoulder, her dark eyes on Blythe. "Take your time."

With that, everyone began to file into the castle. Blythe saw Nyxa staring at Brock conspicuously as she walked by, her eyes not leaving him until she disappeared inside the castle. Rohan walked by with his arm securely around Serendipity's waist, as though showing his ownership of her. While Blythe could understand his statement, it bristled her feminine pride to see it.

She stared after Lucian and Liam as they walked away, both turning around briefly to grin and wave at her before heading inside. Her hand shot up to wave back and she fought back the urge to cry again. Damnit, she had never cried so much in her entire life. What the hell was it about this specific occasion that was turning her into a blubbering fool?

"So, how've you been?" she tossed her hair back and turned to her father, forcing herself to act casual.

"Fine…I've been fine." Brock glanced around the courtyard, marveling at nothing in particular. "Much better now, though."

"I bet." She smiled, only to have it vanish the moment he pulled out a flask from his suit jacket and took a long swig. "I'm going to guess that isn't orange juice."

He stared at her a moment and then burst into laughter. The raw, rough sound echoed through the now empty courtyard. She waited until he finished, tears in his eyes from laughing so hard.

He patted her on the back roughly as he grinned. "That's funny, babydoll. Real funny."

"I wasn't trying to be funny." She shook her head, trying to understand him. "I get it, okay? You're an alcoholic. That's fine, we'll work on it."

Insult flashed in his eyes as his smile faded. "I am not an alcoholic. A man's got a right to have a drink now and again."

"Sure, but most people I know don't carry booze around in their pocket." Annoyed, she fisted her hands on her hips and stared him down, which was comical since she was much shorter and petite than him. "I don't want to fight with you, but you're gonna learn something real fast about me. If something bothers me, I speak my mind. And right now, this concept of you being an alcoholic bothers me. I missed out on having my father around for fifteen years, and now you're basically ensuring that I'm only gonna get another ten years out of you before you croak from liver disease."

He laughed again, amused by her. "Don't worry about me; I can take care of myself. Now, tell me what you've been up to. Did you miss me?"

"Well, let's see," Blythe began, feeling more than a little vicious as her temper sparked. "I suppose it would have been foolish to miss a man I was convinced was responsible for my good friend's disappearance and her mother's death. So no, I didn't really miss you. And what have I been up to? Well, my mother disowned me because I look way too much like you, which now I can see is definitely true. Rohan hates me because I act too much like you, which I can also see is true. Hardly anyone respects me or gives me the time of day because of what you supposedly did. My entire future was essentially blown to pieces the moment you were banished, and everyone is waiting for the day that I follow you down to Hell. So, to sum it all up, life hasn't been peachy, but I've done alright."

She regretted her outburst the moment misery flashed in his eyes. Cursing herself and her temper, she exhaled a whoosh of breath and slumped her shoulders.

"I'm sorry, that was uncalled for." Gritting her teeth, she looked at him again. "It's been tough, okay? And I get that it's probably been tough for you, too. I suppose I just really wanted you to know what damage this whole bullshit has caused."

"There wasn't anything I could do, Blythe." His voice was low, the pride and power diminished. Now he had the appearance of a helpless and miserable man. Seeing it, knowing the true face behind the mask he wore, humbled her. "Damnit, that night I didn't even think about why Balgaire was in the courtyard, I just assumed he was fighting the demons, too. It never occurred to me that he was the one responsible. And when the demon they captured confessed that it had been me who let him onto the grounds, I had no defense other than my word. And with Rohan and Balgaire so eager to place the blame on me, citing my weakness for demon liquor and black market weapons, I had even less of a chance to prove my innocence. I didn't see any way out of it; no one would believe for once that I had been in the dungeon working." He paused, bitterness in his eyes. "The one and only time I chose to work over going to a party."

"So you left, because you felt that was your only option," Blythe murmured, feeling sick to her stomach.

"If there had been another way, I would have fought for it. But there wasn't. My fate was sealed. I'm sorry you've had to go through all this shit on account of me, babydoll, but I'm home now, and I intend to make things right."

Biting the inside of her lip, Blythe considered his words. He sounded like he meant it, so she supposed she'd have to take him at his word.

"Alright. But I want you to cut back on the daily drinking, okay? It's not good for you, and I want you to live a long time."

She cocked one eyebrow at him skeptically, then grinned and wrapped her arms around him. "I know I can be difficult. But you'll get used to me."

"From one difficult person to another, I think we'll get along just fine." Holding her close, he sighed deeply. "Now, let's get some of that fine Euphorian dinner I've been missing these past fifteen years."

If she had any doubts about her father's charisma and ability to light up a room, they were squashed within seconds at dinner that night.

The stories the man told were vulgar, crude, and unapologetic, but they were damn entertaining. It seemed as though most of the people present had missed Brock's antics, given the way they were laughing and cheering him on. And she loved watching Lucian and Clynn reminisce with him about the old days when they had all been young men, pursuing women, practicing their powers, sneaking vodka onto Euphora and getting piss drunk in the courtyard. Seeing her foster father light up with genuine happiness at having his old friend home made her feel much better. Maybe Brock wasn't perfect, but just like when Capri had come home, Brock's homecoming was filling a hole in many of their lives.

"This one time we were in Vegas for Clynn's bachelor party, and Lucian and I take off to get a drink at the bar, and it's got to be four in the morning by the time we head back to the hotel room. When we turn the corner of the hallway we see Clynn sitting against the wall in goddamn handcuffs, blood all over his face, and a shit ton of cops standing around. Lucian and me, we're ready to get the hell out of there because we're drunk and the last thing we want is to be interrogated by a bunch of human cops, but of course Clynn sees us and calls out to us, and so the cops flag us down. Turns out, we leave Clynn alone for less than an hour, and he manages to get into a fist fight with Roarke, which was a bad idea to begin with. And of course Roarke kicks his ass and now Clynn's outside in handcuffs and Roarke's sitting on the bed in the room holding his head because he just threw up all over the carpet. Damn good time, wasn't it boys?"

"Clynn got into a fist fight with Roarke?" Blythe snorted, staring at Clynn incredulously. "What the hell were you thinking?"

Clynn flushed bright red, obviously embarrassed. Capri was watching him, amused. "Well, it was a long time ago…and if I remember correctly, he had called me a *pansy* for not wanting to get a prostitute, so I corrected him and told him that I didn't think it was fair to my fiancé for me to sleep with another woman."

"Aw." Capri beamed and patted his arm, obviously pleased. "That's sweet."

"So you went to blows over that?" Blythe still looked bemused, even as Clynn sighed.

"I don't really…remember, exactly."

Brock and Lucian broke out into raucous laughter and many around the table joined in.

"It was certainly a memorable trip," Lucian mused, looking nostalgic. "Things have definitely changed since those times. We can't handle our liquor like we used to, can we Clynn?"

"Definitely not," Clynn chuckled, toasting with his glass of apple cider. "Those were the days."

"The four of you were probably the biggest handful I'd ever had in a Dryad group," Thea chimed suddenly, her eyes dancing as she looked around at them. "It was like you were made for causing me trouble and headaches. Thank goodness the new generation is much more mature."

Blythe snorted again. "I'm not very mature."

Thea focused her eyes on Blythe, tilting her head slightly in acknowledgement. "No, I suppose you're not."

"Yeah and we know how to party," Liam countered, looking insulted. "We can throw down with these old guys any day, huh Blythe?"

"Duh. They're old, Liam. They need canes and walkers and stuff."

"Now, wait a minute." Brock wagged his finger at Blythe from across the table, a challenge gleaming in his eyes. "I'm willing to take you kids up on that bet. Whaddya say, boys? Can we party with the young crowd?"

"Actually, we probably can't," Lucian pointed out, smirking at the way Brock's face fell. "But there's no reason why we can't give it our best shot."

"Hah! Good man, Lucian, good man." Patting the Water Dryad on the back, Brock grinned wickedly at his daughter. "Once dinner's over, babydoll, we're on."

"Alright, old man." Blythe returned his grin and the similarity between the two of them had never been more clear.

It pleased her immensely that the first thing Brock did the moment they all headed outside to the patio was to pull her close for a dance.

"You're a real funny girl, Blythe. Take after your old man."

She rolled her eyes, but the pleasure showed on her face. "I suppose. Though I think I'm funnier than you."

"Maybe so, babydoll." He grinned as he twirled her, while in the background Eric Clapton sang about a girl named Layla.

"It was fun to hear about all the old stories you have with Lucian and Clynn," Blythe commented, gazing up at him. "I've always known both of them to be pretty mature and fatherly…so to hear about them when they were my age is bizarre."

"Those were the best years of my life." Brock sighed, a hint of regret in his voice. "When Thea and Sebastian showed up at my apartment yesterday and explained everything to me, I think the thing that hurt me the most was to know that those years had ended much sooner than they should have."

"I think I was happiest then, too," she said, watching him closely. "I don't know if you noticed, but Rhiannon doesn't speak to me. We haven't been friends since you left. So that's another thing you and I have in common…we drive the Earth Dryads crazy."

He laughed loudly, his smile bright. "Damn right."

He twirled her again and when the song ended, he led her over to a table where Lucian, Liam, Clynn, Capri and Rian were all sitting.

Brock sat beside Rian and turned to him, holding out his hand. "I didn't get a chance before to thank the two of you," he began as he shook the Fury's hand, nodding at Capri as well. "I owe you both for what you've done for me."

"I was only doing my job," Rian told him, his serious blue eyes locked on the older man's tawny ones.

"If you and Capri hadn't done what you did, I may have rotted down in that dingy apartment for the rest of my life," Brock acknowledged, his expression unusually somber. "I don't know how I can ever repay you."

"By being a good man to your daughter. That is enough repayment for us."

Capri nodded in agreement, smiling sweetly at Brock. "Everyone is so happy you are home. They missed you so much."

"And I missed all of you, too." He returned her smile, but it faltered a bit as he stared back at Rian. "I'm sorry to hear about your dad. Roarke was one of my best friends, and one of the few who defended me after the raid. He was a good man and a good friend to me."

Rian nodded, but didn't say anything. Capri's hand sought his under the table to comfort him.

"By the way, dad, we might as well get this conversation out of the way now before I forget," Blythe began, waiting for him to turn and acknowledge her. "I'm going after Dante."

Everyone at the table went silent as they stared at her, disbelief on their faces.

"Blythe, you told us you wouldn't go. The bounty hunter is handling it," Lucian protested, eyeing her worriedly. "There's no need for you to get involved."

"This is a joke, right?" Brock grinned, glancing around at everyone. "You're all messing with me."

"No, they're not. I'm completely serious," Blythe told him, eyebrows raised.

"When did you decide this?" Liam asked her, the look of concern on his face identical to that of his father.

"Just now." She beamed at all of them, finding it humorous that they were all so shocked. "C'mon, hearing about all the good times you guys had back in the day, and knowing that Capri's mother and Roarke died because of this bastard...I made up my mind. I'm going to get justice, and I'm too damn impatient to wait for some bounty hunter to find a man who shares my blood. I bet I know more about what Dante's thinking than that human does."

"Blythe, he's dangerous." Brock suddenly looked very much the stern father as he stared at her in disbelief. "Stay away from Dante. You're letting your ego get the best of you. Trust me, you don't know what he's capable of or what he's thinking."

Pride bruised, she looked at him with hurt eyes.

"I'm surprised that you're not siding with me on this. Better yet, why aren't you offering to come with me? Don't you want to find him, to take him out?"

He stared at her, and she saw a flicker of fear cross his face before his own pride kicked in and reared up to take on her own.

"I just spent the last fifteen years in a crappy apartment in goddamn Las Vegas, penniless and alone, and the only thing I want right now is to relax and enjoy being home. Sure, I want revenge on that cocksucker, but I'm gonna leave that up to the man who's already on the job. I'm content to let him take care of it."

Blythe stared at him for a moment, chest heaving as she fought back all the angry things she wanted to shout back at him. They could have a shouting match, then and there, and they'd most likely resolve the issue. But something inside of her was far too hurt to muster the energy for it.

"I thought you were like me, dad," she murmured, disappointment on her face. "But I guess we're nothing alike."

With that, she stood up and raced off toward the castle, confused and hurt.

Back at the table, Brock stayed where he was for a moment, unmoving. After a second, he turned and smiled at everyone.

"Maybe I'll go find another female that I can piss off," he said in a cheerfully sarcastic voice, rising from the table and stalking off to where Nyxa was seated with the other Fates.

Lucian stared after him, disapproval clear on his face.

"I'll be back," he muttered as he stood and ran after Blythe. When he found her, she was pacing back and forth in the corridor, her hands clenched and glowing bright red as she held in the fire she desperately wanted to unleash.

When she heard him approaching, she turned, ready to shout again, until she noticed it was Lucian and not her father.

And seeing him, seeing the remorse and the understanding on his face, destroyed her resolve. She stood motionless until he wrapped her in his arms, and then she crumbled against him and wept.

"It's okay, honeypot," he cooed, his voice soothing her. When she was all cried out, she sighed so deep it ached in her ravaged chest and shook her bones.

"God, I have high expectations," she confessed, turning her eyes to look at him. "I haven't gotten off to a good start with him. This is the second fight we've had and he's only been home a few hours."

He smiled at her and chuckled, his hands cupped gently over her shoulders.

"This is rougher on you than you've let on, isn't it?"

She shrugged, averting her eyes from his. He knew her better than she knew herself sometimes.

"I just…" She stopped, feeling her throat tighten again, and she cursed herself for being weak. "I just wanted to believe that I needed him to support me and be with me…but the more I think about it, I really don't need him at all. I never did."

"Every child needs a father," Lucian reminded her, his eyes kind.

"I know that…but even though he was gone, I had you." She felt a tear slip down her cheek despite her attempts to fight it back, and her lips trembled slightly as she watched him.

His face softened as he hugged her again, squeezing her tightly. "I must confess, honeypot, I may have used you to fill a gap in my life as well."

He pulled away and kept his eyes on hers. "Clarity kept Cilla to herself, even though she was just a baby at the time. But I'd always wanted a daughter, and I would watch Brock play with you and I was always envious. And then when you were all alone, I took the opportunity and snatched you up for my own." He cupped his hand around her cheek and smiled. "It was the best decision I ever made."

"Thank God you did." She threw her arms around him and held on for dear life. "I don't know who that man is out there, Lucian. But I hope things get better than they have been tonight."

"They will be. He's a lot to handle all at once, but then again, so are you."

"Damn right," she agreed with a shaky laugh.

"Let's get back out there. We haven't danced in awhile; maybe we should show them all how it's done."

Arm in arm they walked back out into the courtyard, where many people were already dancing. Blythe saw Capri and Rian, Rohan and Serendipity, Thea and Sebastian, and Rhiannon and Brogan all swaying to an old Temptations tune.

She glanced around but didn't see her father.

"I wonder where he went," she murmured as Lucian led her onto the dance floor. The song switched to an up-tempo jazzy beat, and she quickly forgot about her father as she and her favorite person in the world did what they did best. They danced.

Out of breath and exhausted, she slumped against him after the song was over. "Damn, we're good."

Lucian chuckled, wrapping his arm around her. "I taught you well. One day you'll dance circles around some lucky man who's going to fall head over heels for you."

"I wouldn't hold your breath on that one." She laughed breathlessly, grinning at him. "I'm going to be a crazy cat lady, you watch."

"Nonsense, you're beautiful, honeypot." He paused, noticing something that he hoped to God Blythe wouldn't see. He was about to turn her away, but her eyes caught sight of it before he could. And when he heard her sharp inhale and felt her tense against him, he knew the damage was done.

Brock and Nyxa were walking arm in arm, practically leaning against each other for balance, both looking more than a little breathless and disheveled, with pleased looks on their faces. Blythe had a distinct feeling that they hadn't been dancing, at least not in the literal sense of the word.

"Figures," she spat, tearing her eyes away from them. "We have an argument, I leave all pissed off, and what does he do? Oh, that's right, he goes and bangs my whore mother."

"They were married once, Blythe. It wouldn't be unusual for them to want to get back together," Lucian reminded her, though she wasn't having it.

"I don't care. That woman disowned me, and instead of being disgusted with her over that, he's all over her. He clearly doesn't care about my feelings at all. I'm his child, his blood! He's mine, not hers."

When Brock and Nyxa got within a few yards of where Blythe and Lucian were standing, Brock beamed like a cat that had just devoured an entire bowl of cream.

"Hey, babydoll. You feeling better?" he asked, his arm still around Nyxa. Nyxa rolled her eyes and refused to look at Blythe, who was glaring at her with similar disdain.

"I was. But I'm going to refrain from saying what I really want to say right now because I feel we've gotten off on the wrong foot here. I'm just going to distance myself from you and enjoy the rest of the party, and then I'm going to bed. We can get a fresh start in the morning, okay?"

He looked momentarily taken aback, but he smiled anyway. "Whatever you want, sweetheart."

With that, he sauntered off, Nyxa at his side, to one of the empty tables near the back.

"Now just what in the hell am I supposed to do about that?" Blythe said angrily, turning to Lucian.

"Exactly what you said, love. Try for a fresh start tomorrow."

She was annoyed, but knew he was right. Until then, there was nothing left to do but shine on.

Chapter Three

Despite her frustration with the events of the night before, when morning came she did precisely what she did every day: she ran.

Her sneakers pounded the soft ground as she jogged through the forest surrounding the castle. The hazy morning sunlight cascaded through breaks in the trees above her, sending shimmering beams of light down to highlight the ferns and moss growing wild there. Birds scattered overhead, startled by her intrusion into their world. She hardly noticed, her mind as fine tuned in the moment as her body was. She was all focus, all strength, and pure energy.

She had headphones in her ears blasting Zeppelin, Springsteen, ACDC, and Queen. She loved rock music, especially the classics, because it had just the right amount of attitude and power. The rock gods didn't ask you politely to listen to them. They commanded it. It was a sentiment she found she agreed with wholeheartedly.

She kept her breathing steady as she rounded a turn and emerged out onto the cliffs' edge of the island. Following the strip of land that extended beyond the forest, she kept moving, her mind focused intently on the task at hand.

Her muscles felt warm, strong, and powerful. The wind from the ocean blasted her face, but she embraced it. It only made her feel freer. In her mind, this was the next best thing to flying.

The song changed and she picked up the pace, her lips curving into a smile as *Highway to Hell* lifted her spirits.

She made the entire loop around the island, then headed back through the trees toward the meadow and the entrance gates. It was a long, satisfying run, and in her eyes there was no better way to start the day. Other than coffee, of course, but she'd already had that.

Pleased with herself, she paused just inside the courtyard to stretch, pulling her right leg up behind her to soothe her quad muscle. She grabbed the water bottle she'd left sitting beside the gates and gulped down nearly the entire thing as she walked to the castle.

Today was going to be their fresh start. It was good to go in feeling positive, empowered, and focused. Exercise was good for all of those things.

Upstairs she showered and dressed, and, feeling genuinely optimistic, she headed downstairs to meet her father in the dungeons. She had no idea what the day held for her, but she was feeling pretty damn good about it anyway.

The dungeon had, for whatever reason, seemed an appropriate place for Thea to put the Fire Dryads, even though it didn't really make a difference if they were underground or not. Perhaps an ancestor long ago had been a recluse and had preferred the cool, stone floors and walls of the dungeon, where there were no windows for sunlight to shine.

It didn't really bother her, she was happy just about anywhere. Besides, when she'd been younger and it had been Thea who had taught her the ways of Fire, she had appreciated having the seclusion to practice her craft. She had her pride, after all.

She opened the heavy wooden door at the bottom of the stairs and walked into the dungeon, only to find her father there already, standing over the large stone fire pit in the center. She watched him for a moment as he stared at his hands, looking lost.

"Is everything alright?" she asked. He jumped and stared at her, his mouth open slightly as though he was about to say something. Instead he grinned at her, replacing his mask.

"How's my girl?" He had dressed in faded jeans and a white t-shirt, and seeing him look so casual made him appear more innocent than he was.

Nonetheless, she was here for a fresh start.

"I'm fantastic. I got my caffeine and my run in this morning, took a nice hot shower and I'm ready to go through a refresher course for you." She smiled warmly.

"Oh, yeah, I guess it has been a long time since…" he paused and stared down at his hands, as if he'd forgotten what they were for.

Feeling sorry for him, she walked over and grasped his hands in hers. "It's like riding a bike, right? It'll come back to you in no time."

"Yeah…yeah I'm sure it will." He looked happier as he glanced around at the dungeon, drinking it all in.

The walls, floor, and ceiling were all made of hard gray stone. The room was circular and large, roughly twenty feet in diameter, with flame torches lining the walls every few feet. The dungeon glowed with vivid, orange light, with dark shadows dancing off the walls.

The entire room smelled of cool smoke.

Despite the vastness of the room, the only fixture was the fire pit in the center of the floor. It was about five feet wide and sunken into the ground, exposing the raw dirt beneath the stone. Thea had once told Blythe that a Fire Dryad centuries before had used the fire pit as a portal into the Underworld, where he had frequently gone to fulfill his darkest desires. She wondered briefly if her father had once used it as a gateway to the Underworld as well, despite it being expressly forbidden. But hey, who was she to fault someone for breaking the rules? She could understand healthy curiosity. Though the one time she had considered attempting to open the portal to see what all the fuss was about, Thea had interrupted her. She'd never tried again, mostly out of a guilty conscience.

But the fire pit had other purposes, the most important of which was to monitor every aspect of fire on Earth.

"I'll bring up the globe, and then we can start from there, 'k?" She glanced at her father briefly, who nodded and stepped back, before she raised her hands and focused her attention on the fire pit.

She could feel her palms heating as the power she held pushed through her and expelled out toward the pit in the form of a tiny white light, which quickly grew and caught fire. What then began as a spinning ball of fire hovering just inches above the dirt slowly transformed into a model of the globe as it rose into the air. By the time it was roughly three feet off the ground, the globe was three feet in diameter and slowing until it spun no more.

Pleased, she looked at her father, who was staring at the globe in awe. It had been years since he had used his gift, and so to once again witness the sheer power that was possible with it must be baffling to him.

"So, you probably remember most of this, but what I usually do first is divide the globe in half to see the layers inside, then I follow my checklist to make sure nothing is out of whack or in need of urgent attention."

"I can do that," he assured her, stepping forward, chest out as he raised his right hand and focused his attention on the globe.

She watched as the globe cracked in half, part of it crumbling to the ground in ashes. What was left of the globe was jagged edged and unbalanced, but it would do.

"Okay, good," she encouraged, noting the determination in his eyes. "So the first thing to check is—"

"I got it...I got it," he interrupted, both hands raised now as he focused on the gaping half of the globe. It showed all the layers of the Earth, including the jet black inner core, the liquid hot outer core, the unstable mantle, and the outer crust. Because the globe represented the actual world in real time, they could observe exactly what was happening at the precise moment where no living creature had ever been able to go. It gave her a sense of real power that she knew came with real responsibility.

And because she knew the weight of that responsibility, she watched her father with wary eyes. Thea had long since warned her of the dangers inherent with making a drastic mistake in regards to the core.

After he'd scanned the many layers of rock, magma and minerals, he let his hands fall as he turned to her.

"Done."

Raising an eyebrow at him, she smirked. "Already? Did you check the temperature at all the layers? We have to make sure there's no sudden increase or we could have a real mess on our hands. And did you check the pressure levels? Or the viscosity of the magma in the mantle?"

He let out a huff of breath as he laughed. "Well, I did it the way I used to always do it, and it didn't involve any of those scientific terms. Thea must have been the one to teach you everything, huh?"

"Seeing as there was no one else around who knew, Thea was the obvious choice." She tilted her head up as she considered him. "So if this is not how you are used to doing it...what is?"

He winked at her. "Much simpler. Your grandma taught me to check for three things when looking at the globe. If all three things are in order, then you're good to go." He turned and faced the globe again, demonstrating to her. "First is to check the coloring of the layers. As long as the inner core is black, the outer core white, the mantle gray with orange lining, and the crust brown, then your temperature is good. Second is to check for cracks between the layers. If there aren't any, then the pressure is good. And lastly, ask Earth, aka Rohan, if he has any earthquakes planned that may happen in an area where lava is too close to the surface. Of course, I never really did that part since we're not on speaking terms, so I just assume we're all good on that one."

"You have got to be kidding me." She shook her head as she doubled over with laughter, mostly in astonishment at how nothing catastrophic had ever happened under his watch. Out of breath, she looked up at him and saw with bemusement that he was smiling at her.

"What's so funny?" he asked, eyebrows raised.

"Was that seriously all you ever did? Just check those three things and then call it a day?"

"Well, yeah. That's all I was responsible for." He looked taken aback for a moment by the disbelief he saw in her eyes. "I'll have you know that my method worked just fine. Under my watch we never once had a volcanic disaster."

"Only because of dumb luck." She sighed, shaking her head at him. "Alright, so tell me how you monitored fires."

"If there was a brush fire, I'd—"

"What do you mean, *if?* You never enacted any preventative measures? Or created a fire when an area had too much foliage that was stifling the ecosystem?"

"What? No. Why would I?"

Exasperated now, she threw up her hands and groaned. "Yikes, okay. I guess I'm going to have to show you all of this ASAP. Might as well get started now, we have a lot to cover."

It was the most exhausting three hours of her life, but it was also probably the most rewarding. While her father had been reluctant at first to learning anything new, he eventually gave in and was actually an avid student. She gave him all the books she had on understanding the Earth's core and all the important terms he would need to know. She walked him through the steps, breaking it down just like Thea had for her, even going as far as to give him all of her old notes.

She understood his initial frustration completely, and she didn't hold it against him. If someone younger than her had claimed her methods were old-school, she'd be pissed too. But he had to learn these things if they were going to work together. You couldn't have two people who didn't understand each other's methods. It just wouldn't work.

But thankfully, he picked up on the basics pretty quickly, and she hoped that after he read through the material she gave him that he would familiarize himself with all the details.

They had an important job to do, and if he was going to be a part of it, she needed him to commit to it. Otherwise, she'd have to tell him to butt out and she'd have to do all the work alone again.

Not that she minded it so much, she thought with a sigh as she hefted a large pastrami sandwich onto her plate at the dining table. She had been practicing her craft alone for so long, carrying the weight of responsibility by herself ever since she could remember. She didn't really need him to help out, but it would be nice to have more free time like the other Dryads did. Besides, she didn't want him to get out of his responsibilities altogether. He was a Fire Dryad, and therefore he had to act like one.

Crunching down on her sandwich, she nearly moaned at how delicious it was. Pastrami was a favorite of hers, especially when accompanied by pickles. She loved pickles.

She really just loved food. Any kind of food, she wasn't picky. She could gorge on a big juicy steak one minute and then sample a tart grapefruit the next. She'd tried tofu, sea eel, rabbit, bison, alligator…you name it, and she'd had them all, and virtually loved them all.

Except peas. For whatever reason, she couldn't stand peas.

"You know, you could have been nice and saved me half of that sandwich," Liam chided as he settled down beside her, running a hand through his dark hair. Because he had a goofy, lovesick grin plastered over his face, she knew he'd just been out with Rhiannon.

"Well, if you'd hauled your ass in here like I did, you might have gotten a sandwich before they all got eaten. It isn't my fault you would rather flirt with the devil incarnate."

"Ouch, harsh." He chuckled, reaching over to grab a tuna sandwich on wheat. He was used to the feud between Blythe and Rhiannon at this point, so he rarely let it get to him. "So how'd training with daddy go?"

Blythe swallowed and rolled her eyes. "We fought at first, of course. Seems like all we can do is bicker at each other. In all honesty, I think we're both a little too hot headed. Anyway though, get this. I start showing him how I like to do things, you know, the way Thea taught me. And then he interrupts me and spouts off about his simplified method which, honestly Liam, scared the living daylights out of me."

"Not that I really understand any of what you do, but what was it that scared you?"

"For years he had barely been monitoring anything. He was doing some half ass thing where he'd check the color of the crust and check for cracks or something. God, do you understand what could have happened with only that basic observation?"

"Nope." He grinned at her as he bit into his sandwich.

"Ugh, hopeless. You're all hopeless." She sighed as she bit into a pickle, crunching on it as she thought. "Disaster, Liam. The end of humanity as we know it. That's what could have happened."

"But you showed him the right way to do things?"

"Yeah, and I gave him books on it and stuff so we'll see. I just wonder why Thea never trained him or my grandmother this way. I guess she had no idea how lax they had gotten through the generations."

"Look at you, all concerned about responsibilities. This is a new side to you." Amused, he patted her shoulder.

"Shut up." She laughed, batting his hand away. "I guess when you're around an adult who acts more like a child than you do, you automatically assume the grown up position."

"In all seriousness…are things going okay with him?" He watched her closely, his dark blue eyes kind.

"Yeah, we're fine. I have issues I have to get over I guess regarding him and my mother, but whatever."

"It hurts you to see him with her." He touched her arm gently, wanting her to know he understood.

"Yeah, only because I know the person she was when he was gone. She was terrible, Liam, you remember. She did everything she could to make me feel like I was responsible, like I was evil in some way. And then she dumped me like I was yesterday's garbage. It was cold and it was heartless. I just can't figure out what he sees in her."

"Maybe it's just a physical thing, ya know?" He took another bite and grinned when she shuddered. "Old people have sex too, Blythe. It's not that weird."

"Ew." Her appetite gone, she pushed her plate away and rested her elbows on the table, planting her face in her hands. Exhaling deeply she tilted her head to look at him. "It's not really that part that bugs me. I mean, it does bug me, but not that bad."

"You're upset because the time he spends with her takes away from time he could be spending with you?"

"Exactly." Pursing her lips, she reached for her glass of lemonade and took a long drink. "It sounds petty, I know."

"Yes and no." His lips curved as he studied her. "You should be his priority, no doubt. And I know you could care less about your mother's feelings, but she has a right to spend time with him too."

"I guess." Feeling glum, she pondered grabbing a chocolate chip cookie, but decided against it. Even chocolate wasn't going to help. What she needed was time alone. "I'm gonna go to the library and try and find this book Capri keeps bugging me to read. I'll see ya later, 'k?"

"Take care." He watched her as she got up and left, unable to hide his uneasiness about the whole situation. He wished there was more he could do for her, but he knew that this was a battle she was going to have to face on her own.

Blythe walked through the corridor, making her way to the library. She hummed *Highway to Hell* under her breath, her footsteps echoing off the stone walls. When she reached the library, she shoved open the door and stopped just inside, almost walking right back out.

Seated on one of the many sofas were Brogan and Nova, heads together, deep in discussion. The second the door opened they both looked up like guilty children, only to have the surprise on their faces replaced with disdain. It was a look she was well accustomed to from both of them.

Deciding it satisfied her mood better to interrupt them than hightailing it out of there, she walked forward, head held high and a mocking grin on her face.

"Don't let me interrupt your little book club meeting," she said sassily, even though she noticed neither of them had been reading a book. Curiosity almost had her ask what they were up to until...

"You are such a bitch!" Nova exploded, jumping to her feet and pointing an accusing finger at Blythe. Brogan instantly jumped up and restrained her, even though she had made no threatening move toward Blythe. Yet.

Torn between utter shock and a tinge of amusement at seeing her quiet, dark haired little sister have a passionate moment, Blythe stopped dead in her tracks and fisted her hands on her hips defensively.

"What the hell is your problem?" she countered, temper flaring as one eyebrow cocked indignantly.

"Your father is a horrible man! He's going to take advantage of our mother! Do you even care about that? Does it even bother you that he's using her again?" Nova managed, tears now streaming down her thin face out of dark eyes.

"Maybe she's getting what she deserves for being a rotten whore," Blythe spat, trying not to care about the despair and anguish on her sister's face.

Brogan didn't say a word, he simply pulled Nova against his chest to comfort her, his dark eyes locked on Blythe. The cold disgust she saw in them chilled her to the bone. What the hell was wrong with these two?

Deciding it wasn't worth getting the damn book, she turned on her heel and stalked out of the library, not wanting to see her sister's tears any longer. Why it had affected her she didn't know, but she couldn't get the image out of her mind as she raced down the corridor toward the living quarters.

Nova didn't mean anything to her; she was just another girl living on Euphora. They'd barely spoken to each other, much less even *looked* at each other. But there was something about seeing her cry that hit a chord deep in her heart.

Knowing it was easier to be angry than it was to dwell on the sadness she felt, she pounded up the stairs and raced to her room, slamming the door behind her. Once inside, she turned toward the flame retardant dartboard Lucian had given her for her birthday and proceeded to hurl darts of fire at it.

They erupted from her wrist and shot through the air, and she felt a stab of satisfaction every time one burst against the board. She didn't even care about accuracy, it just felt good to throw something. Especially when she had the pleasure of seeing an explosion of fire at every impact.

After what must have been forty shots fired one after another in rapid succession, she crumbled to the floor, gasping for air. Exhausted, she curled into herself and reveled in her momentarily empty mind.

Minutes later, she sprawled on her back and stared up at the ceiling of her room, trying to focus on her breathing. And as her heart rate and her breathing slowed, the thoughts returned.

Why was Nova so convinced that Brock was using their mother? The man had only been back one full day, they couldn't possibly know his intentions yet. And if they were just making assumptions about him, then they were fools. They knew nothing about him, other than what Balgaire had told them since they were children, and she could only imagine what that bastard had to say about his rival. Not a single kind word about Brock had ever come out of Balgaire's mouth, that she was sure of.

She took a deep breath and hefted herself up off of the floor, feeling better than she had before. What did she care what Nova and Brogan thought, anyway? It was useless to worry about things she couldn't do anything about.

And if Brock was just using Nyxa, she didn't really see how it was any of her business.

Chapter Four

Maybe her expectations were too high. Or, maybe her father's standards were just too low.

Whichever way she looked at it, as the days progressed she noticed him getting more and more distracted with his work.

The first couple of days he was reading the books she'd given him, and when she'd quiz him on the terms he was doing fairly well. Not perfect, but good considering the man hadn't learned something new in twenty, maybe even thirty years.

But then it was like a light bulb switched off in his head. He started coming in later than their usual meeting time, nearly always dragging his feet like she was forcing him to be there or something.

When she'd ask him a question, he'd get frustrated and annoyed with her, as if the last thing he wanted to do was actually work.

And to top it all off, she could smell women's perfume on him. He really just didn't care about working, and the fact that it had taken only one week for that to happen led her to believe she'd be working by herself after all.

Deciding she wasn't going to let him off the hook that easily, she left him alone with explicit instructions not to touch anything, and she went to see Thea.

Ready to vent her frustrations, she burst into Thea's lofty garden room, prepared to unleash all matter of indignities. But the moment she came in, she heard a polite "shush" from Sebastian, just in time for her to notice Thea was talking to someone through a device resting on the small table beside her.

Sebastian was relaxing on one of the nearby chaise lounges, a glass of raspberry tea in his hand as he eyed her, amusement clear on his face as he noticed the waves of frustrated energy she emanated.

Resigned that there was little she could do but wait, Blythe trudged over and plopped down beside Sebastian.

Smiling serenely at her, he lifted a small plate crowded with tiny cookies and offered her one.

Sighing, she grabbed two and settled down to wait.

It wasn't until she heard the man's voice that she actually paid attention to Thea's conversation.

"I've got three demons and several humans who say they saw Dante at the Bellagio just two days ago. Now, I've checked the records and if he was there, he was checked in under a fake name. I also got a lead on a Mercedes Benz that was stolen out of the Bellagio lot just yesterday morning. I watched the security camera footage, and it's our man."

He had a slow drawl to his voice that gave a southwest flavor to every syllable he uttered, making the matter of fact way he told his tale all the more alluring. Blythe found herself leaning in closer, her interest piqued.

"Excellent. Do you have a lead on where he's headed?" Thea looked immensely pleased as she tossed back her dark curls and winked at Blythe.

"My gut tells me he's heading west. There's not much to the east or to the north, and Phoenix is the only big city south of here. So west makes the most sense."

"I trust your judgment one hundred percent, Jax." Thea smiled, clearly trying to hold back a laugh. "Have you been keeping your distance from the tables like a good boy?"

The man on the receiver chuckled before he spoke. *"Yes ma'am. I keep my money firmly tucked in my wallet these days. I'll let you know if I hear any more details, but until then, I'm heading west."*

"Safe traveling, darling." She pressed a button on the receiver, ending the call, then turned to face Sebastian and Blythe. "How nice of you to come visit with us, Blythe. I know you must be very busy."

"Was that the bounty hunter?"

"Yes, Jackson Murphy. He's on Dante's tail. It should only be a matter of days now." Stretching her arms over her head, Thea yawned and sighed before looking back at Blythe. "Was there something you wanted to talk about?"

Warring between curiosity over the bounty hunter and her frustration with her father, Blythe decided it was better to push curiosity aside in place of more pressing matters.

"It's my dad, Thea," she began, running her hands through her hair as though all she wanted to do was pull it all out. "He's distracted, disinterested, and ridiculously careless. I've had to give him all my old books and notes from when you taught me so he could learn the proper way to do things, and he's barely looked at them. I mean, the first couple of days he seemed to be committed and excited, but now it's like he doesn't even want to be there. I keep pushing him, scolding him, whatever it takes, but he isn't responding to me. I'm at my wit's end here."

"Blythe…" Thea leaned over and patted her arm sympathetically. "Brock has never had a very good work ethic. I'm sorry you're frustrated, but there's really not much I can do."

"Can't you tell him to get off his ass and get to work?" Irritation flickered in her eyes at Thea's nonchalance.

"I suppose I could, but if I'm speaking honestly, which I always will with you, then I need you to know that I'm hesitant to push him right now. Because of my decision he lost years of his life here. I don't have any way to make it up to him except to give him time to adjust and to find ways to get those years back. That includes spending quality time with you, dear."

"Well that sounds great, only he doesn't want to spend much time with me." Annoyed that she was being petty, she rubbed her face before looking at Thea again. "Look, I knew what to expect, alright? I knew he'd be difficult, I knew he'd be obnoxious, and I knew he would have a hard time keeping away from the ladies, namely my mother. But I guess I also expected him to give a damn about working with me, or even talking with me. God, he hasn't even asked me if I have a boyfriend. Shouldn't all dads want to know that about their daughters? He's so goddamn self-centered he can't see anything beyond what applies directly to him. It's frustrating, Thea."

Thea was silent for a moment, her gypsy eyes locked on Blythe's. When she spoke, there was unmistakable pride in her voice. "Of all of you kids, you have undoubtedly been dealt the hardest hand, Blythe. But instead of crawling into a hole and wallowing in your misfortune, you stand tall and make life work for you. I admire your tenacity, your determination, and your strength of will. I know you're frustrated and more than a little disappointed in him, but give it time. I'm sure you'll pull some trick out of your hat that will turn everything around."

"I feel like my hat is running a little short on tricks these days," Blythe muttered, though Thea's words made her feel more optimistic.

"It may help to keep something else in mind, darling, as you decide how to handle your father," Sebastian said suddenly, looking cool and composed as he nibbled on a lemon cookie, his soft gray eyes echoing with wisdom.

She often forgot just how long Father Sky and Mother Earth had been around…how many times had they had virtually this same conversation, but with one of her ancestors?

"When Brock was growing up, he didn't have the same support system that you have. He had the other Dryads, but they were young and easily influenced by him, making him their natural leader. But he never really had a father figure, or a mother once Bristol left. And I suppose at that time we didn't realize just how badly he needed guidance and authority to push him in the right direction. But you…you've had Lucian, and Liam, now Capri. And this time we knew we needed to take a more hands on approach so we were more involved in your upbringing as well. So you see love, you can't fault him too much for being what he is. All you can do is try and see things from his point of view and then use it to your advantage."

"That's a good point," Blythe conceded, sighing. "Alright, I'll give it another shot. But if he screws up I'm going to flip my lid and you can damn well believe I'm not giving him a second chance."

"Hey, wait up!"

Turning around in the corridor on her way to dinner, Blythe saw Capri running up to her, her smile cheerful and glowing. Stopping mid-step, she waited for her friend to catch up.

"Hi, honey," she greeted as Capri fell into step with her, attempting to smile in return despite her sour mood.

"I haven't seen much of you lately. How's everything going?"

Shrugging, Blythe kept her eyes focused ahead as they walked, unsure if she felt like discussing it at that moment.

"Things are going good. I'm sorry I haven't had time to see you…I've been busy."

"It's okay. Liam told me you had to fully retrain your dad on everything. I know firsthand how long that can take."

"Yeah, it's a pain in the ass. But what can I do?" Chewing her bottom lip, she tried to push away the agitation she felt. It wasn't going to get her anywhere.

"Have you had a chance to read *Jane Eyre*?" Capri asked, her hands in the pockets of her dress. She could tell Blythe was in a mood and she didn't want to perpetuate it. She had learned in the months of knowing the Fire Dryad that sometimes she preferred to handle things on her own without the help of others. She respected that.

"No, honey...I'm sorry. I haven't yet." Scolding herself, she turned to look at Capri, sincerely sorry. "I was going to, really, but then..."

Seeing her friend's questioning look, Blythe made the instantaneous decision to confide in her. She slowed to a stop, glancing around the corridor to make sure they were alone. She could see Rohan and Serendipity entering the dining hall several yards away, but knew they were out of earshot.

"Well, I went to the library to get the book, and I ran into Nova and Brogan. We had some words, the little brat called me a bitch, and then she said something that bothered me."

"What was it?"

"The gist of it is that they both feel my dad is going to take advantage of our mother. Now personally, I don't really care what happens to that monster, and I especially don't know what he sees in her to begin with. But she was crying, Capri...my stupid little sister who I've barely even spoken to in my entire goddamn life was crying and it irked me in a way that wasn't just anger. It made me sad, too. And I have no idea why."

Capri studied Blythe's face, pulling her hands out of her pockets to rest on her friend's shoulders.

"I think the reason it bothered you is that somewhere inside you know how you would feel in her place. If it was Lucian who was being taken advantage of would you feel helpless and miserable?"

"I would exhaust every option available to help him, and if none of those worked, I'd fight to the death to protect him." She felt her chest tighten at the very thought of it, knowing exactly how she would react. "But yes, I'd be miserable every step of the way."

Capri smiled consolingly, pulling Blythe into her arms. "You feel sorry for Nova. There's nothing wrong with that. And it doesn't make you weak."

"No, but it does make me feel like a fool."

"It shouldn't." Capri pulled away, sorrow in her eyes. "And you should consider that your father returning has meant something much different to Nova than it has to you. She had to sacrifice her father for you to have yours, whether she wanted it that way or not. She had no choice, no say. Now she's trying to protect the only parent she has left against a man she despises."

"Damnit." Cursing herself, Blythe tilted her head back and groaned. "I didn't even think about that. Why the hell didn't I think about that?"

"You were excited about your own father. There's nothing wrong with that. But it might be time to try and mend things with her, let her know that you understand how she feels. It might help you to at least talk with her."

"Yeah, maybe it will." Sighing deeply, Blythe put her arm around Capri and began walking toward the dining hall once again. "C'mon, let's go eat. I want to forget about all of this for awhile."

Her intention had been to clear her mind for the evening and relax with her favorite people, but it was becoming utterly impossible considering the lovely display her father was putting on for the entire group.

Actually, it was more like revolting.

As the whole group gathered in the parlor after dinner like they always did, Blythe seated herself beside Lucian on her favorite comfy sofa and jumped into a debate with him over the true message behind the film *Citizen Kane*. Liam was busy chatting with Clynn about some storm system they were working on, Capri and Rian were snuggled together in the back,

Rhiannon was playing a game of chess with Brogan, Thea and Sebastian were pouring more wine for the Fates, and Brock was busy entertaining the three Muses.

With anyone else it would have been completely innocent, but Blythe knew the moment she heard the burst of giggling laughter that rang like choir bells throughout the room that he wasn't just telling jokes. He was flirting with them. And from the way his arm was draped over Serendipity's shoulders, it looked like his main focus was on her.

Irritated, Blythe scanned the room and spotted Rohan hovering in the corner, nursing a glass of brandy and pretending to read a book, though his eyes were locked on his wife and Brock. His face was flushed red with indignation, and for the first time in her entire life, Blythe found herself in complete sympathy with him. What a shock that was, she thought with an astonished laugh. To know that she actually sided with Rohan on something was revolutionary. Even if she didn't like it, she couldn't help but feel it. It was absolute bullshit the way her father was blatantly hitting on three happily married women. Though he wasn't touching the others the way he was with Serendipity, Blythe vowed at that moment that if Clarity, Lucian's wife, made even one sniff in Brock's direction, she would personally flay her alive.

But, until she saw evidence, she could only stand by and observe. And then she noticed her mother. It wasn't hard, since Nyxa was standing three feet away from Brock with the other Fates, her wine glass clenched so tight that her knuckles were bright white. Her pale face was flushed and her dark eyes looked madder than usual. But that didn't startle Blythe. That was normal and easily handled. No, what startled her was the blatant longing mixed with the anguish in her eyes.

Nova was standing beside their mother, her eyes shifting to Blythe's when she noticed her staring. She did little to hold back the bitterness upon her face.

And those eyes, dark and round and melancholy, held hers for several long moments before Lucian touched her arm, startling her.

"Are you alright, honeypot?" he quietly asked her, his hand resting on her forearm.

"You know what? No, I'm not," she said suddenly, her mind instantly made up on what she wanted to do. "Excuse me."

She rose from the sofa and walked purposefully toward Brock, her head held high. When she reached him, she had to nudge herself by the Muses to put herself in his line of sight.

"I'm sorry, ladies, but I need to have a word with the gentleman. If you'll excuse us," she said regally, smiling as she grabbed her father's arm and proceeded to tug him out of the room.

"Babydoll, can't this wait until later? I was halfway through my joke about the elephant and the mouse."

"Nope, it can't wait." She shut the door to the parlor so they could be alone in the empty dining hall. Whirling around to face him, she jabbed a finger into his chest, her eyes on fire. "You need to shape up. I'm tired of training you and expecting things of you and not having you deliver. Either you give it one hundred percent or you give it nothing. I'm not going to play this game with you. And, to answer the question I know you're dying to ask, I'm not joking."

"I've been trying, Blythe, Jesus. Don't you think maybe you've been pushing me too hard?" Anger flashed in his eyes, coupled with the annoyance on his face. She could tell he thought she was being overdramatic. Well, if he didn't want to take this seriously, then he was going to see just how overdramatic she could be.

"You know, I don't think that asking you to show up on time and actually give a damn about learning the important stuff is really asking all that much. I get that you want time to relax and enjoy being home, but we only meet for five, six hours out of the day. You have plenty of free time as it is. You seriously can't devote even five measly hours to the purpose of your existence?"

"You know, kiddo, I love you, but you're one tough cookie. Maybe it's best if we put this work stuff on hold for awhile. I'll get the kinks out of my system, and then we can get back to work. Is that alright with you?"

She was silent for a moment, fighting tooth and nail to hold back the barrage of unpleasant comments she wanted to hurl his way. Teeth clenched, she sucked in a breath and slowly exhaled before speaking again.

"Fine. One week, no more. Goodnight."

She turned on her heel and left the room, leaving him behind looking both pleased and confused by how easily she had given in.

The truth was, she was worn out. Worn out from him, worn out from worrying about her sister, worn out from trying to understand everyone else's feelings while ignoring her own. But it was just downright impossible for her to ignore her own feelings, her own heart. She was too damn stubborn to let that happen.

She slammed the door to her bedroom and threw herself down upon the bed, praying for sleep to come quickly so she could just stop thinking.

Sleep was not restful. In fact, her dreams were perhaps more chaotic than her reality. In them she was a warrior, a general perched on a regal black horse decked out in all kinds of shiny, glittery chains and armor. She wore war paint all over her body and her red curly hair circled her face like a bloody halo.

Around her, men screamed while other men died. Her soldiers, her warriors, fought valiantly at her command, hurling their wicked swords into the fray with violence in their eyes. She herself was fighting, lashing out with a whip made of fire, scorching any who dare come close to her. Her battle cry rang out against the smoke filled sky, the flag of her allegiance billowing beside her like a beacon. Yes, this was her fight, her battle, her legacy. She would do everything she could to protect it.

But when a dark black mass of smoke approached from over the horizon, coming closer at speeds that seemed impossible, she heard her men scream in terror instead of exhilaration as they turned and ran. Determined to stand her ground, she kept her frightened horse in place and faced the onslaught of mysterious darkness alone.

And when it swallowed her whole the last thing she heard was her own scream.

Jolting awake, she clutched at the blankets around her and panted, her chest heaving uncontrollably as she fought to regain control of her mind. Sweat dripped down her face and her back, causing her shirt to stick to her skin. Real terror gripped her heart and it took all the strength she had to fight it back.

Chilled to the bone, she collapsed against her pillows and covered her face with her hands, her breathing shallow and her throat tight.

She had never in her life had a dream quite like that. Correction, she had never in her life had a *nightmare* quite like that.

Repulsed by the images of death and destruction that kept replaying over and over in her mind, she threw off her blankets and padded into her bathroom, splashing cold water on her face and neck.

Stripping off her shirt, she threw it on the ground and quickly grabbed another, wanting to rid herself of the sweat. Annoyed that she was still shaky, she headed back into the bedroom and paused in front of her clock.

Midnight. The witching hour.

Because she no longer felt tired, she threw on her robe and decided to go outside for some fresh air. Maybe a walk in the moonlight would help clear her mind.

Quietly shutting her bedroom door, she padded down the hallway, passing Liam's and Capri's rooms as silently as she could so as not to wake them. She went down the stairs and out into the main corridor, her eyes adjusting to the darkness.

At night only some of the torches were lit so most of the lighting came from the moonlight. The white beams cascaded through the stained glass windows at either end of the corridor, making the stone castle seem mysterious and more than a little eerie.

Clutching her robe tighter around her, she headed toward the atrium. When she heard a shuffling sound and a muffled giggle, she paused, instantly thinking of Capri and Rian.

Curious, but not wanting to disturb them, she leaned around the corner carefully, just enough so she could see into the atrium.

At first she couldn't see much of anything, but then she saw two figures pressed up against the stone wall, silhouetted in the moonlight. When she looked closer, she was momentarily confused. Rian wasn't that tall...

And when she heard the man's murmuring voice, and the woman's delighted giggle, she felt her heart fall straight to the floor even as her blood began to boil with fury.

Incensed, she lifted her palm and shot fire into the torches, igniting them with flames that matched her anger and instantly chased the shadows away.

Now she could see more than just the silhouettes of her father and Serendipity, and she noted with disgust that he had one hand up the Muse's blouse and the other hiked up high on her thigh as he pressed against her.

They jolted apart, both staring in disbelief at Blythe who now stood at the head of the corridor, her hands on her hips and her head shaking in revulsion.

"This is just terrific, isn't it?" she snarled, her eyes on fire.

When she saw Serendipity struggle to fix her clothing and smooth out her hair, unbridled fear and embarrassment on her face, Blythe couldn't help but think of Rohan and what this would do to him.

Brock glared angrily at Blythe, his hands lifting and lowering. When she saw him clench his fists, she silently dared him to try.

"This is none of your business, Blythe. Go on up to bed."

"You know what? This is my business, dad. You want to know why?"

When he didn't say anything, she continued.

"I never thought I'd say this, but you're fooling around on my mother, and it pisses me off. And Serendipity's fooling around on Rohan, which also pisses me off. Funny, because I can't stand my mother or Rohan, but I'm going to have to tell them both in order to have a clear conscience."

"You can't!" Serendipity shrieked, her face drained of color as she jolted toward Blythe, her arms outstretched in an urgent plea. "Please, don't tell my husband. This was a onetime thing, it doesn't mean anything."

But now that Serendipity was closer, Blythe could easily smell her perfume. "Liar. I've been smelling you on him for days. God, you're both so pathetic."

Shaking her head, she turned away, not able to look at them any longer. This was the last nail in the coffin. The straw that broke the camel's back. The shot that stopped her heart. She had no reason to trust him now. In only one week he had obliterated any faith she had in him. And, even though it both terrified her and repulsed her, he had recklessly broken her heart.

Chapter Five

When morning came, she was thousands of miles away.

In one of her admittedly weaker moments, she'd decided the only thing she wanted to do was get the hell off of Euphora. She didn't want to face her father again or see her mother when she heard the news. Nor did she want to see Rohan have his greatest fear confirmed. She didn't want to be comforted by those who loved her, nor did she want to have to retell the story a dozen times as the gossip mill ran its course.

And so she had done the only logical thing. She'd written a long letter to Thea, explaining what she had witnessed and that she needed to get away for awhile as a result of it. She didn't say how long.

Although she still felt the anger and betrayal in her heart, she knew she couldn't stay away for long. Lucian, Liam and Capri would be worried about her. She couldn't let them down.

But she couldn't ignore her own needs either.

Sunny skies welcomed her as she walked the streets of Hollywood, clad in a summer dress the color of ripe yellow squash with a thin rainbow scarf draped around her neck and strappy silver sandals on her feet.

Hundreds of people walked the streets with her, chattering amongst themselves, laughing, smiling, enjoying the sunshine. Californians were always happy, it seemed. It must be all that vitamin D.

Determined to soak up some rays for herself, she shaded her eyes with big, rounded glasses and tilted her face towards the sky.

Cars honked from the street, music warbled out of a nearby sidewalk bistro, Spiderman and Jack Sparrow took pictures with the tourists, and giant gold stars glittered in the sunlight at her feet.

What a magical place this was, she thought, feeling content for the first time in days. What a relief that life was being lived, glamorous and untamed, by those who couldn't give a damn what else was going on in the world. They lived here, in this paradise, where bad things never happened. War never reached the star studded hills of Hollywood, and people rarely discussed anything more than the latest film, fashion trend, or hip dance song.

It was all so fast paced...so anonymous and thrilling. No one knew her and no one cared. She could roam the streets for hours, explore the shops, and maybe catch a movie at the theater. Or she could take a bus and hop on down to the beach, where she could mull around the pier or lay in the sand and really soak up some sun.

Here the world was her oyster, and it was no wonder she felt so at home.

But this wasn't her home, and she knew she couldn't stay. But that didn't mean she couldn't enjoy herself while she was here.

And that, she thought with a devious grin, meant she was going to hit up the clubs and indulge in the nightlife.

He knew her the moment she entered the room. Not only could he feel it in his blood, but he could see it in her face, her hair, her eyes. Those amber eyes, so cocky and defiant, glowing impossibly bright despite the darkness of the club. Oh, yes, he'd known it was her within seconds.

But what to do about it, he wondered as he watched her tease some poor fellow by lighting his cigarette with her thumb. How to approach her...how to make himself known without endangering himself.

He was a wanted man, after all. Not that it meant much to him. He'd considered himself a wanted man for a long time now; it made life a lot more thrilling when you lived on the run.

He knew Thea wanted his head, however, he wasn't going to give her the satisfaction. He wasn't going to give *any* of them the satisfaction of seeing his demise. No...he was leagues beyond them, wiser despite his "handicap" as they so generously described it.

What they didn't understand was that being part demon didn't hinder the Dryad in him...no, it only enhanced it. He was powerful, intelligent, and wicked. And because he saw all three of those things in the eyes of his niece, he felt instantly drawn to her.

He couldn't resist, couldn't help himself...he had to have a piece of her, had to gulp down her brilliant vitality like water until he had soothed this ache of longing in his blackened heart.

He sincerely hoped she wouldn't mind.

His name was Duncan. A silly name for a guy, she thought with a smirk as she watched him stare at his cigarette with baffled eyes. But he was cute, and he and his friends were buying the drinks, so what did she care what his name was.

"Honey, it was just a trick, don't look so frightened," she cooed, stroking her fingertips down his tanned cheek. When his eyes met hers, she saw him forget all about the cigarette. He shifted his hand until it rested suggestively on her thigh.

"Girl, nothing scares me. Why don't we go dance?" Duncan winked at her out of clear blue eyes.

"Sure, why the hell not." Blythe shrugged as she gulped down the last of her appletini, letting him lead her onto the dance floor.

The song was a fast paced hip hop beat that pounded through her entire body, skimming through her veins and shuddering in her heart. Above her, lights shifted and circled and zoomed in all directions, so that they flashed and highlighted every single person moving in this sea of wild and untamed beasts.

She let Duncan put his hands on her hips and grind against her, the vodka she'd just finished leaving her feeling loose and reckless and free. This was exactly what she had needed, a superficial human ritual that meant so little in the grand scheme of things...yet felt so exhilarating.

Feeling someone in front of her, she opened her eyes and saw a man dancing with her. He was a bit older, but he had moves. Her eyebrow cocked as she smirked at the dark haired stranger, who pulled her away from her previous dance partner and into his arms. The move was rough—a bit rougher than she liked—but she figured what the hell. She was here to have fun, wasn't she?

And he was a terrific dancer, much better than Duncan. He turned her around so she was facing away from him, and she felt his hands running up and down her body. Pursing her lips, she decided that despite his talent for dancing, she didn't appreciate being man handled quite to this degree. She turned around, prepared to casually say goodbye and slink off to get another drink, when he pulled her against him again and this time clamped his mouth down upon hers.

Indignation tore through her as he kissed her, but even though she tried to pull away, he was much stronger.

Fear joined her rage, but when she suddenly felt his tongue inside her mouth begin to shift and change, something much deeper and darker than fear hit her.

She could feel his tongue split at the tip and slim down until it was snakelike, coiling inside of her mouth. Disgust and terror had her shoving as hard as she could against him, and she would have bit him if he hadn't suddenly been thrown to the floor.

Gasping and furious, she was prepared to kick the creep's ass when she realized he had disappeared into thin air. The man who'd thrown him suddenly grabbed her roughly around the arm and dragged her out of the club.

It wasn't until they'd reached the exit doors that she came to her senses and kicked him sharply in the foot with her stiletto heel.

He stumbled a bit, grunted in pain, but didn't let go.

"*Back the hell off!*" she screamed, swinging with her fist this time, barely missing the man's face.

"Goddamnit, will you stop resisting? We need to get the hell out of here."

"We?" Blythe tried to dig her heels into the ground to slow him down, but he was already dragging her into a cab. "I don't even know you!"

Without responding, he squeezed in beside her and slammed the car door.

He gave directions to the cab driver, then tilted his head back and rubbed his face, looking incredibly stressed out.

Wondering how in the hell she had ended up in this situation, she tapped the shoulder of the cab driver as they pulled away from the curb.

"Excuse me sir, this man has kidnapped me. I need you to call the police."

She was about to smack the cab driver upside the head when he didn't answer, only to have the stranger stop her.

"Do you have no appreciation whatsoever?" he said, staring at her indignantly. "I just saved your life."

"Oh, excuse me if for some reason I don't constitute punching some guy caveman style and then dragging me off like the winning prize to be saving my life. I was handling the situation just fine by myself." She tossed her hair back before giving him a good, long look. In the darkness of the cab, she couldn't make out much of his face. "Who the hell are you, anyway?"

"It was a demon, not just some guy," the man corrected her, crossing his arms across his chest and stretching out his long legs as best he could. "And it sure didn't look like the situation was handled."

"Screw you, asshole! I don't need some man coming to my aide. I was about to bite that creep's tongue and…" Her thoughts smacked right into a solid brick wall as the memory returned fully. Her face paled and her eyes widened in horror. "Holy shit, demon? Snakelike tongue…oh, goddamnit!"

Feeling her stomach revolt in disgust, she covered her mouth and closed her eyes, fighting to forget just how horrible that tongue had felt. She was grateful that the man next to her kept his mouth shut. She needed time to compose herself.

As the sharp edges of shock dulled, she took a deep breath and looked at him again.

"You didn't answer my question. Who are you?"

He tilted his head to stare at her, his mouth forming a knowing smirk. His left eyebrow cocked and he made a motion of tipping a non-existent hat.

"Jackson Murphy, ma'am."

Surprise flickered over her face but delight warmed her eyes. It was nice to see the face behind the voice that had so intrigued her.

"Well, well. We meet at last, bounty hunter." She stretched out her hand to shake his. When he took it, she couldn't help but notice the calluses on his skin.

He had nice hands. Long fingered and wide, rough but clean cut. They spoke of a man accustomed to hard laborious work, but who could appreciate the need for presentation in an environment that required it as a standard. That made him adaptable, but she had the distinct feeling he was only that way when it suited him.

The cab passed under a bright intersection and she briefly caught a flash of his face. Well, hello there, handsome, was the first thing that came to her mind. Now she knew why Thea took such a particular liking to this particular bounty hunter…he was quite easy on the eyes. At least, if you were into the rough and tumble cowboy sort.

He had a hard face, more lines and edges than curves, with sharp green eyes housed under a brow currently creased in irritation or amusement, she wasn't sure which. His honey blonde hair was combed back in waves streaked liberally by the sun, ending in a curl at the nape of his neck.

"I'm taking you back to my hotel," he began, releasing his hand from hers and focusing his attention on the outside view through the window. "We'll stay the night and then tomorrow morning I'm taking you back to Euphora."

"Hmm…that sounds nice, but I'm going to have to regretfully decline," Blythe replied politely, turning to look out her window.

"Unfortunately, you don't have a choice."

"Fortunately, I do."

"No, you don't."

"It's a free country, I can do whatever I want."

"You're not a citizen of this great country, so no, you can't. You are technically an illegal alien with no paperwork or identification and so help me I will take you to I.C.E., tell them you're from Canada and have you deported. Not much fun up in Canada, but the demon problem isn't so bad."

"Just who do you think you are?" She turned to face him, eyes narrow and temper flaring.

"I'm the man Mother Earth asked to find and bring home her Fire Dryad. That is you, right?" Amusement flashed in his eyes as his head tilted in her direction.

"Thea asked you to find me?" Now she was really pissed. Apparently her explanation about needing to get the hell away had been blatantly ignored.

"Yes'm. Now, we can do this the easy way and go back to my hotel, get you your own room, and leave bright and early tomorrow morning for Euphora. Or, we can do this the hard way and I'll handcuff you to the nice comfy chair beside my bed, and tomorrow morning I'll drag you kicking and screaming back to Euphora."

With a snort, she rolled her eyes. "You think you have this all figured out, don't you? And what if I just burn the shit out of that handsome face of yours and run away? Does that fit under the 'hard way' category?"

Chuckling, he shook his head and reached down toward his feet. Blythe watched him as he sat back, and then calmly and steadily aimed an old west style .44 revolver at her heart.

She kept her eyes trained on his, not glancing at the gun glinting silver in the glow of the passing streetlights. It didn't scare her; in fact, he'd just earned her respect.

"Well played, cowboy." She grinned, shifting to rest her elbow on the top of the seat so she could get a better view of him as he slipped the revolver back into his ankle holster. "So, how did you happen to find me in that nightclub?"

"Coincidence. I followed Dante there."

Her breath caught and she gave him a bug-eyed stare.

"He was there? So close? Why didn't you catch him?"

"Yeah, he was there. You should know, you were kissing him." He glanced back out the window as the cab parked in front of the hotel. "Let's hold off on making a scene until we're safely up in the hotel room."

He held open the door of the cab for her to follow. It took every ounce of control she could muster to clear the red from her vision so she wouldn't scream. Of all the low, disgusting, vile…

Cursing herself, she took a deep breath and climbed out of the cab, refusing to accept his hand even when she nearly tripped over her own two feet from her trembling knees.

Shrugging, he paid the cab driver and led the way into the hotel, where he proceeded to book a room for her. Leaning against the counter, she rested her chin in her palm and watched him.

He had an efficient, businesslike way about him that intrigued her. She decided to focus on that, and other things about him, to take her mind off the horror she knew she was going to have to come to terms with at some point in the near future.

"You certainly are a tall, cool drink of water, cowboy." She managed a grin as she watched him slip his wallet out of the back pocket of his faded jeans and pull out cash for the room. He ignored her statement, but she thought she saw a hint of a smirk cross his face.

"Here's your key. I have a copy as well. The room is right across from mine," he said curtly, slapping the key card in her hand before turning around and leading the way to the elevators. She rolled her eyes as she followed him, then leaned against the carpeted walls of the elevator as it took them to the fifth floor.

He was silent as he led the way toward their rooms, his pace brisk but not rushed. His black leather boots thudded against the carpet, and she found herself disappointed that he wasn't wearing spurs. It would have suited him so well.

He paused in front of her room and slipped the key card into the lock, pushing open the door so she could enter. She whisked past him and examined the room.

It was relatively small, but seemed cozy enough. The large king bed was covered in white linens and had an oversized mahogany headboard with matching end tables. A matching armoire sat across from the bed, housing a flat screen television set and a mini bar she expected would be stock full of all kinds of goodies she imagined would cost him an arm and a leg if she decided to take advantage of them.

She crossed the room and peered out of the hanging curtains, watching the city lights shimmer in the darkness of night. All around her, Los Angeles pulsed with life. Just how close had she been to losing hers?

"So that was Dante," she murmured, mostly to herself, her unfocused eyes staring out the window. She heard Jackson come into the room and shut the door before approaching her.

"That is why you need to go home, Blythe. It's not safe for you or any of the others while he knows we're after him," he replied, his voice steady and even. She shifted her eyes to watch him in the reflection of the glass, wondering if he expected her to rage and hiss and throw something. The truth was, while she certainly felt like doing all of those things, she couldn't quite muster the strength.

"How did he get away? It was like one minute he was there, and the next, poof, he was gone," she asked, turning to face him, her eyes sharpening.

"He transformed." Crossing his arms over his chest, he watched her with a guarded expression.

"He changed into a demon." Understanding dawning on her, she tried to grasp just exactly what that meant. "Did you lose him in the crowd?"

"Unfortunately. But he'll be back now that he knows you're here. He won't be able to resist seeing you again, especially since your earlier rendezvous was so rudely interrupted."

"So then why send me away? Why not use me as bait?" She stepped toward him, the idea taking root. "In fact, we should go back to the club right now, see if he's still hanging around."

She was already halfway toward the door before he grabbed her arm to hold her back.

"Just where do you think you're going?" he asked as he whirled her around to face him, impatience flashing in his eyes.

"I'm going back to the club to find that bastard and make him pay. You can either come with me or not. I can handle this by myself."

She tried to wrench her arm free from his grasp, but his hold only tightened.

"And just what are you going to do if you find him?"

Glaring up at him, she couldn't help the sneer that came from instinct. "I'm going to flay him alive while he begs me for a mercy that I will never give him."

Impressed more than he wanted to admit, he released her. "As much as I can appreciate the violent nature of your ambitions, the likelihood of you getting the upper hand on him in a fight is slim to none. He's extremely dangerous."

"Oh, but a big strong man like you is perfectly suited to take him down," she spat, fisting her hands on her hips. "And a poor little girl like me has no place taking on a sadistic half demon, is that right?"

"You can pull the feminism card if you want, but I'm still going to stick to the cold, hard facts here. He's dangerous and you're not trained in fighting demons. Much less a Dryad/demon hybrid who is capable of much more than you can even imagine."

"So, because I'm not *trained*, I get packaged up and shipped back home like some helpless, fragile child? I'll have you know that I'm a hell of a lot tougher than I look, and I'll take you or anybody else on without a moment's hesitation. So go ahead, give me your best shot."

Cocking her chin up in challenge, she stared him down, her lips curled in a snarl. She looked every bit the defiant spitfire Thea had warned him she would be. Tough, stubborn, argumentative and feisty. Not exactly what he felt like dealing with at two in the morning when his head was pounding and he was craving a hot shower to clear his mind.

"Alright, if you want to do this the hard way." He stood still for a moment, his eyes locked on hers before he suddenly moved toward her, attempting to pull her arms behind her so he could cuff her. Instead, she swiftly dodged out of the way, jumping onto the bed much quicker than he'd had given her credit for. Before he could do more than duck, she'd shot a fireball the size of a basketball straight at his face.

"Damnit woman, are you crazy?" he shouted, feeling his head to see if any hair had been singed by the flames. Behind him, a gaping hole smoldered in the wall.

To his amazement, she immediately doubled over with laughter, the husky sound filling the room as she collapsed onto the bed.

Glaring, he checked the hole in the wall, wondering how in the hell he was going to explain it to the hotel.

When she only continued to laugh, he whirled around, beyond irritated with her.

"What in God's name are you laughing about? You could have taken my head off!"

"I told you…not to…mess with…me," she managed between laughs, clutching her stomach as she lay on her back. "God, your face was classic!"

"Well I hope you're proud of yourself because not only have you shaved years off my life, you'll also have to explain to Thea why she has to reimburse me for the charges the hotel is going to force me to pay for this goddamn hole in the wall!"

"Oh, calm the hell down, cowboy." She chuckled, rising to a sitting position. "It's not that big of a deal."

He only stared at her, wondering how the hell he'd let Thea convince him he needed to bring this psycho back to Euphora. "I'm going to go because I don't think I can stand being in this room with you for another second. Don't bother trying to sneak out. I'll be watching. See you in the morning."

He stormed out of the room, slamming the door shut behind him.

Smirking to herself, Blythe laid back down and pictured him going into his own room, all pissed off and fussy.

She liked seeing him all riled up. He was much more interesting that way. Though she had to admit, he'd caught her interest from the start even when he'd been efficient and boring.

Too bad she probably wouldn't ever see him again, she thought as she rose and checked outside the window again, scanning the streets below. He was a fool if he thought she was going to just hang out till morning and let him drag her back to Euphora.

Whirling around, she grabbed her purse from the side of the bed and peered out the peep hole in the door. Seeing no sign of him, she slowly inched the door open, wincing at the slight creak it made, before slipping out into the hallway.

Biting her lip to hold back a grin, she slowly closed the door behind her and eyed the room directly across the hall, where she imagined he was checking for burns so he'd have more to bitch about.

Sorry cowboy, she thought wistfully, blowing a kiss toward the door. Until we meet again.

With that, she took off down the hallway, not even bothering to look back.

Chapter Six

She stepped out of the elevator and made a beeline toward the exit, head held high with a distinct feeling of success.

It was too bad she couldn't hang around with the bounty hunter any longer. But she now had a purpose greater than the one that had brought her to Los Angeles in the first place. She was going to find Dante. And when she did, he better pray that he died quickly.

She reached out to push open the large, glass doors of the hotel, only to stop short as she noticed Jackson standing outside, leaning against a streetlight pole, arms crossed over his chest.

Cursing under her breath, she had a brief thought of trying to slip past as quickly as possible just in case he didn't notice, but all hope was squashed the moment his eyes met hers.

"Clever, but not clever enough," he drawled, his head now covered by a black Stetson that shadowed his face. "You didn't really think I was that dumb, did you?"

"I was hoping," she told him as she sauntered over, feeling more amused than angry. Perhaps she hadn't given him as much credit as he deserved. "So were you gonna hang out here all night?"

"No." He smirked, eyeing her from under the brim of his hat. "Because I knew it wouldn't take you more than ten minutes to try and vacate the premises."

She opened her mouth to speak, only to realize he was dead right. She hadn't given a single thought to waiting a few hours until he might be asleep to sneak out. She had just gone for it. Acknowledging how easily she'd been played, she couldn't help but laugh.

"You're good, cowboy. Very good." On impulse, she reached over and tipped up his hat so she could see his eyes better. He stood still as a statue, though his lips curved just slightly as his eyebrows lifted in amusement.

"Does my hat bother you?"

"Not at all, I just wanted to see that handsome face of yours better." She bit her lower lip in consideration as she stared at him. "Why don't we get a drink at the hotel bar? I'm not very tired and I could use some company to take my mind off things."

For a moment he didn't say anything, he just watched her with eyes that seemed to penetrate right through her, as if searching for an angle he didn't like.

"I'm going to have to pass," he said finally, his expression casual as he tilted his hat back into place. "But you run along and have fun. I'll see you in the morning."

Sincerely disappointed but determined not to show it, she flashed a bright smile.

"Perhaps. Goodnight, Jackson Murphy."

"You can call me Jax."

Charmed, she studied him. "Alright. Goodnight, Jax."

"Goodnight."

He watched her walk away, hips swaying in that tiny figure of hers, that shock of red hair glowing in the light of the hotel lobby as she headed toward the bar, alone.

She was a spitfire, alright. A crazy, arrogant, careless and undeniably sexy spitfire.

She awoke the next morning to loud banging that thundered in her head and rattled her weary brain. When she realized it was someone knocking on her hotel room door, she got out of bed and threw it open, prepared to rip the asshole's face off.

"What in God's name do you want?" she growled, glaring at Jax through gritty eyes.

"Get dressed. I'll go check us out, we'll have some breakfast and then we're out of here," he ordered, trying to ignore the fact that she was clad only in her undergarments. Her hair was a mass of tangled curls on top of her head, and her foxy eyes were glaring at him as though she wanted to chop him up into little pieces. Despite the threat, he was particularly amused by it, and her.

"Fine. Get out of my face. I'll meet you downstairs."

"Don't keep me waiting," he called out as she slammed the door in his face.

Fortunately for him, she wasn't one to waste time. She took a quick shower, let her hair air dry and slipped into the extra cotton dress she'd packed in her purse.

Within fifteen minutes, she was downstairs on the hunt for the breakfast buffet.

When she found it, she could have wept. There was a full coffee bar, pancake and waffle center, muffins galore, scrambled eggs, hash browns, crispy bacon, succulent ham, sausage links, all kinds of toast, yogurt, orange juice…

When she sat down beside him at the table he'd chosen near the back, he stared at the mounds of food on her plate in pure shock.

"Lord, you got enough food?"

She grinned at him. "I couldn't decide. So I got some of everything. I have a big appetite."

"Little thing like you?" He gestured to her trim physique, blown away. "It's a wonder you're not eight hundred pounds."

Shrugging, she forked up a bite of pancakes doused in syrup, and nearly groaned. "God, this is good."

Reaching for the giant mug of coffee she'd brought to the table, she gulped down a few sips, and sighed.

"The coffee's good, too."

Lifting his own mug of coffee, he eyed her curiously. "So Thea didn't specify why you left home in the first place."

Blythe hesitated, a piece of bacon halfway toward her mouth. Her eyes narrowed as she lowered it back to the plate.

"That's not really your business," she informed him. "Besides, it's complicated."

"Alright." He cut into the corned beef hash on his plate and scooped some into his mouth, averting his attention from her as he chewed, focusing instead on the morning's paper.

Pursing her lips, she found that his sudden indifference about hearing the story only made her want to tell it more. She waited nearly two full minutes before the urge to share it was too strong to resist.

"Okay, so it's like this," she began, wagging her fork at him as he slowly glanced up at her. "Fifteen years ago my father was framed for a crime he didn't commit, and now, due to recent events that I'm sure you're familiar with, he has been exonerated and has returned home. Well, he's decided that he would rather sleep around with both my mother and another man's wife instead of giving me the time of day, which, as you can imagine, pissed me off. So I left, at least for a little while, to clear my head."

"Doesn't sound so complicated to me," he replied, taking another sip of coffee.

Pushing the eggs around on her plate, she considered his words. "I guess it is kind of straightforward, isn't it? Though it sure seemed like a lot while I was there."

"Have you told him you're upset about it?"

She snorted, her lips flashing in a quick smile. "Trust me, he knows. You seriously think someone like me can hold back when something pisses me off?"

"No, guess not." He smirked as he leaned back, finishing his coffee and watching her casually. "We should head out now."

Sighing, she pushed aside her empty plate and downed her coffee. Setting down the mug, she wiped her lips with the back of her hand and shot him a spry grin. "I guess I don't have much of a choice, now do I?"

Amused, he stood up and threw down a few dollars on the table for tip. "No, you don't."

She followed him outside, marveling at the rays of warm sunshine that shone down around the tall buildings surrounding them. People crowded the sidewalks and cars jammed the streets, making this a Mecca of urban life. She was going to miss it, especially since she had a feeling she wouldn't be seeing it for some time.

He led her to a small cluster of trees that acted as an entrance courtyard for one of the commercial buildings. Approaching one of the more hidden trees in the back, he stopped in front of it and put his hand against the bark.

Without hesitation she followed suit, looking bored as she glanced around one last time at the streets of Los Angeles.

When he started to speak, she found herself almost instantly forgetting all about the city.

"Mother, I am a loyal servant who requests to see you. Grant me entrance, and I will always be true."

Because his words differed from those she normally used, she was intrigued. This was a side of her world that she hadn't experienced and she briefly wondered how someone like him had come to accept the existence of Euphora and those who lived there.

Moments before the flash of gold took them far from Los Angeles, his eyes met hers, cool green into gilded amber, and the impact it had on her was incendiary. Lord, he had this intensity underneath all that cool resolve. The urge to know him, to know everything there was about him, jolted through her unexpectedly, taking her off guard.

And then the world went dark, only to brighten again as the shrouded mist disappeared, revealing the meadow shimmering in morning sunlight.

Tearing her eyes away from him, she glanced toward the entrance gates of her home.

Unnerved, she began to walk toward those gates, Jax at her side. He didn't say anything, for which she was grateful. She was having trouble fighting the whirlwind of emotions coursing through her, ranging from anxious to furious to resentful to relieved. She had missed her friends, that much she could admit to herself. But was she ready to face her father?

She lifted her palm to the entrance gates and watched with unseeing eyes as they melted away at her touch. When at first she didn't move, Jax gently pressed against the small of her back, shaking her out of her reverie. Determined not to sulk, she tried to smile as they walked through the gates, following the cobblestone path.

Thea and Sebastian appeared out of the castle and raced toward them, a few others following close behind.

Preparing herself for Mother Earth's wrath, Blythe dug her heels into the cobblestone walkway and stood her ground, feeling more defiant by forcing Thea to come to her. Stopping beside her, Jax watched her out of the corner of his eye, noting the intensity on her face.

"Blythe, thank God." Thea sighed as she wrapped Blythe into a tight hug.

Shaken and obviously confused by the warm welcome, Blythe hugged her back, her eyes meeting Sebastian's over Thea's shoulder. His were clouded with concern and worry.

When Thea pulled away, she cupped Blythe's face in her hands and studied her.

"Did he hurt you? Jax told us what happened last night."

"No, Thea, I'm fine." Releasing herself from Thea's grasp, she turned to Jax with a nod. "Cowboy here scared him away for me."

"Did you see where he went?" Sebastian asked, eyeing Jax hopefully.

"No, I didn't. But I'm willing to bet he hasn't gone far, not yet anyway. He's hoping he'll see Blythe again."

Before Thea could respond, Lucian and Liam approached. Seeing them, Blythe ran to Lucian and into his arms.

"Blythe." He shuddered once as he held her close, breathing in her scent as if to prove to himself that she was unscathed. Pulling away, he tried to smile. "You had us so worried, honeypot."

"I'm fine, really. It's no big deal." Though the look in his eyes shook her to the core.

"You're such a brat," Liam told her playfully as he grabbed her for a tight hug. She hadn't realized just how worried she'd made them all. It made her feel extremely guilty.

"Shut up, idiot," she replied, punching him in the shoulder when he released her. "I was only gone for one day."

"Yes but you conveniently neglected to tell us where you were going or how long you would be gone. What if something had happened to you down there? I can't protect your stubborn ass when you're God knows where, running rampant with the humans."

"Liam, we've gone over this a million times. I can take care of myself." But even as she said it, the memory of carelessly letting her guard down and Dante getting so close sent a violent chill down her spine.

She noticed his eyes were suddenly staring at Jax, who was speaking quietly to Thea and Sebastian. "You want to meet the bounty hunter?"

"Yes...yes I do," Liam decided, protectively wrapping his arm around her and leading her toward Jax.

"Sorry to interrupt, but everyone wants to meet you," Blythe cut in, her eyes dancing. "Jax, this is my brother of sorts, Liam. He's a Water Dryad."

Jax held out his hand politely, though his eyes were guarded. He didn't like the confrontational way the Water Dryad was staring at him.

Taking the offered hand, Liam smiled coolly.

"So you're the man who saved my sister's life."

"If you want to call it that, then sure." Jax nodded as they released hands.

"I suppose I should thank you."

"No need," Jax replied curtly, crossing his arms over his chest. Blythe watched as he caught a glimpse of something in the distance, and the genuine smile that came over his face startled her. "Excuse me," he mumbled as he suddenly walked away.

Confused, Blythe turned and saw Rian and Capri emerging from the castle, making their way to the gathered crowd. Jax headed straight for them, and to her surprise, shook Rian's hand and gave him a one armed hug. She saw him shake Capri's hand, then launch into some kind of discussion with the Fury.

"Well, well," she murmured, biting her lip as she watched the situation unfold. "I think it would be downright un-sisterly of me to not rescue Capri from what must be dreadfully boring man talk. Excuse me, Liam."

Though he didn't look happy about it, he let her go, keeping a close eye on her. He didn't like strange men on his turf–end of story. And while Jackson Murphy may be a good man, he was still a man. And he had a sister to look out for.

As Blythe approached, Capri smiled brightly and rushed toward her, crushing her in a hug.

"Oh, I was so worried," she confessed, blushing as she pulled away. "I know that I shouldn't have been, but I was."

"I know." Blythe couldn't help but smile as she squeezed her friend's hand. "So, what do you think of our bounty hunter?"

"Oh, well." Capri bit back a grin, trying to contain her excitement. "He seems wonderful, but the best part is how happy Rian is to see him. They're old friends, you know."

"I didn't know that, actually." Intrigued, Blythe watched the Fury and the bounty hunter as they talked. Both were grinning ear-to-ear like fools, which was a marvel in itself. "Wow, cowboy looks real cheerful, doesn't he?"

"They're talking about this new tracking device that Rian's invented," Capri gushed, her smoky eyes lit with pride. "He's going to let Jax borrow it!"

"No shit?" Intrigued, she suddenly decided that she needed to get in on this invention. Especially since she was still determined to find Dante. "What does this device do?"

"Well, I only know the basics, but essentially it does what the Furies can do naturally. It senses the presence of different kinds of beings based upon how you set it. There's a Dryad setting, a Fate setting, Fury, Muse, demon…etc. He invented it for the Enforcers to use, but he's letting Jax try it first!"

"Huh, that sounds pretty cool." She *definitely* needed to get her hands on that device. Blythe grinned conspiratorially at Capri. "You don't suppose he has more than one, does he? Maybe one I can borrow for awhile?"

"No, just the one…but what do you need it for?"

"Because once I figure out another way to get out of here, I'm going to need it to find Dante."

"Blythe!" Startled, Capri pressed her hand to her heart, her soft eyes wide. "You can't! No…no, I won't let you go."

She stomped her foot down as if to make her point, her chin up stubbornly and her mouth set in a firm line as she crossed her arms over her chest in what was intended to be an authoritative gesture. Behind them, Rian and Jax both watched curiously.

"Honey, even you won't be able to stop me." Blythe patted Capri's arm gently, amused by her quiet friend's outburst.

"What's wrong, Capri?" Rian asked, wrapping his arm around his girlfriend and eyeing Blythe distrustfully.

"I told Blythe that I won't let her leave again."

"She's a big girl, she can make her own decisions. Even if they're not in her best interest," he reminded her, still watching Blythe. "And if she chooses not to listen to the advice of those who care about her, then that's her choice."

"Exactly, thank you Rian." Blythe nodded in agreement, beaming at him.

Jax just crossed his arms over his chest and smirked at Blythe, laughter in his eyes as he watched her. She caught his eye and stared him down.

"What's so funny?"

"You just drive everyone around here bonkers, don't you?" he commented, enjoying the way her eyes turned to slits at the insult.

"I do not."

"Seems like everyone was real stressed out because you high-tailed it out of here yesterday," he pointed out.

"Yeah, well, that's because no one around here knows how to take a chill pill," she reasoned, huffing out a breath to blow her bangs out of her eyes. "I was perfectly fine, okay? Maybe I made one itsy bitsy bad decision, so sue me. It's not like I–"

"Blythe? You're back. Who's this?"

Brock appeared behind Jax, his face strained as he walked toward her.

"Shit," she cursed under her breath, averting her eyes from him. "Shit...shit...shit."

Jax noted the pain and fury that flashed over her face the second she'd heard the man's voice, which led him to assume that this must be her father. Giving her time to compose herself, he turned around to face Brock, and held out his hand.

"Jackson Murphy, bounty hunter. And you are?"

"Brock, Fire Dryad." They grasped hands for a brief shake, eyes meeting. The concern and anger he saw struck him as normal for any father whose daughter had run away. But then again, this was the same man who'd sent her running away in the first place.

"Well, I'm back." Blythe threw out her arms melodramatically, as if to show that she was unharmed. "No need to worry anymore. Now, if you'll excuse me, I'm gonna go take a nap or something."

Without a glance at her father, she turned on her heel and would have gotten away if Thea hadn't called her back.

"Blythe, we need to speak with you, please."

Clenching her fists, she whirled around and stalked right past her father and toward Thea. Jax followed her, leaving Brock standing beside Rian and Capri, looking puzzled and frustrated.

"Yes?" Looking bored and irritated, she planted her fists on her hips.

"Jax, this concerns you as well."

"Yes, Thea." He came to a stop beside Blythe, his hands tucked into his jeans pockets.

"Based upon the information you shared with us today, Jax, Sebastian and I have made a difficult decision that I think will ultimately lead to us capturing Dante sooner rather than later." She paused, acknowledging the doubt that came into his eyes. He wasn't going to like what she had to say, but the decision had been made. "Jax, we want Blythe to join you in locating Dante."

"*Whoa*," Blythe gaped, eyes wide. "You're joking, right?"

"Damnit, Thea." Jax clenched his teeth, unpleased. "Why?"

"Because when you told me about the way Dante targeted Blythe, about how drawn he was to her, I decided it would be beneficial to us to have her with you to attract him. Obviously, I will expect you to protect her one hundred percent, and if anything happens to her I'll never forgive myself, but…"

"We've considered the risks, and we've considered the benefits," Sebastian continued, wrapping his arm around Thea to comfort her. "This scenario, however dangerous it may be, may just be the key to getting him. He clearly has some kind of attraction to Blythe. We should use that against him."

"Hot damn, you are serious!" Blythe hooted, fist pumping the air. "Just think of how much fun we're gonna have, cowboy," she added as she turned to Jax, grinning ear-to-ear.

"You always somehow get what you want, don't you?" he grumbled, looking extremely unhappy. But, an order was an order, and you didn't question the person paying your salary. "Alright, well, we should probably leave soon then. Go say your goodbyes. There's no way of knowing how long we'll be on the hunt."

On impulse, Blythe hugged Thea and Sebastian, beaming at both of them. "Thank you, I won't let you guys down."

Whirling around, she practically skipped off to where her family was waiting so she could tell them the good news.

Chapter Seven

No one was happy about it. But she was getting exactly what she wanted, so she didn't really dwell on their feelings too much.

Besides, it was Thea's idea. If they had any concerns or doubts, they could take it up with Mother Earth. It was no longer her problem.

Though saying goodbye to Lucian had been tough, she tried not to focus on it. Nothing bad was going to happen to her. They'd probably be gone less than a week because the plan would work so flawlessly that Dante would fall right into it. Then all of their worrying would have been for nothing.

Her father would have to keep up with the Fire duties while she was gone, a fact which amused her more than worried her. Not only was he pissed off about her leaving Euphora, but he was also now forced to work, largely under Thea's supervision. And his two girlfriends were angry with him. In her mind, it was karma at its best. He was just sleeping in the bed he'd made.

When they arrived back in Los Angeles that afternoon, Jax took her to a different hotel located closer to the night club, hoping that Dante was still in the area. He booked a room for each of them, then led her to the hotel restaurant so they could work out their plan.

The restaurant was crowded with the lunch rush, so they were forced to settle down at a tiny two person table in the corner while they waited to order.

As they sat down, Jax reached into his back pocket and pulled out the tracking device Rian had given him. It looked exactly like an iPhone, only a little bit larger, with a screen that lit up at his touch. On the screen were six buttons labeled: Human, Demon, Dryad, Fury, Muse and Fate.

"Guess we should find out if this thing works," he commented, pushing the Dryad button. Blythe leaned over to get a better look at the screen, noticing with wonder how it suddenly looked like radar, a series of circles representing the area around them with a line scanning clockwise. When the line reached where Blythe was sitting, a red dot appeared.

"Is that me?"

"No, it's Elvis."

"Ha, ha, very funny." She grabbed the device out of his hand and began playing with it, hitting the Human button. "Oh, look, there's you and all the other silly humans. Only…geez, what are all these other dots?"

She tilted the device so he could see the screen.

"The device senses the presence of the being you request, and depending on how recent the being was in the area, the dot will be a different color. Red means the presence is very strong, as in the being is definitely still in the area. Yellow is recent, but the being has likely moved. Green is even older, and blue is the oldest. Therefore, many of the dots you see on there are people who have come and gone from this restaurant throughout the day."

"Wow. That's so cool." Grinning, she switched back to the home screen and pressed the Demon button. The radar popped up, and the scanner line began its curve around. When she saw a red dot appear toward the bottom, representing what was behind her, she whirled around in shock.

"It says there's a demon sitting right back there!" she whispered, her eyes wide.

He scanned the back of the room, but it was impossible to tell from the dozens of people which one was the demon. The radar was accurate to within a three foot radius, but the area it was suggesting housed a demon was currently a ten person table full of normal looking people.

Without missing a beat, he unclipped his cell phone from the holster on his belt and immediately launched into a screen which showed a long list of names. He selected the name on the top, and then aimed the phone's camera toward the back table. Taking a picture, he then looked back at his phone as it processed the image. Within three seconds, the word NEGA-TIVE in big, bold letters popped up on the screen.

Huffing out a breath between disappointment and relief, he began to put his phone away before Blythe interrupted him.

"What is that? What did you just do?"

"I checked to see if Dante is the demon possessing the human back there. It's not him, so no need to worry about it." Nonchalantly, he took a sip of the ice water the waitress had just dropped off.

"How?" She leaned toward him across the tiny table, her eyes bright with exhilaration and intrigue. "Tell me how you did that."

He leaned back in his chair, watching her carefully. He wasn't sure how much information he should share with her, since the less people who knew about his methods the better. After all, if it came out that he had such a device, then the demons would find some way to be one step ahead of him. And he was a cautious man. But, then again, perhaps she had a right to know as she was now waist deep in this operation with him.

"It's something the Enforcers recently created, a program we install into our cell phones so it doesn't raise suspicion. How it works is you take a photo of the demon you want to keep tabs on, and it registers their unique signature. You see, Rian's device only shows one type of being at a time, so if Dante was in demon form while he was here, we could easily confuse him with another demon. But with this, I can see exactly if it is him based upon his signature. The only downside is that if he is in Dryad form, this device won't pick up on him because it only registers the demon components of his genetic makeup. Which is why Rian's device is so useful."

"When the hell did you get the chance to take a picture of Dante?" she demanded, more out of curiosity than irritation.

"At the night club, just before he approached you. I didn't even realize you were there until I saw him watching you from the bar. I wanted to be sure just in case I lost him, I would have the ability to find him again."

Impressed, she leaned back in her own chair and eyed him, chewing on her bottom lip as she thought. "When were you going to let me in on this useful little tool of yours?"

"I had no reason to share any more information than was necessary with you before. But, now that I'm forced into using you as bait, I guess it doesn't hurt none to show you."

She rolled her eyes and snorted at him. "Whatever. Okay, so that demon back there isn't Dante. Aren't you still going to kill him or something?"

"That's not my job," he replied simply, cocking one eyebrow at her. "I'm employed to hunt down one demon at a time."

"Yeah, but they're evil…shouldn't you do something about it? I mean, he's back there possessing a human, he needs to be stopped."

His eyes narrowed as he leaned toward her, his voice lowered conspiratorially. "Darlin', just how many demons do you think there are in this world?"

Cocking her chin up defensively, she smirked. "I don't know, a few hundred?"

"Try nearly three million." He felt his own lips twitch into a self-satisfied grin, watching her mouth fall open in shock.

"You have to be kidding me." She couldn't believe it. Why had no one ever told her this before?

"Your education in the ways of demons is obviously lacking." He saw her rev up in indignation at his words, and found he couldn't help but enjoy the crease that formed angrily between her eyebrows as her eyes fired up with deadly heat. "Before you attack me, let me fill you in."

She let out a breath as she crossed her arms over her chest, her initial anger sizzling into irritation. "Alright, fine. Educate me, cowboy."

"You see, most of the demons that come to the surface from the Underworld are not worth taking the time to worry about. They usually are just trying to sell their wares, whether it be weapons, drugs, or alcohol to the willing human masses. Where do you think methamphetamine came from? Or absinthe? They've been running that crap up to the surface for hundreds of years, and there's not much we can do about it. However, there are very dangerous demons out there who come to the surface to wreak havoc. They've influenced nearly all the evil that has occurred to the human race since the dawn of time. Hitler, Jack the Ripper, most recently Saddam Hussein. All possessed by demons, all committed terrible crimes against humanity."

"So you're saying that all those guys did bad things against their will?"

"Not necessarily. A demon can only possess someone who is in a weak emotional state, whether it be grief, anger, despair… they have to have something to latch onto. Hitler was already teetering on the edge because of his anger, so he was an easy target. And that demon was particularly evil. Notice they never found Hitler's body? That's because the Enforcers had to destroy every bit of it so they could be sure the demon was obliterated for good."

"Wow." Taking a deep breath, she tried to digest everything he had told her. She had never realized the magnitude of the demon influence on the human population. Sure, she'd known about demon alcohol and weapons because she had been told that her father had enjoyed them, which had been one of the many reasons she had despised him as a child. But maybe she had been too sheltered all her life about the truth.

The waitress suddenly approached to take their orders before rushing off to get the meals that were waiting for the table in the back. Glancing over her shoulder, Blythe scanned the faces at the table, wondering if she would notice some quirk, some sign that would let her know who the demon was. But they just looked like normal, happy people—smiling and laughing with each other. It alarmed her that they had no way of knowing that evil resided among them, hiding out in the body of one of their own.

About an hour later they headed over to the nightclub to see if they could find any sign that Dante was still in the area.

They walked along the sidewalk, Blythe in jean shorts and a bright yellow tank top, her wine red hair glowing hotly in the bright sunlight and her eyes shaded by jet black sunglasses. She kept in step with Jax despite her legs being much shorter, as he walked steadily and efficiently in boots, faded jeans and an equally faded plaid shirt rolled up at the sleeves. His sharp eyes were glued to Rian's device as they walked, searching for any sign of Dryad or demon.

Anticipation was building inside of her as they approached the club, joining the thrill of the hunt that she recognized as pure bloodlust. She wanted so badly to take out Dante. And while she would have preferred doing it solo, having the bounty hunter around was proving to be more useful than detrimental. After all, he was the one with the fancy gadgets and the knowledge of demons. And she was the one with the thirst for revenge. Coupled together, she had a hunch they'd make an excellent demon hunting team.

"Don't you think someone's going to notice you staring at that device and think you're up to something?" she asked him suddenly, glancing around at all of the people who were walking the streets with them.

He actually stopped and stared at her, eyebrows raised. "Trust me, being glued to various devices was perfected on the streets of Los Angeles. I thought you were savvy to the human world?"

"I am." She pouted a bit as she saw a group of teenage girls breeze past them, all clutching their cell phones and chattering away at each other. "At least, I thought I was. I've never used a phone before."

"You're not missing out on anything, trust me. More trouble than they're worth, most of the time." Beginning to walk again, he widened the scope on the device to a half mile wide as he switched back and forth from Demon to Dryad, hoping to catch something. He began to turn down the alleyway to the side of the club, when suddenly he got a hit.

"There's a demon around the back of the building." He walked swiftly down the alley, Blythe in his wake.

"Right now?" she asked, excitement blooming within her.

"Stay behind me," he told her as they approached. He slowed, peering around to try and catch a glimpse of the being his radar was picking up.

"I don't need protection," she snapped as she tried to round the corner, hands held out ready to destroy whatever it was that lurked just out of sight.

"You will do what I tell you." Jax grabbed her arm and pulled her back, keeping her at his side. He glared at her, the scolding look in his eyes making her feel like a bad child. "Wait until I can determine the full scope of the situation before you go charging in, alright?"

"Fine." Rolling her eyes, she waited for him to glance around the corner. When he pulled back, his eyes were sharp and focused, but she could feel the adrenaline pumping through him. He was just as excited as she was at the idea that they could be within feet of their target.

"There's a human beside one of the dumpsters, he looks like he's been freshly possessed," he told her as he pulled out his phone and reached around to snap a quick photo of him. They both held their breath, waiting for the device to determine if the demon was Dante.

When NEGATIVE flashed over the screen, they both cursed under their breaths.

"Well, shit. Now what?" Blythe asked, disappointment clear in her eyes.

"We go talk to him, see if he knows anything." After putting both devices away, he reached for the revolver in the ankle holster housed in his right boot. "Don't do or say anything unless I tell you to, you hear?"

"Yeah, yeah, whatever." Still annoyed that they hadn't discovered Dante, she followed him as he rounded the corner of the building, revolver pointed directly at the demon.

Blythe's eyes widened in shock as she stared at the man as he writhed and trembled against the side of the dumpster, clutching his head and muttering words she didn't understand. When she heard the word "diablo", she felt a cold chill run down her spine. The man fought against the possession, sensing the demon's attempt to get inside his mind. He was chanting what she assumed were frantic prayers in Spanish. Anger built up within her at the sight of it, but as she stepped forward to do something– anything–Jax held out his arm, stopping her and shaking his head.

"What did I say?" he growled, the look in his eyes frightening...somewhere between frustration, fury and pain. He didn't like what he saw either.

She stopped in her tracks, holding eyes with him until he turned at the sound of a brutally disturbing noise.

She jolted and looked at the man who now stared directly at her. His dark eyes were wide and his mouth was opened in a snarl, baring teeth that looked unnaturally sharp. The sound had been a frightening mix of a hiss and a guttural growl. There was only one word to describe it. Evil.

"I have no business with you except to ask questions. I am not an Enforcer, I am a bounty hunter. I demand you vacate that human immediately," Jax ordered, his revolver still pointed at the man.

The man shifted to stare at Jax, crouching in a defensive and inquisitive position, his hands and feet both touching the concrete. Suddenly, the man began to tremble again, his face going blank with horror, as thick black smoke began to seep out of every orifice on his face...his eyes, ears, nose, mouth...it poured out of him and gathered to form something long and slender on the ground. The man collapsed, his head banging hard against the side of the metal dumpster.

Blythe almost stepped forward to help, but the sight at their feet stopped her.

The black smoke had swirled together, creating a serpent figure—shadowy and larger than any snake she'd ever seen. It was about five feet in length and three inches in diameter, and seemed to shift and shudder like a flickering movie image in front of them. It was almost as if it wasn't fully solid, but a wispy mass that contorted and exuded waves of smoke around its body. When it lifted its head to face her, she saw large, glowing red eyes that pierced through her. She could sense the unbridled hatred, and against her will, felt her body instinctively edging away from the creature.

"Thank you." Jax kept his revolver aimed as a precaution. "We're looking for a demon with Dryad blood. Have you seen him?" The snake hissed again, and then began to "speak" in guttural, whispery sounds. Jax listened intently and Blythe wondered if he could understand it. When the demon fell silent, she turned to look at Jax, who looked disappointed.

"Alright. Thank you." He grabbed her arm and pulled her away, leading her toward the alleyway.

She yanked her arm free, glancing back at the demon, who continued to stare at her with those horrific eyes. The only thing she knew for sure was that the demon wanted her dead.

She rubbed her arm where he had grabbed her, glaring up at him. "Can I go back and torch that demon? He wants to kill me and I think it's only fair that I set him straight."

"No. Now come on." He led the way back out onto the street, heading away from their hotel.

Rolling her eyes, she tried to keep pace with him. "So what did the bastard say, anyway?"

"He says he saw Dante last night at the club, that he threatened him, but he didn't see Dante leave. We're back at square one." He veered left suddenly into a large parking lot, and made his way toward the back. Blythe followed, eyeing the junk cars surrounding them.

"I didn't know you had a car."

"Most people have cars, Blythe," he said gruffly as he stopped in front of an older looking jet black two door with sparkling chrome rims. Pulling keys out of his pocket, he shoved them in the lock and opened the driver side door. She waited while he climbed inside and unlocked the passenger door for her.

"This is nice." She grinned as she stared around at the leather upholstery. "What kind of car is this?"

"1968 Chevelle." He slipped the keys into the ignition and turned it on, revving the engine. "With a 5.7L V8 engine, 450 horsepower."

"Cool, I guess." She smirked at him as he reached into the backseat and pulled out another Stetson, this time in white. When he slipped it over his head, she couldn't help but laugh. "Got a hat for all occasions, cowboy?"

He didn't say anything, but she saw his lips curve just slightly at the edges. With a sigh, she sat back against the seat as he drove them out of the lot and onto the street.

"So where are we going now?" she asked, staring out the window at the people walking on the street.

"We're going to meet with a few of my contacts here in L.A. If Dante's still in town, we'll know by the end of the day."

Unfortunately for them, by the end of the day they knew for certain that Dante was indeed not in Los Angeles. As it turned out, the plan to lure him using Blythe had not gotten off to a good start. In fact, it appeared as though they were dead in the water.

Jax's contacts had been two arms dealers on opposite ends of the city who were demons possessing humans. Because of what she was, Jax forced Blythe to stay behind in the car, which she didn't like one bit. But when he assured her he would get more reliable information out of them if they weren't distracted by her, she gave in. Each time he left to speak with one of the contacts, he was gone for less than twenty minutes. And each time he returned, he looked even more irritated.

According to Jax, they had heard that a demon with Dryad blood was in town, but no one had seen him since the night before when Blythe had encountered him in the club. He had not gone in to purchase weapons, nor had he discussed his plans with anyone. According to them, he'd kept to himself while in the city. Which was probably for his own benefit, because Blythe had come to realize that other demons despised Dante nearly as much as she did. They didn't like that he had Dryad blood, something they deemed disgusting. So he was not only an outcast by everyone on Euphora, but he was also an outcast by most of the demon population as well. If he wasn't a murderous bastard she might have felt sorry for him.

They returned to the hotel as night fell over the city, exhausted and frustrated, both unsure where to look next. They sat together in the hotel restaurant, this time much quieter than the lunch rush had been, as the city lights flickered on outside the open windows.

Blythe pushed around the mashed potatoes on her plate, her mind elsewhere. She felt disheartened, which only made her more annoyed. They needed a new plan or some hint of Dante's whereabouts. Something so they could do more than just sit there immobilized. It was making her agitated and restless, and she could tell it was taking its toll on Jax.

He sat across from her, barely touching his grilled chicken as he sipped quietly on a bottle of beer. The phone call he'd made to Thea just an hour before still resonated painfully in his mind. He'd hated telling her that they were at a dead end, that using Blythe hadn't worked. That fact had surprised him. He had been convinced that Dante was after Blythe in particular and that he would have a hard time avoiding her if she were thrown back into the mix. Maybe he hadn't analyzed the situation closely enough and now it had cost valuable time and energy.

"What do you think happened with that guy the demon was trying to possess earlier?" Blythe asked suddenly, the thought just occurring to her. "Do you think he got away?"

"I don't know." Jax studied her, noting the concern in her eyes. "You can't save everyone, Blythe."

"Obviously." She sighed, twirling the straw around in her glass of Coca-Cola. "That was the first demon I've ever seen. I didn't know they were like that."

"Like what?"

She met his eyes, her lips curling with disgust as she remembered what she had seen, what she had felt. "Evil. God, I've never felt so exposed, so vulnerable to that evil in all my life."

He tilted his head as he set down his beer. "You didn't look scared."

With a snort, she drank some soda to steady herself. "I told you I can handle myself in tough situations. I wasn't gonna show that bastard any fear. Especially because I knew deep down that he wanted me to be scared." She slammed her fist down on the table, rattling their plates, almost causing him to flinch. "Damnit, you should have let me kill him."

"You wouldn't have been able to."

"Why not?" One eyebrow raised as she eyed him incredulously.

Smirking now, he lifted his beer to his lips. "Demons don't fear fire. It doesn't hurt them. The only way to kill them is to freeze them and then smash them to pieces."

"Huh." Honestly taken aback, she chewed her bottom lip in thought. "So that's why the bullets in your gun look so funny, they're not normal bullets, huh?"

"Why the hell were you looking at the rounds in my revolver?"

Blythe shrugged. "I was curious and you left the gun sitting out while you were taking a shower earlier. What is that silver liquid inside of them?"

"Liquid nitrogen," he replied, still irritated that she had been nosy enough to check the rounds in his gun. "It freezes the demon on impact, then you can crush them to pieces, destroying them for good."

"Can you get me a gun, too?" Eyes lit up now at the prospect, she started to reach down toward his boot to grab his. "Or maybe I'll just try yours out for awhile."

He caught her hand halfway under the table and wrestled her back up into a sitting position. "Stop it. There's something called gun laws in this state and you can't just pull out a gun in a crowded restaurant."

She supposed that he probably knew best. Apparently she knew less about the human world than she had thought.

"Fine, whatever. Can you get me a gun, though?"

"Do you know how to shoot?"

"Sure. How hard can it be?"

This time he rolled his eyes, a movement that amused the hell out of her. "Unless we get a new lead on Dante, you're going home. So until we find out anything new there's no point in me wasting time teaching you how to shoot."

"Heaven forbid we waste more of your precious time," she mumbled sarcastically, going back to pushing the food around on her plate. For a few moments she was silent, her mind drifting back to the demon. When she spoke again her voice was much softer, as if speaking more to herself than to him. "Why would my grandmother sleep with a demon? After seeing one today…after feeling that evil…"

"Maybe there's more to the story than what you know." He could tell she was troubled and it irritated him that he cared enough to notice.

"Even if there is, it doesn't change the fact that she did it, and consequently gave birth to the monster that destroyed my life and countless other lives."

"Excuse me, Mr. and Mrs. Murphy?"

Blythe couldn't help but break out into laughter at the waiter who had just approached them, a small package in his hands.

Jax sighed and accepted the package from the waiter, who flushed red with embarrassment and retreated back into the kitchen. "Are you finished?" Jax asked her, looking annoyed as he eyed the package skeptically.

"Oh, God, that was hilarious," she managed, gasping a bit for breath, a big grin on her face. "Your face when he said Mr. and Mrs., it was priceless."

"I guess the thought of you being the Mrs. was what threw me off," he grumbled, tossing the package at her. "It's for you."

"Ooh, I hope it's chocolate. I've been craving some like you would not believe." She grinned, winking at him as she tore open the packaging, only to pause as she held a necklace in one hand and a letter in the other. "This is beautiful." She sighed, eyeing the brilliant amber stone the size of a quarter set in bronze. It hung from a bold and bulky chain and she felt a strange heat radiating from it, almost as if it had just been dipped in flame.

"Read the letter, Blythe," Jax ordered her impatiently.

Her smile faded the moment she set the necklace aside and focused her attention on the letter. Her eyes jolted up to meet his as her stomach fell damn near to her feet.

"It's from Dante."

Dearest Blythe,

I hope you enjoyed your stay in Los Angeles, just as I did. I apologize for having to desert you so abruptly last night, but you see, I am a wanted man on the run.

Even without ever seeing you before, I knew you the moment I saw you. Did you feel our connection? My blood, your blood...we're kin, darling, and were bound together by a force deeper than any other. I cannot wait till we meet again, as I am certain we will in due time. Until then, I have a project for you that will keep you occupied and entertained.

I am aware that you are in the company of the bounty hunter. While I would have preferred you to go on this journey alone, I think your bounty hunter's skills will add an intriguing danger to the mix. I do love danger...just as I know you do. You see, we are so much alike, you and I.

If you follow my instructions, then at the end of your journey we will meet again. I am going to give you a clue and a gift. The clue will guide you to where I will be and the gift is for you to enjoy.

Here is your first clue, darling: Follow the highway to the city of the fire bird. If you get there in time, you may catch me. If not, then I will leave you another clue and another gift. Happy hunting.

Dante

P.S. The necklace was your grandmother's, a Fire Dryad heirloom. I know you will look radiant when you wear it.

Later, it would occur to her just how eerie his words were. But until then, she could feel nothing but fury.

Chapter Eight

He's playing a goddamn game with us." She tossed the letter to Jax, covering her face in her hands and trying to breathe.

Connection! Just who did he think he was? And giving her a necklace that had been her whore grandmother's? Was that just some ploy of his to win her sympathy? Well, he obviously thought he knew her better than he actually did, because knowing what the necklace was only made it revolting to her, not priceless.

Irritated, she picked up the necklace once more, eyeing it with disdain instead of admiration. It really wasn't all that pretty, now that she really looked. The stone had a couple of nicks on it and looked faded from time. It was just junk, that was all.

She impulsively wrapped it up in her napkin and shoved it aside so she wouldn't have to look at it any longer. She watched Jax pore over the letter, devouring every word like it was scripture. Because she didn't consider Dante's writing to be anything more than bullshit, she felt annoyed that he was taking it so seriously. When he finished, he set the letter aside, leaned back in his chair, and reached for his beer.

"Phoenix," he said suddenly as he took a swig from the bottle.

"Phoenix, what?"

"That's where he's going. Phoenix, Arizona."

Annoyed with him for no real reason in particular, she felt her temper flaring. "And how do you know that? He might just be screwing with us."

"Doubtful." Sipping again, he continued to watch her. "Looks like he wants you, after all."

"If he wanted me, he would just come and get me. I don't understand why he's trying to get us to play this stupid game."

"Because it amuses him." He picked up the letter and read it over again. "He's like a cat with a mouse. He's going to play with you before he destroys you, all for the fun of it."

"That's all very cute, but why do you think he's going to this Phoenix place?"

"I don't know about you, but the only bird of fire I know of is the phoenix. And there just so happens to be a city named that within driving distance, which would be why he said to follow the highway."

Pursing her lips, she resigned that his logic made sense. "So you think we should go along with this?"

"Unless you have a better idea," he drawled, smirking at her. Suddenly, his cell phone began to ring beside him. He glanced briefly at the Caller ID before answering it with a grin. "You're never gonna guess what I just found out."

"Dante's in Phoenix." Rian's voice came through the phone in his matter of fact tone.

Jax frowned. "Now how the hell did you figure that out, son?"

"You're not the only one with connections. My grandfather on my father's side retired down there, and I asked him awhile ago to keep an eye out. Turns out he spotted Dante about an hour ago at a convenience store on Van Buren Street right by the airport. He would

have tailed him but Dante got in a Mercedes and drove off, and my grandfather had walked there."

"Well, shit." Pleased, Jax winked at Blythe. "Blythe just received a letter from our demon leading us on some wild goose chase to Arizona."

"Looks like you're going to Phoenix, buddy."

"Looks like it. I'll keep you posted." Hanging up the phone, he focused his attention back on Blythe. "Go on upstairs and get your stuff. We should be able to make it to Phoenix in about five hours."

"So Dante's really in Phoenix, huh?" Hearing the confirmation from Rian regarding Dante's whereabouts perked her up a bit. Maybe this was for real, after all. "Lucky guess on your part, cowboy."

He grinned at her, the thrill of the hunt back in his system. He had a wicked gleam in his eyes as he spoke.

"Girl, lucky might as well be my middle name."

Despite the adrenaline she had felt upon leaving Los Angeles, by the time the drive was done she had fallen fast asleep in the passenger seat of his car.

Jax couldn't help but watch her for a moment as he pulled into the hotel parking lot and turned off the ignition. She was curled up into the corner with her head resting on her arms and her legs tucked up against her chest, her breathing slow and steady.

She looked so innocent while she slept that it took him off guard. That sharp, foxy face seemed soft and childlike when it wasn't lit up with that vixen grin of hers or fired up with her quick temper. A face like that could be misleading to a man who didn't know better, he mused. Good thing he did know better, and knowing better kept his priorities from wandering into dangerous territory.

Not only was she six years younger than him, she was also one of Thea's prized Dryads and therefore extraordinarily important to the world as a whole. And that fact put him in an awfully shitty position, as he was the one now entrusted to protect her. And despite how fervently she denied it, she was vulnerable and constantly in danger here. Though he knew for damn sure that she would put up a hell of a fight if given the chance.

He nudged her softly, his own exhaustion wearing down on him so his eyes felt heavy and his mind numb from hours of staring at nothing but dark, empty highway. When her eyes fluttered open and met his, her lips curved into a soft, sleepy smile.

"God, you're handsome," she mused, still half asleep. She could see his face, half bathed in the yellow light of the hotel, stubble shadowing the hollows of his cheeks and his chin. He looked dark, dangerous, and much too sexy for his own good. Her eyes fell closed again as she felt herself drifting back to sleep.

The husky, throaty way the words had poured out of her mouth had him straining against his own self control. Mentally slapping himself in the face, he sat up straight and nudged her again.

"Wake up, we're here." He pushed open the car door and climbed out, stretching his legs momentarily before reaching in the back for his duffle bag, trying hard not to look at her again.

"Mmm." Stretching her arms up over her head, she yawned deeply and slowly unfolded herself out of the car. "What time is it?"

"One in the morning." He slung his bag over his shoulder, tossing her own bag to her before locking up the car. "We'll go inside and get a few hours sleep. I'll come wake you up at six."

Too tired to complain, she followed him into the hotel so he could get the keys to their rooms. He did all the talking while she nearly fell asleep again at the lobby counter, her eyes drooping against her will.

He grabbed her arm, much gentler this time, cupping his hand under her elbow to keep her going as he headed down the outdoor corridor toward their rooms. He slid the keycard in himself and propped open the door for her.

"Goodnight, Blythe," he muttered as she slid out of his grasp and stepped forward into the room.

She dropped her bag just inside the door and turned, facing him before he could walk away.

"Jax?"

He didn't say anything as he turned and watched her, the dim glow of the outside lights highlighting the angles of his face. Because she could see he was as exhausted as she, if not more so, she decided against what she was going to say. He didn't need to know that while she had been sleeping on the drive over, she'd done nothing but dream of him. Besides, she wasn't sure she was even ready to think about just how badly that complicated everything.

"Thank you for driving." With a smile that didn't quite reach her eyes, she backed into the room and shut the door behind her, trapping herself in darkness.

"You can't keep leaving me out of the loop. Whether you like it or not, I'm a part of this and I should get to go wherever you go."

"This is about your safety, and as your temporary guardian I don't feel it is in your best interest to go along."

They were both standing on opposite sides of the car, currently parked outside the store of Jax's only demon contact in Phoenix. The sun had barely been up two hours, and already it was rapidly nearing ninety degrees.

"Bull." Indignant, Blythe tossed back her hair and stared him down. "I think you just want to maintain some semblance of this being your solo gig."

Because it was close to the truth, Jax merely shrugged. "I'm sure you'd rather take on this expedition solo too, sweetheart."

"Aw, but then I'd lose out on all the fun bickering we do." She smiled at him, a teasing light coming into her eyes. "C'mon, cowboy. Let me come play with you in the big boy leagues."

Despite knowing it would probably be a big mistake, he sighed and gestured for her to follow him.

"Fine. Come along then, we don't have all day."

She bit back a triumphant grin as she followed him toward the store.

He pulled open the glass front door and motioned for her to enter in front of him, his eyes immediately scanning the dimly lit room full of display cases housing hunting and fishing gear. She kept close to him, which he appreciated, as he could only do so much to protect her if his demon contact decided to attack. The last thing he needed was her wandering around out of sight.

As they approached the long, glass counter, a man stepped out from the back room. His polite smile faded the moment he saw Jax, a tinge of fear replacing it.

"Jackson Murphy," the man managed, wiping his suddenly damp hands on his khaki pants before reaching out to shake Jax's hand. "Long time no see."

Blythe eyed the man curiously. He was tall and slender, with a nerdy looking face and dark hair combed over to one side. His eyes had a panicked look to them, making him appear completely out of place amongst all the testosterone infused hunting gear.

Suddenly, as if an electric shock had pulsed through his body, his bony back seemed to cringe as he turned to face her, his nostrils flaring and his eyes wide with revulsion. A low hissing sound escaped from somewhere deep in his throat.

Jax stepped in front of Blythe, his hands held out peacefully. "Lenny, you need to calm down. She's with me."

"A Dryad. A Dryad is in my store." Lenny's hands clenched anxiously together as he backed away, bumping into the wall behind him.

"You and I both know this isn't the first time." Jax tucked his hands into his jean pockets, a grin playing over his face. "Brock's one of your best customers."

"I don't know nothing about that," Lenny choked out, looking timid and scared again. "Must be someone else your thinking of."

"Are you really lying to me now, son?" It wasn't said in a threatening way, but Blythe could hear the authority in it. Apparently the demon could, too.

"Alright, fine. Maybe one time I did business with him. I don't want no trouble."

"Good, neither do I." Jax grinned again and pulled out his phone, taking a moment to bring up an image before showing it to Lenny. "You seen this fellow around here lately?"

Lenny's Adam's apple bobbed as he stared at the picture. "Maybe."

"Why don't you come on over here and get yourself a better look." Waving him over, Jax held the phone out so Lenny could look closer.

"Nope, ain't seen him."

Blythe watched Jax take a deep breath and slowly exhale. Then he suddenly grasped Lenny's shirt front and dragged him halfway over the counter.

"I thought we were past the lying bullshit, Lenny," Jax grunted, bringing Lenny's terrified face close to his. "Now I want the truth. Have you seen this fellow around here, or not? He's half demon, half Dryad. I know you can tell the difference."

"Yes...yes, he was here last night," Lenny stammered, shaking head to toe as Jax released him.

"Did he buy anything?"

"Just a demon blade, is all." Lenny fingered the collar around his polo shirt, fighting to get his breathing steady. "I didn't want to sell it to him, on account of his tainted blood and all, but he paid double for it. In cash." He shrugged defensively. "I run a business, after all."

"Did he say where he was heading?"

"No, didn't say much of anything, really. He was driving a silver Mercedes Benz, though. Acted all high and mighty like he was hot shit."

"Nevada plates?"

"Nah, Arizona plates. Probably stolen, I imagine."

"Interesting." Jax paused as he considered this new piece of information. So Dante had switched license plates on the stolen Mercedes...smart move since he was a cop magnet with that stolen car.

"So you sell demon weapons?" Blythe asked curiously, unable to resist. After all, this was a whole new world to her, and she was especially interested because apparently her father was a customer here.

Lenny's head whipped around at her voice, his face tightening with barely restrained fury. At first he looked like he wasn't going to answer her, but then his eyes suddenly narrowed to slits and he stepped toward her.

"Who wants to know?" he spat, eyeing her with disdain.

Her temper sparked as she instinctively straightened up to her full height, a meager five foot four compared to his towering six foot two. But the attitude she exuded made her seem much more intimidating then she actually was.

"I happen to be Brock's daughter. You know what they always say, the apple doesn't fall far from the tree. Maybe I would like to purchase something from you."

His face softened as he pondered, but his eyes never left hers. "Brock's daughter, huh?"

"That's right. Now what can you offer me?"

He smiled and she saw a brief, momentary flash of red in his eyes that caught her off guard. His nerdy demeanor hid it well, but she knew the demon inside was wicked.

"Come on back, I'll show you around."

An hour later, they walked out of the store, Jax looking more than a little frustrated and Blythe patting the new semi-automatic pistol tucked into the holster on her waist, a brand new carton of ammo in her purse.

"I don't know how you did that," Jax murmured bitterly as he climbed into the car and slipped the keys into the ignition. He reached in the backseat for his Stetson as she sat down beside him.

"Did what?" She beamed, still admiring her new gun.

"Manage to convince that demon not to kill you." He began flipping through the radio stations, his hat hiding his eyes from her. "Your dad was the only other Dryad I've heard of who could actually make friends with demons and not get himself killed."

"Really?" She sat back in her seat and stared out the window. "Once we got past the initial 'ew you're creepy and disgusting' stage, Lenny was a pretty cool guy. I'd do business with him again."

Jax glanced up at her and grinned. "Especially the moment he saw that wad of cash you carry around with you. His eyes damn near bulged out of their sockets."

One of her eyebrows cocked haughtily at his words. "I think it was my charming personality that won him over, not my money, thank you very much."

"I'm sure it was, darlin'." Finally settling on a radio station, he sat back and put the car in drive. "Rian's grandfather said he spotted Dante by the airport. I want to head on over there and use the tracking devices and see if we come up with anything."

"Okay. God, seriously? What is this crap?" She wrinkled her nose at the music coming out of the stereo. Beside her, Jax was busy beating his hands against the steering wheel in time to the music.

"Waylon Jennings. And it's not crap." He glanced over at her dangerously, as if daring her to say it again.

She just rolled her eyes. "I don't know why I'm surprised that the cowboy likes country music."

"Lemme guess, you're an N'sync girl yourself."

He managed to catch a glimpse of the horror on her face before he had to watch the road again. God, it was entertaining to rile her up.

"Look here, country boy," she began, turning in her seat to face him. "Give me the Stones, Joplin and Hendrix, and you can refund the cheesy boy band."

"I guess I could see a girl like you enjoying Woodstock."

"Sure, though I'd have to pass on the drugs and the anonymous sex. The music's enough of a high for me." She grinned then as he chuckled, shaking his head. "So what's your idea of a good time, cowboy?"

"Kickin' back on my front porch after a long day, a beer in my hand and my dog at my feet, listening to the crickets and the coyotes as the sun sets over the horizon."

Because she could picture it so clearly, could see him sitting on some porch with the damn beer and a big, yellow dog so vividly in her mind, she found herself momentarily at a loss for words. He was suddenly quiet, too, as if he was taking the time to build back up the wall that he had briefly let down.

She opened her mouth to ask him another question, only to have him interrupt her.

"Take a look at the radar and call out if you spot anything." He pulled out the device from his pocket and handed it to her as he pulled onto Van Buren Street, where Rian's grandfather had spotted Dante.

She took the device and immediately began scanning for both demon and Dryad, though her mind was elsewhere.

It was best that they refrain from getting too personal with each other, that much she knew. They had a business relationship and a common goal. And his reluctance to share more about himself told her that he wanted to maintain a safe and comfortable distance.

That was just fine, she reassured herself. They had very little in common anyway. He was bossy, distant and way more intelligent than she had given him credit for. And she was temperamental, blunt and not nearly as smart as she'd given herself credit for.

No way in hell would the two of them ever really be friends. And it was a damn shame, she thought wistfully as she glanced at him out of the corner of her eye. He was so cute when he hummed along to that steel guitar.

Because their search around the surrounding neighborhoods of the airport turned up nothing, and the continued search down the main strip of hotels and night clubs also turned up nothing, they decided to head back to the hotel room and regroup.

Blythe was starving. They hadn't even stopped for lunch and it was already nearing seven o'clock at night. Consequently, she had big plans for the vending machine just outside her room. Thinking about Milky Way bars and potato chips made her stomach grumble longingly as they walked down the corridor toward their rooms.

"You should order a pizza while I tide myself over with a candy bar." Blythe stopped at the vending machine and slipped in a few quarters, punching the buttons for the chocolate and watching it eagerly as it fell into the catch below.

"Alright, just don't–" Jax stopped mid-sentence, noticing a small package resting in front of Blythe's door. He raced toward it and held it in his hands, already knowing they were too late. The bastard had slipped just out of reach, once again.

Biting into the candy bar, Blythe sauntered over and, noticing the package in his hands, felt her face drain of color.

"Is it from him?" she asked, already knowing the answer from the look on his face. He nodded and tossed the package to her.

"Might as well see what it says. I'll be inside ordering the damn pizza." He left her and disappeared inside his own room, needing to vent his frustration in private.

Her hands trembled as she fumbled to open the package, hope combating with the dread she felt. She pulled out the letter and began to read as she entered her room and shut the door behind her. She sat down on the bed and laid back against the comforter, her eyes scanning Dante's all too familiar handwriting.

Blythe,

Congratulations on making it to Phoenix, darling, but you are too late to find me. As you read this, I am no doubt on the road, thinking of you. I hope you enjoyed the necklace I gave you in Los Angeles. Perhaps when you see your newest gift, you will appreciate the necklace even more.

You look so much like her, it's uncanny. There is very little of your disgusting Fate mother in you, and not much of my scumbag brother, either. No, you are like Bristol incarnate, darling. I love seeing her live on in you.

Though I won't be seeing you this time, perhaps you will catch me at my next stop. I'll be "stepping" swiftly on down south, where a big river passes on its way to the sea.

With love,
Dante

She set the letter aside and reached into the package, pulling out a single, aged photograph. Despite all the anger, frustration and bitterness she'd felt after reading her uncle's letter, the moment she saw the photograph she was consumed by a devastating emotion that tore through her, leaving her raw and exposed. She sat up as her breath caught in her throat and her mind searched for any reasonable explanation other than what was absurdly obvious. The photo was of Bristol, her grandmother, and it was the first time she had ever seen the woman who had destroyed everything.

She was standing on the beach with the ocean at her back, clutching a straw hat against her mass of curly hair against the sea breeze. She was smiling brightly, her face glowing with youth and promise. Her bathing suit was a modest one piece, with the exception of a daring diamond cut around her navel. Despite the photo being black and white, Blythe knew her hair was the same wine red, her eyes the same gilded amber, her skin the same sun-kissed ivory scattered with freckles. Dante had been right, the resemblance between her and her grandmother was uncanny.

If someone hadn't scribbled Summer 1966 on the back, Blythe would have sworn she was looking at herself. Her grandmother would have been eighteen at the time of the photograph, which was only one year younger than Blythe was. It disturbed her to see how vibrant and happy her grandmother had been all those years ago.

And around her neck hung the heirloom necklace, the amber stone catching the light.

Chapter Nine

Jax stood in the blistering hot spray of water from the hotel shower and desperately tried to clear his mind.

He had almost let his frustration get the best of him at a time when he needed patience in order to complete his job. Thea was counting on him, and he hadn't made his reputation by being careless and unreliable. No, he'd carved a niche for himself as a bounty hunter known for delivering fast and effective results. He was ruthless, unrelenting, and had an avid and quick mind.

So why the hell did he feel like he was missing some important piece of information, some key to getting one step ahead of Dante?

Sure, the girl was a distraction of sorts, but he had a pretty good handle on how to deal with her by now. And it didn't hurt that she was not only committed to their cause, but also an important link to Dante. The bastard was obsessed with her, that much was obvious. He wasn't sure if she realized just how crazy her uncle was, but he could see it. And it disgusted him down to the very core.

He'd seen the glaring possessiveness in Dante's eyes when he had been watching Blythe in Los Angeles. Just as he'd stood and watched as Dante had approached her, started dancing with her. She hadn't even realized who he was, but Jax had known. And he hadn't thought to stop it until the timing had been right and Dante nearly distracted enough for Jax to catch him. It hadn't even occurred to him how she might feel afterward, because he hadn't cared about her then. She had just been another person for him to catch and bring to Thea. So what was she to him now, if not a means to an end?

Nothing. She wasn't anything to him; just a girl who was assisting him in the capture of a fugitive. He had to convince himself of that, and keep his head clear for the remainder of their journey together. A journey that unfortunately had no clear end in sight.

He toweled off and dressed before heading outside to knock on her door. It was time to read the newest letter and figure out where the hell they were off to next.

He wasn't sure what he expected from her. Probably rage, frustration and irritability. But what he saw on her face when she opened the door was unbridled vulnerability.

Her eyes were wide and blank, staring but not really seeing. Her face was pale and hollow; the same sharpness that gave it vitality now casting a haunted look. He saw her bottom lip tremble as she handed him the letter.

"I'm going to take a shower," she said numbly, her mind and body drained of all emotion at this point. All she wanted to do was sink into nothingness. "Come on in, I won't be too long."

She turned around and disappeared into the bathroom. He shut the door and wandered over to sit on her bed, noticing the photograph resting on the nightstand. His heart sank as he picked it up.

No wonder she was upset, he thought glumly as he examined Bristol's image. The granddaughter was a spitting image of the grandmother. Even the eyes. If he hadn't known better, he'd swear those were Blythe's eyes. But they weren't and this wasn't Blythe. This was a woman who was dead now, who had posed for this photo decades before Blythe or he had been born.

He felt a hatred building inside of him as he realized what Dante was trying to do. He was using his dead mother to not only lure Blythe, but to also hurt her so deeply that she would never be the same. She had already gone through enough on account of her father's carelessness and now Dante was trying to use a dead woman to damage her even further.

Furious, he contemplated tearing up the photograph, only to think twice. Knowing her, she would want the honor of tearing it to pieces herself if she saw fit. And the fact that she hadn't done so meant that she had decided not to. He knew it wasn't his place to interfere, so he set the photo aside and proceeded to read the letter.

Blythe felt like she was cleansing herself, not only physically but spiritually. She wasn't going to let Dante get to her this way, not ever again. She knew what her grandmother had done and seeing some old photograph of her looking young and happy didn't change anything. She still screwed up and was selfish enough not to care about anyone but herself.

There was no reason to feel this aching sense of loss, none at all. Bristol was already dead, so there was no pressure to try and reconnect. It was all just some disgusting game that Dante was playing. Well, she wasn't going to play along.

Feeling marginally better, she stepped out of the shower and wrapped herself in a towel, realizing suddenly that she had left her clothes in her duffle bag by the bed. Tucking the towel around herself tighter, she stepped out into the room where Jax was still busy pouring over the letter.

At his side were two boxes of pizza.

"My hero." She smiled fondly at him as she walked over, not noticing the surprise that flashed over his face at seeing her in nothing but a fluffy white towel, her damp hair grazing the freckled skin of her shoulders.

She opened the top box and lifted out a slice of pepperoni pizza, biting off the tip indulgently. Her ravaged stomach begged for more as she took another bite, all but purring in satisfaction.

"You feeling better?" He watched as she polished off the first slice and immediately reached for a second.

"Much. So where do you think he's going now?" she asked as she chewed. He noticed with relief that the color had returned to her cheeks.

"I'm not sure." He paused, weighing whether or not he wanted to ask her about the photograph. She saved him the trouble.

"Did you see my newest present?" she asked dryly, motioning to the photograph. He could tell she was trying to not let it bother her, but it was still there, lingering in her eyes.

"I did." She saw his pity, but she also saw his outrage. Knowing he understood what that picture meant to her brought her an odd sense of relief.

"You look like her."

"Yeah, I do," she murmured, her eyes still glued to his. "But it doesn't change anything. She's the reason we're here, Jax. It's because of her that Dante exists, and just because some stupid photograph shows our obvious relation doesn't mean I'm going to forget what she's done."

He got to his feet slowly and approached her, his eyes never leaving hers. Placing a hand on her bare shoulder, he watched the awareness flash across her face.

"Get some sleep, Blythe," he murmured, twining his fingers in the damp ends of her vivid red hair, the urge to touch more of her almost overwhelming. Her body stayed perfectly still, but he heard her breath quicken as his fingers roamed down the back of her neck. "Leave the worrying to me for the night."

Entranced, she felt her eyes close as her head tilted toward the palm of his hand, his fingers softly kneading the curve of her neck.

"You really do have nice hands." She sighed as he pulled away from her, her eyes fluttering open to watch him. "You look real beat up about something, cowboy. What is it?"

You, he wanted to say. But he knew that neither of them could use that complication. Before he could respond, his phone started to ring. He frowned when he saw Rian's name on the Caller ID.

"Yeah," he answered, moving to sit back down on the bed. Blythe reached for a third slice of pizza and sat beside him, trying to listen in.

"I just got off the phone with the Enforcers. Looks like a human highway patrolman pulled over a silver Mercedes Benz SL600 traveling southeast on I-10 near the border of Arizona and New Mexico. A red flag went out when the description matched the stolen vehicle we know Dante has been using, but because the plates didn't match he got away. But the name on the license matches one of Dante's known aliases."

"Well, this is convenient." Jax rubbed his chin as he considered the new information. "Dante just left us another note. Said he was heading south."

"I've never been down there, where does the I-10 go?"

He knew where it lead, alright. And a sinking feeling of dread and fear came over him as he began to wonder if this whole game wasn't just about getting to Blythe. It was about getting to him, as well.

"El Paso? What's El Paso?" Blythe scrambled to her feet as Jax said goodbye to Rian and suddenly stormed toward the door, the look in his eyes frightening.

"Pack up your stuff, we're leaving," he ordered as he swept from the room and slammed the door behind him.

If she hadn't been so uneasy from the utter fury she'd seen in his eyes, she might have stormed after him, demanding he apologize for being so rude. But even she knew better than to confront the bull when it was in the mood to charge. So she packed up her things as quickly as she could and met him in the corridor.

He had his phone to his ear as they walked to the lobby, and when it didn't pick up he shut it off angrily and tried again. After three tries, he shoved the phone back in his pocket.

Within five minutes they were checked out of the hotel and climbing into his car. When he started it up and pulled onto the highway, Blythe decided it was time to ask for an explanation.

"Can you tell me what's going on?"

He took a deep breath to calm his nerves as they merged onto I-10. It was just past nine o'clock and he was pleased to see very little traffic. Hopefully they could make it in five hours. He had to pray they had that long.

"The I-10 leads straight to El Paso. El Paso in Spanish means 'the step', and the Rio Grande, or Big River, runs right through there on its way to the Gulf."

Blythe glanced down at the letter. "I'll be stepping swiftly on down south, where a big river passes on its way to the sea. Well, well...another lucky guess. You should be happy we have a direction again."

"Not when that direction is leading right to my hometown." His lips pulled back in a sneer as his hands clenched tighter on the steering wheel.

"You live in this El Paso place?"

He nodded solemnly, his face stonily blank now. "My mother's ranch is there. She isn't answering my phone calls. If he's hurt her, you won't get your chance to kill him, because I will."

"I'm sorry, Jax." She reached over to lay a comforting hand on his shoulder, true fear and remorse in her eyes. "We'll get there in time, I promise."

By midnight they'd reached Lordsburg, New Mexico. They pulled into the local gas station, and as they stopped, his phone rang.

Blythe watched his expression go from tense to relieved, and knew that it was most likely his mother on the line. Smiling, she patted his arm and headed inside the convenience store to get something to eat.

When she came out a few minutes later with two Cokes and a couple of sandwiches, he was busy filling the car with gas.

"Everything okay with your mom?" She leaned against the side of the car as she handed him the food.

He set the sandwich aside and popped open the top on the Coke. "She's fine. I told her to keep her shot gun next to the front door and to not let in any strange men. She reminded me that the shot gun is always by the front door and that she only lets in strange men who bring her flowers."

Blythe grinned. "Sounds like my kind of lady."

"She can handle herself, but I still worry." He leaned against the car beside her, setting the Coke on the roof before crossing his arms over his chest. "I want to stop in on her, give her a picture of Dante so she knows who to look out for."

"How much does she know? About your job, I mean?" Blythe asked curiously.

"Nothing about demons…she thinks I'm just your good old fashioned bounty hunter." He tilted his head to look down at her, his lips curving slightly. "I'm gonna have to figure out how to explain why I have you with me."

"We'll just tell her that I'm helping you on this particular case. It's not really a lie so much as an omission of key information."

"True."

"Besides, I'm excited to see that porch you were talking about. It sounds nice." She took another swig of soda before setting it aside, amused at the doubt that flashed over his face.

"It is nice, but probably too boring for your taste." Instinctively, he reached out and brushed a strand of her hair behind her ear that had blown free in the wind. She reached up and held his hand there, cupped against her cheek.

"Tell me what your dog's name is, cowboy." She bit her lip as she watched him, suddenly aware they were so close their hips were touching. She angled herself closer as her hand trailed down his arm and felt her own resistance crumbling. She was only fooling herself by pretending she didn't want this, want him.

He watched her eyes light up and her lips curve in that distinctly feminine grin that had his gut clenching and his control shattering. Damning the consequences, he shifted until he was pressing her up against the car, his hands fisted in her hair, his mouth inches from hers. Her eyes held his, the heat in them scorching.

"Cooper. His name is Cooper." He inhaled sharply as he crushed her mouth with his, nearly groaning as her hands instantly came up to rake her nails down his back. The heat he felt from her consumed him until he felt like he was diving into a pit of flames, but he didn't care. On the contrary, he'd never wanted to burn so badly in his life.

The thrill shot straight through her like an arrow as she arched against him, her mouth cruising skillfully over his. Never had she felt so much power, or felt so powerful, just from a kiss. But he was nothing like the others she'd had. He took what he wanted without apology and nothing had ever turned her on more.

He pulled away, fighting for air as his forehead rested against hers, his hands now gripping her waist. His eyes were closed, so she took the opportunity to skim her lips over them, and over his entire face, soothing and sensual. The effect it had on him was like gulping down cool water after a blistering hot summer's day.

"Christ, girl," he whispered, slowly leaning back to look at her. Her answering grin was just cocky enough to remind him of who he was dealing with, and the dangers that were inherent with what they had just done. It also struck him that it had all been worth the risk.

She touched her fingertips to her lips, leaning back against the car, watching him. He had that dark, dangerous look again, and she wondered briefly if he was considering assaulting her senses one more time. Part of her sincerely hoped he would.

"That was interesting," she mused, reaching behind her for her sandwich and unwrapping it slowly without taking her eyes off him. She took a tiny bite and chewed.

"We should get going," Jax said gruffly, tearing his eyes away from her to put the nozzle back into the gas pump. From the flatness of his tone and the systematic way he moved, Blythe could tell that the moment had passed.

Shrugging, she grabbed her soda and skirted around the front of the car to climb into the passenger seat.

He said nothing as he got in beside her. Instead he flipped on the radio and George Jones tenderly crooned about wine colored roses as they continued on to El Paso.

The next thing she knew, she woke up in a soft, comfortable bed with smooth cotton sheets and mountains of pillows with the early morning sunlight beaming in from the window. She instinctively burrowed into the warmth and comfort of the bed, sighing contentedly. Then it occurred to her that the last thing she remembered was being in Jax's car.

Jolting awake, she stared around at the strange room, her eyes sharp and questioning. She noticed her duffle bag resting on the chair beside the bed, and a doorway leading to what she assumed was an adjoining bathroom. Slipping out of bed, she tip-toed toward the only other door in the room, and opened it slightly so she could peer out.

Just outside the door was a long, wood paneled hallway, and at the end of it she could hear two sets of hushed voices. One was a woman and the other she recognized as Jax.

Realizing that she was probably in his mother's home, she hurriedly shut the door and went into the bathroom to take a quick shower. Hell if she was gonna meet his mother looking like a train wreck, she thought as she glanced at herself in the mirror and groaned.

After her shower, she dressed in jeans and a faded red t-shirt and attempted to tame her hair into a less unruly state. As she began to dab on blush and mascara, her hand paused halfway to her cheek. Her eyes widened and she stared down at her hand incredulously.

What am I doing, she wondered, looking up at her reflection. Since when do I care about making a good first impression?

But she knew the answer. It came to her as instinctually as putting on the makeup had. This time everything was different. This was Jax and his mother, and for some reason she gave a damn what they thought. Knowing that, accepting it, she finished putting on the makeup and briskly left the room, partly ashamed at the odd feeling of butterflies in her stomach.

She shut the bedroom door quietly behind her and padded down the hallway toward the voices.

When she emerged into the kitchen, she saw Jax sitting at the dining table with a beautiful blonde woman. They were both smiling and she immediately felt as though she were intruding on some special moment.

He glanced up when he saw her, and the way his eyes sharpened ever so slightly reminded her of how he had looked at her just hours before. And then, just like that, the naked desire was gone and replaced with cool concern.

"Good morning, Blythe." He got to his feet, and as he did so his mother whirled around, her smile bright.

"Oh, honey, would you look at that!" The woman jumped to her feet and rushed forward, planting her hands on Blythe's shoulders. "Aren't you just the prettiest thing?"

She was at least five foot nine, with generous curves and a slender waist. Bombshell blonde hair curled around her face and down to her shoulders, pristine and perfectly in place. Her eyes were the same vivid green as Jax's, but softer and friendlier, set in a face that was movie star beautiful, with skin that had been meticulously maintained all her fifty years.

Blythe stood, stunned, as the woman lushly kissed both of her cheeks, leaving what was sure to be two giant red lip marks. Like any good mother, the woman fondly brushed at the rouge on Blythe's skin and smiled.

"Jax has been telling me all about you, sugar. I'm his proud mama, Loretta Murphy." She backed away and held out an expertly manicured hand covered in glittering silver rings.

"Pleased to meet you." Blythe shook Loretta's hand and grinned. "Thank you for letting me stay last night. Cowboy didn't tell me we would be imposing on you like this." She angled her head to wink at Jax, who simply raised one eyebrow at her and smirked.

"Darlin', I don't think a bomb could have woken you up," he retorted, even as he tried to forget how it had felt to lift her into his arms to carry her inside, and how she had curled against him. It had been one of those rare moments where he had been given the chance to take care of her, where she had let him witness this vulnerable side she kept so rigorously under wraps.

"Honey, you must be hungry!" Loretta said suddenly, her hands on her hips as she eyed Blythe's trim figure skeptically. "Has my boy been feeding you right? Let mama fix something up for you. Come on now, sit down and tell me all about yourself. The stuff Jax doesn't want me know," she added with a wink as she turned and headed toward the fridge.

Blythe eyed Jax apprehensively as she sat down at the table, wondering what the hell she was supposed to say. He just shrugged and sat across from her, leaning back comfortably in the chair, interested to see how Blythe handled his mother's questions. He'd seen her handle herself under pressure before, but could she handle this?

"Well, Loretta, I was born in…" She bit her lip as she tried to remember names of cities in the United States. She rattled off the first one that came to mind. "Miami, but grew up in the Keys. My dad was a fisherman and my mom a waitress at this diner that served the best key lime pie you ever tasted. I have an older brother, Liam, and a younger sister, Capri." She winked at Jax, who was watching her with laughter in his eyes. "When I was four, my parents died in a car accident, and so my siblings and I were raised by our uncle Lucian. He's the greatest man I've ever known."

"Aw, honey." Loretta stopped chopping onions and stared at Blythe sadly. "That must have been hard on you."

Blythe shrugged, then realized that if she had loved her parents in the first place and had lost them in a horrific accident, she probably wouldn't be shrugging. So she fought to bring tears to her eyes, at least a little bit, just to up the believability factor.

"It was hard, but having Lucian made life better again." Thinking of him brought a poignant and very real ache to her heart, so she kneaded it with the palm of her hand, trying to will it away. Jax noticed the real pain on her face and regretted that he hadn't even given her a chance to call home. She obviously missed her family more than she had let on and the fact that she had never once asked to use his phone humbled him. In fact, the only thing she had really ever asked him for was a gun so she could fight alongside him.

"Mama, you got any bacon?" he asked, hoping to give Blythe time to recover or whatever she needed to do.

"Why, I sure do," Loretta replied as she bustled around the kitchen. About ten minutes later, she put out plates piled high with bacon, hash browns, scrambled eggs, sausage, and toast onto the dining table. Blythe's eyes watered with joy at the sight of all the food.

"Loretta, you are now my favorite person," she declared as she began piling food onto her plate.

"Blythe thinks with her stomach most of the time. Don't expect to be her favorite person forever," Jax told his mother teasingly.

Loretta smiled. "I want you to finish every last bite now, you hear?"

"Don't worry, mama. Blythe's notorious for not leaving a single crumb behind."

Amused, Loretta stared at her son as if seeing him for the first time. Had she ever heard her baby boy talk about a girl so fondly? And the way he watched her, so much warmth in his eyes…it was enough to make her speculate that there was much more to their "partnership" then her son had let on.

"So you two are working on this case together?" Loretta asked politely, stirring more sugar into her coffee.

Blythe nodded as she swallowed. "The guy we're hunting down is my uncle. My other uncle," she added, grinning at the startled look in Loretta's eyes. "My uncle Dante is a bad man who's done some bad things. And he's a bit obsessed with me, so cowboy here is using me as bait."

"Good heavens, Jax, I hope you gave this girl a gun." Loretta pressed her hand to her heart, looking aghast at the idea of any woman possibly being unarmed.

"I bought my own, semi-automatic .38 special. Haven't gotten to use it yet, unfortunately."

"I have some tin cans out back, we can target shoot if you'd like," Loretta offered, perking up a bit at the prospect. "C'mon, honey, it'll be a bit of girl bonding time."

"That sounds fun." Turning to look at Jax, she grinned. "Run along after breakfast, cowboy. Your mom and I are going shooting."

About an hour later, Blythe was standing beside Loretta in the wide open field of her backyard, aiming her new gun at an old tin can on a fence some ten yards away.

The Texas sun was already high in the sky, despite it being mid-morning, and the heat was already sweltering. But since she was no stranger to heat, it didn't bother Blythe one bit. In fact, she considered the welcoming heat a good omen for things to come. She would learn to shoot, they would find Dante, and then they would kill him. Case closed, mission over, justice served. It was all just a matter of getting the shot down.

Which, she had to admit, wasn't as easy as she thought. She'd gone out there, head cocked arrogantly and ready to go, only to discover there was much more of a kickback from her gun, and a lot more to it than just pointing at the target and pulling the trigger.

Loretta showed her how to hold the gun properly, with one hand cupped beneath her other to steady it, and how to look down the sight at her target. Standing was also something she hadn't realized played such an important role. In the movies, it seemed like people just flung their guns out and shot at random, miraculously managing to hit something. But in reality she discovered it wasn't like that at all, especially since she didn't manage to hit a single can until she'd fired five times, and even then she just clipped it.

But after some practice, she found she was getting the hang of it.

"Good job, sugar!" Loretta gushed, clapping her hands together giddily as Blythe shot an old coffee can to the ground.

Pleased with herself, Blythe turned and hugged Loretta. "God, it feels good to finally hit something," she laughed.

"I think you're doin' great, honey." Beaming, Loretta pulled away and gestured out to the fence. "Why don't you put the safety on that thing and come help me line up those cans again?"

"Sure." Turning the safety on and slipping the gun into her holster, Blythe followed Loretta out toward the fence, feeling accomplished. She'd never realized just how good a release it was to fire a weapon, to feel the power and the punch behind it as it fired, and then the thrill of hearing the clink of metal on metal and seeing the can fly into the air. She'd have to set up her own target shooting area back home once this was all over. Then she could teach Liam and maybe even Capri.

Thinking of them brought an ache back into her heart, so she tried to push it aside. But the fact was she missed them all so much. Even though it had only been four days since she'd had her encounter with Dante in the nightclub, and three days since she had last seen her family.

Yet for reasons she couldn't quite identify, being there on Jax's mother's ranch with its acres of land dotted with grazing horses and stables, and its big white house shaded by dozens of trees felt safe and comforting. Almost like home itself, even though her home was so different than this place.

Loretta's house, while charming and beautiful, was nothing compared to the castle back home. And the land, while so expansive and flat to the point that you could see for miles to the horizon, had nothing on the lush gardens of Euphora. And yet, this place felt right to her, just like Los Angeles had felt right to her, at least before. She wondered how she would react to the bustling city streets when she had now experienced the vastness and freedom of the southwest.

And Jax's mother was so warm and inviting, unlike any mother she had ever known. Probably because she never really had a mother, at least not one who cared to be one for her. But Loretta was everything that Nyxa was not. She fretted, cooked, laughed, and loved. Blythe realized that she would have given anything to have a mother like that.

And the moment she realized that, she also had another sharp and disappointing realization. She could never, ever share who she truly was with Loretta Murphy. Even if somehow Jax let her correspond and come visit, she could never let Loretta know the truth about her. Knowing it broke her heart.

"Somethin' wrong, sugar?" Loretta asked as they replaced the cans on the fence, spacing them out every foot or so. Her warm green eyes found Blythe's and held, polite but worried.

"Nope, I'm fine." Blythe smiled, determined to push aside any negative thoughts for now. "So how long have you lived here?"

"Oh, about twenty four years or so." Loretta led the way back toward their earlier spot, her blonde hair glowing in the sunlight. "I don't know if Jax told you much about me, but I was a dancer back in the early '80s here in El Paso. I made the mistake of fooling around with a married man and I got pregnant. Though, in retrospect, it was the best thing to ever happen to me." She smiled, pausing to place her hand on Blythe's shoulder.

"Because you had Jax." Blythe reached up to cover Loretta's hand with her own, understanding in her eyes.

"Yes, because I had Jax. And Larry, that was Jax's daddy's name, he was a big shot CEO of some company up in Dallas so he gave me a settlement to make sure I never bothered him again. I suppose I should have insisted on him being a father to my son, but I was young and scared, so I took the money and bought this ranch. I've lived here ever since, raising horses. After Jax was born I never danced again."

"So Jax has never met his father?"

Loretta sighed, sadness clouding her eyes. "No, he hasn't. When he was fifteen he had it in his head that he was gonna go on up to Dallas and hunt him down, make him pay for abandoning us. But by the time he got up there Larry had already passed away a couple years earlier from a heart attack. So he came on back home and never once mentioned it again."

"God, that's horrible." All the times she had complained about her father and Jax had never once mentioned his own, even though his situation was worse. But then again, he had barely told her anything about himself in their time together. Maybe it was time she changed that.

"Why don't you take another shot, sugar?" Loretta said suddenly, nodding toward the fence and smiling. "I bet you take one down this time."

"Let's hope so." All concentration, Blythe took her stance, feet slightly apart, elbows locked straight ahead, her eye on the sight as she took aim. Biting her lip she pulled the trigger, used to the kickback by now, and watched as the can shot into the air and onto the ground.

"Hot damn, I got it!" Blythe cheered, fist pumping the air with her free hand. She turned when she heard clapping behind her and saw Jax watching, his head covered by his black Stetson. Her face automatically lit with a smile. "You see that, cowboy? I'm gonna be a better shot than you."

"Doubtful," he drawled, walking toward them.

Loretta had begun to fire with her own pistol, knocking the cans off like they were nothing until she used up her rounds. She put down her weapon to reload and glanced over just as her son approached Blythe. Her eyebrows raised at the casual way he touched Blythe's shoulder, slipped the gun from her hands, and brushed against her softly to take her place in line of the target. Oh yeah, there was definitely something going on between them. And seeing it, knowing it, made her ridiculously happy. She really liked the girl. She had fire and spit to her, something she admired in a woman. A girl like that would be good for her son, who seemed to always date the cool, reserved types with their noses in the air. About damn time he found someone with some sense.

"I must congratulate you on doing so well your first time out," Jax told her as he took aim at the target, his eyes shaded by the rim of his hat. Blythe watched as he shot three rounds in quick succession, making three cans fly off the fence and into the air, one right after another. He flipped the safety on the gun and handed it back to her, his lips curving in a cocky grin as he spoke. "But I am still better than you."

Pursing her lips, Blythe eyed him in challenge. "That's just that lucky streak of yours again. I bet I can hit three cans in a row by dinner."

"If you can, maybe I'll give you a congratulatory kiss," he murmured, leaning in close, his voice low enough for only her to hear. She tilted her head and smiled coolly.

"Maybe that's not what I want," she replied, noting the easy way he shrugged and stepped back from her.

"Too bad." He smirked before loping off toward his mother, who Blythe suddenly realized had been watching the whole thing. Fighting back a surge of embarrassment, she took aim with her gun once again and fired.

Chapter Ten

By the time they were ready to call it a day, Blythe had, much to her pleasure, managed to hit four cans in a row, beating Jax's earlier attempt. She wasted no time boasting to him about it as they packed their things to head over to his house. In response, he simply slipped his white Stetson onto her head and patted it down.

"There you go. Now you're officially a cowgirl." He smirked, turning away to say goodbye to his mother.

He left before she could even respond, and Blythe grumbled to herself about how she thought she was supposed to get a kiss. Even though she'd teased him about not wanting one, the truth was that she did. Quite desperately, actually, a fact that bothered the hell out of her.

If Capri could only see her now, she mused as she slipped her duffle bag onto her shoulder, holding the hat to try and keep it on her head. Fawning over some guy, just like how she had said she would never do. Best to keep that on the down low for now, she decided. Not like anything could ever come of this little crush she'd suddenly developed for him, they were just too different. And once they caught Dante, they would probably never even speak again. So it was definitely in her best interest to ride this one out and keep it on the light and fun side, just for her own protection.

She walked down the hallway and paused just before the kitchen. She found Jax hugging his mother and seeing it made her heart flutter. What a guy, she thought with a sigh, only to catch herself and curse inwardly. No, she wasn't going to fall for him. Nope...nope...nope.

"Ready to go, cowboy?" She burst into the room, a cheerful smile on her face as she watched Loretta and Jax part and turn to her.

"Sure am, cowgirl." He chuckled, enjoying the way her fiery curls spilled out from under his hat, paired with the cocky grin she always wore and the gun holstered on her belt. She looked like a fiery pixie who'd decided to try her hand at gun battles in the Wild West. It suited her more than he'd ever thought it could. But then again, she was often surprising him by being more than he expected her to be.

"You make sure you come back and visit now." Loretta hugged Blythe, smelling like lilacs in spring. When she pulled away, she smiled warmly. "I know you will, but take good care of my baby boy."

"I'll protect him." Nodding her head, Blythe shifted her bag on her shoulder to redistribute the weight, and as she did so, the picture of Bristol slipped out and drifted to the floor.

"Oops. I'll get that," Loretta chimed, reaching down to pick up the photo. She paused as she stared at it, her eyes widening. "Why, that's Miss Bristol," she murmured, her brow creasing as she lifted her eyes to Blythe's. "Why do you have a picture of her?"

"You knew her?" Blythe asked, astonished.

Loretta turned to her son, who was watching her curiously. "Yes...yes I knew her. I met her when I was seventeen and started working at the club. She looks quite a bit younger in this picture than she was when I knew her, but it's definitely her." Then she looked back down at the picture, and back up at Blythe, and her mouth opened in surprise. "Goodness, Blythe, you look just like her! I didn't even notice before. Are you related?"

"I'm her granddaughter," Blythe managed, her thoughts racing as she tried to figure out the logic of it all. "So she worked at the club with you?"

"Yes, but only for a few years. Then one day she and her little boy were gone." Misty eyed at the memory, Loretta sniffled. "She was such a nice woman, so lovely and kind. She took good care of me when I started out. I was so sad when she left, without even a note or a goodbye."

"Mama, you remember her son?" Jax asked, his hand resting on his mother's shoulder in comfort.

"Barely, he was just a little thing, maybe six or seven, but she brought him around every day. I didn't pay much mind to him because I was busy doing my own thing, but I do remember him being there. Cute boy, black hair, light brown eyes. Quiet and well mannered as far as I remember." She handed the picture back to Blythe, and then suddenly pressed her hand to her heart. "Lord, is he the uncle you're looking for? The one who did bad things?"

"Yes." Blythe frowned at the picture, a sick feeling in her stomach. She glanced up at Jax, who was watching her, a strange mix of uncertainty and dread in his eyes. "Do you remember where they lived?" She turned back to Loretta, who still looked shocked and dismayed.

"I believe they lived near the airport in a little house she rented. I might still have the address in my book."

"See if you can find it." Jax turned to Blythe as Loretta rushed out of the room, his face grim. "Well, that literally was lucky."

"Tell me about it." Blythe huffed, blowing at her bangs as she pondered. "God, that means he lived in El Paso for awhile as a kid. I wonder why Bristol would have come here of all places. And no offense, but why was she dancing?"

"Back then it was one of the only ways to make decent money as a single mother." Jax rubbed his chin in thought. "This puts us one step ahead of him now. I don't think he intended on us finding out about this. If she has the address then we need to go there immediately and see if he's there."

"Sounds good to me," she agreed, rubbing her arms to chase away the chill that suddenly raced over her.

Their luck held out. Loretta had the address where Bristol had lived all those years ago with her son. With their devices on and ready, they pulled up to the house and parked on the street. Together, they stepped out and leaned against the car to get a better view.

"This looks like a really old neighborhood," Blythe observed as she stared around at the quiet street cluttered with tiny, nondescript houses that were, in most cases, worse for the wear. She spotted an elderly man mowing his lawn several houses down, and a few beat-up pickup trucks drove by as they got out of the car.

"This isn't the best neighborhood, but it's certainly not the worst," Jax commented as he looked at the house that Bristol had rented over thirty years earlier. "She cared about where she raised her son, she wanted him to have a decent shot at a decent life."

Snorting, Blythe eyed the petite house with its peeling beige paint, ancient shutters, and weed infested lawn. "Too bad he didn't get the message."

Ignoring her sarcasm, Jax used the scanner to look for a demon presence, only to have it turn up nothing. Immediately he switched to Dryad, and when the radar line wound around the circle, it picked up two dots, one red, one green.

The red dot beside him was Blythe. But the green dot was near the front porch, as if he had been sitting there for awhile, waiting. "He was here, probably only a few hours ago, but we've missed him." Shutting the device off, he slipped it into his pocket. "I thought he led us to El Paso because of me and my connection to this town. But now I know he led us here because of his own connection."

"At least you know he's not going after your mom," Blythe reminded him, patting him on the shoulder. "So what now?"

"Since Dante lived here for a few years, there's a chance he discovered some of the other demons who live here. He might have paid them a visit."

"Oh, but it's much too difficult to locate every demon here because there's almost three million demons on this planet," Blythe rattled off mockingly, only to glance at him with a grin. "Right?"

He snorted and shook his head, amused. "True, but odds are he knows who the hot shots are in this city, just like I do."

"Well, what are we waiting for then? Let's go." She punched his arm playfully and began to climb into the car, only to have him snag her back and pull her against him.

His face was just inches from hers, his eyes intense but his smile teasing. "I forgot to give this to you earlier, even though you claimed you didn't want it." He gave her a fast, hard kiss then released her, stepping back to round the front of the car toward the driver's seat door.

She stood where she was, biting her lip against the need that was pulsing through her. The fact that he could incite it within her with something so simple as a quick, meaningless kiss meant she was in deep trouble.

Frowning, she got into the car and for once found she had nothing clever to say.

They pulled up to an old, run down bar on the outskirts of town beside the border. The white stucco of the building had rust stains on the sides where nails had been exposed and bled in the rain over the years. There were no windows except a couple of boarded up ones near the back, and only one small, barred door off to the side. A sign above the door read *Ricky's* in faded red and green print. Despite it being only four o'clock, there were already four or five cars parked out front.

"Lemme guess, we're going in to see Ricky?" Blythe joked, hoping to God there were no cockroaches inside. She already felt apprehensive about the cleanliness of the place since the sidewalk and asphalt around the building had cracks in it with weeds joyfully growing. In her experience, that was never a sign of a well maintained establishment.

"He's a good guy," Jax easily replied, opening the door for her to enter. She rolled her eyes and slipped past him, her hand itching for her gun hidden in her waistband. Now that she knew how to shoot, she was dying to have to chance to actually use it.

The inside of the bar was dimly lit and cluttered with tables, chairs, a pool table, darts, and a few ancient arcade games. A long, wooden bar stood at the far end, with bar stools beneath it already occupied by a few shady looking bastards. Over the bar hung an old television set, switched to a baseball game. Other than the cheering sounds from the crowd on the TV, the bar was silent as a tomb.

Jax pressed gently into the small of her back to edge her further into the room to the bar. She noticed a door off to the right that she assumed led to the backroom. Out of that door came a man and when he saw them he stopped in his tracks.

"Jackie!" He smiled, giving Blythe a good view of a few gold teeth as he opened his arms wide and then held out a hand to shake Jax's. "How long's it been, ah? One year, two?"

"One, I think." Jax grinned as he shoved his hands into the pockets of his jeans. "You're looking good, Ricky. Your old lady treating you alright?"

"Nah, I caught the bitch cheating last year so I kicked her ass out," Ricky laughed, the movement shaking his belly. He was a bit shorter than Jax, but a big man nonetheless, with broad shoulders and large hands, and an Italian looking face with a generous nose and thick eyebrows, all under a balding head with dark strands of hair combed to the side. His eyes were dark and calculating, despite his overtly welcoming demeanor. When those eyes shifted over to meet hers, she saw them narrow in suspicion. "Well...well, what have we here? Jackie, what're you doin' bringing a Dryad into my place of business, huh? I do somethin' to piss you off?"

"She's helping me find someone, Ricky," Jax said simply, keeping the mood light and casual. "In fact, that's the reason I'm here."

"And I'm always here to help, aren't I?" Ricky smiled again, though it didn't reach his eyes this time as he turned to look back at Jax. "C'mon back, Jasper and me were just putting away our latest shipment."

He turned around and headed back through the door he'd come out of, beckoning Jax and Blythe to follow.

The door lead to a staircase that went down to what Blythe could only assume was a basement, and part of her was screaming *trap* despite her curiosity and her drive to find Dante. She kept her head up as she headed down the stairs into the dark underbelly of the bar, which smelled of dank wood, bitter alcohol and thick smoke. In the dim single light swinging from the ceiling, she could actually see the smoke hanging in the air, and when she spotted the large metal table in the center with a man seated at it, cigar in his mouth, she discovered the source. Scattered on the table were plastic packages of white powder, which were being cut open by the man and measured out, then placed into smaller plastic bags and set aside. Her eyes widened as she realized what it was but she kept her mouth shut.

Jax had told her there were demons who smuggled drugs in from the underworld and sold them to the willing human masses. So it shouldn't surprise her that Ricky was one of those demons. And judging by the large wooden crates lining the back of the room, she assumed he didn't just smuggle drugs, he smuggled weapons, too.

"Why don't you come back into my office, Jackie. Leave the girl out here, she'll be fine with Jasper."

Ricky chuckled as he made his way back through a door that led into a tiny office at the back of the room. Jax turned to Blythe and placed his hands on her shoulders.

"Be good," he murmured, impulsively kissing her forehead before following Ricky into the office. He shut the door, leaving Blythe alone in the basement with the man named Jasper.

She rubbed her fingers over the spot on her forehead that he had just kissed, troubled. With a sigh, she turned around and faced the table, where Jasper was still seated, busily dividing up the powder.

He was an old man, probably in his sixties, heavyset with graying hair and a ragged looking face with hangdog brown eyes. Beside him, his cigar smoked in an amber ashtray.

He said nothing, didn't even look at her, until she sat directly across from him at the table and smiled.

"Hi, Jasper," she greeted, pleased when he looked up at her and sneered.

"You think I don't know what you are?" he grumbled, his voice gravelly and deep, accented with New York just like Ricky's voice had been.

"I get tired of having to hide it all the time around the humans, so it pleases me that you know what I am," Blythe informed him cheerfully as she eyed the drugs. "Some business you guys got here."

He snorted and went back to his work, hands trembling slightly with age. She watched him, wondering how the hell she was supposed to entertain herself while Jax was busy chatting it up with Ricky. Why did she have to get stuck with the boring guy?

"So how long have you been living up here, possessing humans and the like?" She tilted her head to the side to express her curiosity, hoping he didn't just ignore her. When he looked back up at her again, she saw a flash of red in his eyes, just like she had seen in Lenny's days before. Seeing it unnerved her, but she was determined to stand her ground.

"I've been in this body for damn near twenty five years." He suddenly coughed, his entire body shaking. He slammed his fist down on the table as he fought his way through the coughing spell, his leathery face turning an odd shade of red.

Glancing around, Blythe noticed a bottle of whiskey sitting on a crate behind her. Grabbing it, she handed it to him and he gulped down a few sips gratefully. Exhaling roughly, he set aside the bottle.

"Maybe it's time to upgrade," she mused, watching the way he popped a few pills into his mouth from a container in his pocket.

"Ain't gonna change now. I've had a good life with this body." He stared at her again, noting the sincere interest in her eyes. Humoring her, he continued. "Ricky and me, we've been together since the beginning. We run this town and the border, and because we're smart, we keep good relations with the Furies and the Enforcers. That's how come we're still doin' business after all these years."

"By good relations, you mean you rat other demons out?" Blythe concluded, folding her hands in front of her on the table as she leaned in, intrigued.

"We ain't no rats, we just keep an eye on things," he gruffly replied, puffing out his large chest with pride. "And for doing so, we get left alone."

"I'm sorry, my demon education is ridiculously lacking." Blythe grinned, her eyes sparking with interest. "Can you tell me how you guys get to the surface, from the Underworld, I mean."

"When humans ignorant of the laws of Heaven and Hell open a portal, we come in," he answered, his droopy eyes menacing. "They're fools, which is why we don't have no problem possessing them. Easy, ignorant fools."

"I see…" Because she did, and because the gleam in his eye sent more warning signals off in her brain, she decided to back off of that question. "So where do demons go when they die? You do eventually die, don't you?"

"Eventually." He grinned, showcasing rows of crooked yellow teeth as he reached for his cigar, puffing on it generously before continuing. "But when we do go…let's just say that there's depths of Hell even demons can't escape from."

She had to fight against the shudder that raced over her body at his words.

Before she could ask another question, he leaned in closer to her, until she could see the busted capillaries in the leathery skin beneath his eyes. Around them both, smoke swirled in the light from the bulb dangling over their heads.

"The man you're with…you know what my kind call him?"

She shook her head, eyebrows raised with interest.

"We call him the Reaper Man…he's a man so deadly he makes the true reaper shiver in the bowels of Hell. A man like that, he follows no rules but his own."

She would have laughed had she not seen the seriousness in his eyes, or heard the warning in his voice. What exactly was he trying to tell her?

Suddenly, the door opened and Jax and Ricky stepped out, both grinning.

"Ready to go?" Jax asked her, his hands casually in his pockets. He had the outer appearance of being relaxed, but she could tell by the excitement in his eyes that he had learned something of vital importance from Ricky.

"Yeah, let's get the hell outta here." Blythe rose to her feet, not even looking back at Jasper as she made her way to the stairs.

"Alright, cowboy, tell me what your buddy Ricky told you," she grumbled as she climbed into the car beside him. He flipped on the radio and put the car in drive before heading out onto the street. It was nearly nightfall and the city lights around them glowed orange against the darkening sky.

"Dante was at the bar late last night, and he wasn't alone."

"Who the hell was he meeting with?" Blythe turned in her seat, forgetting all about the bar, Jasper and his dire warnings.

"Ricky didn't get a good look, said the guy was wearing a hooded cloak. The pair of them sat in a booth in the corner and they kept to themselves. After about fifteen minutes the guy with the cloak got up and left and Dante stayed for a few more drinks."

"Wow." Stumped, Blythe sat back in her seat and considered this new information.

"I know. This is huge. If he's working with someone, then he's more likely to screw up. It's hard to control the actions of others, so if we can find out who he was talking to, we might be able to get his whereabouts from them."

"How are we going to find them?" Blythe asked, her stomach suddenly grumbling from lack of food.

"I don't know yet. Let's sleep on it tonight, and we'll figure something out in the morning."

"Alright."

About twenty minutes later, after driving out of the city to the outskirts of town where Loretta's house was, Jax pulled up to his own home.

Blythe slipped out of the car and simply gaped.

The house was enormous—twice the size Loretta's had been. It was a sprawling, single story wood paneled house with desert landscaping and a wide front porch lit by a single, glowing yellow light.

Beside and around the back of the house, Blythe could see nothing but acres of land for miles, lit generously by the pale moon. "This is…amazing," she managed, not even noticing when he took her duffle bag from her to sling over his own shoulder. "And it's just down the road from your mom, how cute."

"When I'm not on a case, I help her out at the ranch," he said simply, leading the way to the house. She followed him up the front steps and onto the porch, noting the hand carved wooden benches and chairs he had placed there. Charmed, she followed him inside, only to be suddenly tackled by something furry. "Oh!"

"Cooper! Down." Jax crouched to gather the wriggling Australian shepherd into his arms, letting it lick his face as he rubbed his hands over the white, gray and black spotted fur.

Blythe watched as man and dog wrestled for a bit, smiling at how happy Jax looked now that he was home. Taking the chance to look around, she glanced at the high ceiling broken up with skylights, and the generous stone fireplace in the corner circled by one large, soft and comfy looking sofa. It was a gigantic great room, with a kitchen and dining area off to the left and the living room sprawled to the right. A hallway led off to what she assumed were the bedrooms just past the living room. The colors were muted earth tones, masculine with straight lines and little artwork or frilly touches. This was a man's room, a man's house, and she respected that he felt no need to let it be more than he was: uncomplicated.

"This is some house." She grinned at him as he stood up and released the dog, which immediately bounded forward to greet her. "Hi boy!" She bent down to rub his body and face, letting him lick her cheek. "He doesn't stay here all by himself while you're out gunning for demons, does he?"

"My mom comes by and takes care of him when I'm gone." He headed off to the kitchen, intending to fix something, only to remember he was seriously lacking any actual food. Knowing her eating cycle pretty well by now, he knew he had to find something to feed her.

"I'm gonna call in for some Chinese food," he told her as he reached for the menu from his fridge and the telephone beside it.

Blythe was too busy playing with Cooper to really care. "Okay, whatever." She laughed as Cooper began chasing his non-existent tail, spinning in frantic circles, his vivid blue eyes wide and focused on something that only he could see. Enchanted, she got to her feet and wandered toward the kitchen, marveling at everything.

A few minutes later she found Jax uncorking a bottle of wine and cocked an eyebrow at him. "Since when do you drink wine?"

He glanced back at her and winked. "Every smart man has a bottle of red on hand for when a lady comes over."

He poured a glass for each of them and turned to hand one to her. She accepted it, tilting her head to the side playfully. "What should we toast to?"

"To finding Dante," he replied, holding out his glass. She tapped hers against his and smirked before taking a generous sip.

She leaned against the counter and watched him, running her free hand through her hair, feeling suddenly edgy. Deciding to just get it over with, she blurted out the words that had been eluding her for nearly an hour.

"Why do they call you the Reaper Man?"

She saw surprise flash quickly over his before he replaced it with nonchalance. "Just a nickname, I guess. I don't know why they use it."

"Jasper said it was because you're deadly." She took another sip of wine, though it didn't taste as good coupled with the bitterness on her tongue. "Should I be worried about you, cowboy?"

His eyes darkened at her words, and the dangerous look he sent her reminded her of the way he'd looked that night in Phoenix. "I would never hurt you," he assured her, though the look in his eyes seemed to contradict the statement.

"I can handle myself, Jax." She frowned, her temper sparking. "That's not what I meant, anyway."

"So what did you mean?"

She took a deep breath, knowing she should tell him. Hell, if anything, at least she could find out where he stood and then she could evaluate her own feelings. That was best, wasn't it?

"What I meant was, should I be worried that I'm starting to fall for the most feared and deadly demon hunter there is? Because, I'm not gonna lie, I kind of like the idea."

He froze, his face stiffening as he processed her words. Then he simply exhaled and leaned back against the counter, lifting his wine and downing the entire glass before setting it roughly on the counter.

"You're not falling for me," he retorted heatedly as the door-bell rang. "That'll be the Chinese."

He stalked out of the room, leaving her alone with her thoughts. She hadn't expected him to be angry. Startled, maybe a little annoyed, but not angry. Feeling more hurt than she wanted to admit, she sipped more of her wine as he returned into the kitchen, setting the bags of food down on the counter.

To her surprise, he suddenly came up beside her and pulled her into his arms, just holding her. She closed her eyes and held on, her heart aching.

"I'm sorry, Blythe," he murmured into her hair, breathing in her scent. "Lord, you scare me sometimes."

She pulled away from him, fighting for nonchalance. "I get it, okay? What's between us has to stay casual, for both of our sakes. I know that. I just...damnit, I don't even know anymore."

"Let's just put this out of our minds for now. Let's eat and then I want you to call your family. You can use my phone." With that, he grabbed the bag of food, the glasses and the bottle of wine and headed into the living room.

"But I don't even know how to use a phone," she managed, fighting back the emotions she felt. God, he could read her like a damn book. He knew, even though she hadn't said a word, that she missed her family.

She wandered into the living room after him, sitting down on the couch as he broke into the boxes of food.

"It's okay, I'll show you." He handed her a box filled with some kind of reddish orange blobs and a pair of sticks. She stared down at them skeptically.

"What am I supposed to do with this?" she choked out a laugh, eyeing him doubtfully. "What is this stuff?"

"Those are chop sticks and that is sweet and sour pork. You hold the chop sticks like this," he grabbed her hands and molded her fingers around the sticks, "and you pinch them together around the food to pick it up."

Snorting, she shook her head. "You're crazy. I'm getting a damn fork."

"Oh no you don't." He pulled her back down as she tried to stand up, causing her to giggle as he wrestled her back into place. "If you're gonna eat Chinese food, you have to do it right. Otherwise it's disrespectful."

She rolled her eyes at him. "Fine, I'll give it a shot. But if it doesn't work I'm getting the fork." She pouted a bit as she tried to maneuver the sticks around a piece of pork, then bit her lip as she managed to grab it. She inched it toward her open mouth slowly, only to have it suddenly slip and fall into her lap. "Damnit!"

He started laughing so hard he nearly cried, and hearing it and seeing it made her start laughing too. They slumped together, both shaking with laughter, her hand finding his knee for balance and his arm winding around her waist. When the humor seemed to slip away, she realized her head was resting comfortably against his chest, and she could hear his heart quicken its pace as she tilted her head back to look at him.

Clearing his throat, he shifted away from her, reaching for the chow mein.

She followed his cue and sat back into the couch with her box of sweet and sour pork, knowing the spark they both felt wasn't going to be as easy to forget as he had made it sound.

"Jax?" she said suddenly, pushing the pork around with the sticks as she glanced over to look at him.

"Yes, Blythe?"

"I realized this morning that I know literally nothing about you, except that you grew up in El Paso, were raised by a single mother who worked at a strip club, had a father who you never knew because he wrote you and your mom a big check and then bailed. You're a bounty hunter who hunts down demons for Thea as a specialty. You have a nice house and a dog named Cooper, and a black Chevelle that you insist on blasting crappy country music in. But other than that…I don't know much else. There's a big chunk missing in between all that stuff. I'd love to hear about it, if you're willing to tell me."

Because his first instinct was to tell her everything, to share all of it with her, he knew that that was what was ultimately going to happen.

He'd fought too long to keep his past under wraps from her, to never let her in on more than what was necessary. But things were different now, and she deserved to know the truth. After all, even before he'd met her he'd known so much about her to the point where she hadn't even had to share anything with him. He'd already known it all, thanks to Thea.

But Blythe had rarely pestered him for information about himself, just like she'd asked him for hardly anything the whole time they'd been together. She didn't require much to be content, but that didn't mean she didn't deserve it.

"When I turned eighteen, I joined the police academy here in El Paso," he began, reaching over to fill their glasses with more red wine. "I guess I had something to prove to myself, that I could protect those around me and take out the bad guys all at once. It was fun and I was a natural." He leaned back and sipped, smiling dryly at her. "When I was twenty two, I was the lead on what ended up being a huge drug bust. It all started out as pretty routine, until I was approached by two men in suits who I assumed were the Feds, come to take charge of my case. Naturally, I was hostile at first as this was my bust and I was reluctant to hand it over to another agency, but they told me they were from an elite, highly top secret unit that specialized in what they called 'the supernatural.' I thought it was all some big joke until they took me into a private room with the leader of the drug ring I'd busted, and the bastard started shaking and black smoke came out of his body, forming what I now know is a demon. I thought I was dreaming; I kept slapping my face and laughing, because I couldn't believe what I was seeing. And then they explained everything to me. They told me about Thea, about the Furies and about demons. They said they were called Enforcers, and that their job was to hunt down demons. They wanted me to join them. I'd get to travel the country, work with a specialized team, and see things that 99.99% of the human population is completely unaware exists. I must of still thought I was dreaming, because I said yes before I'd even given it much thought. The next thing I knew, I was in Washington, DC, training with other new recruits on how to destroy demons."

"That's a long way from home." Blythe sipped her wine. "Is that why you decided to go rogue?"

"In a manner of speaking, but it was mostly because I was given the chance to go solo more than me seeking it out. You see, one of my first major missions with my team was to take out this demon who was mass murdering people in Sudan. We were supposed to go in, capture him, bring him back to our base some five miles away, and destroy him. But what we didn't know was he had taken a hostage, a twelve year old girl, and he was threatening to blow himself and the girl to pieces with a bomb he had strapped to his chest if we tried to take him. So we contacted the Furies and they showed up to try and reason with him. But what we didn't know was that he had never planned on blowing himself up, he had an escape plan. It occurred to me as I was standing there, my weapon drawn and aimed at him as he stood inside the courtyard of his compound. I thought to myself, shit, he's going to start the five second timer on the bomb, possess the little girl and run, and blow his former body to pieces. It was so clear to me that when he suddenly set off the timer and within two seconds released the little girl, I ran for the girl, leaving my post. My commander yelled to me, but I didn't stop. I heard the explosion of the bomb, but I still didn't stop. Rian was there and he must have had the same idea because he was right with me. Suddenly the little girl stopped and turned around, and she had a gun. Lord knows how that happened, but the bastard started firing at us. I grabbed Rian and pulled him behind the side of the nearest building. That was all the time he needed to grab his own weapon and aim it at the demon as he started to run again. He hit the girl with this device that only stuns, not kills, because we knew we had an innocent twelve year old girl on our hands. She crumbled to the ground, he forced the demon out of her, and then destroyed him then and there. The little girl survived, the demon was dead, and Rian and I became friends. He was the one who recommended to Thea that I work exclusively for her. He said that I understood the way demons thought more than any other human he'd met. One thing led to another and I took the job. It worked out better for me, since I could live in El Paso and help my mom on the ranch when I wasn't on assignment for Thea. I've been doing it ever since."

Blythe leaned toward him, a wicked gleam in her eyes. "So how many demons have you hunted down for Thea?"

"Seventeen. Dante makes eighteen." He sipped more of his wine, watching her closely. "I haven't failed yet."

"Did you kill all of them?"

Something dark and haunted clouded his eyes at her question. "Yes."

"So you are deadly." Her lips curved, and he wondered why she was so fascinated by the idea of killing demons. Of course, how could he blame her when it was his life's passion?

"I will stop at nothing and kill anyone who stands in the way of who I'm hunting. That's why I'm deadly." His eyes betrayed nothing as he leaned over to reach for one of the white boxes on the coffee table.

"What's it like?" She couldn't help herself. She just had to know. "To kill a demon?"

"It's not for the faint of heart." He said mildly as he took a bite of orange chicken.

She let out a half laugh at his words. "Well, you know I'm not faint hearted."

"No, you're not." He lifted his eyes to hers, concern edged around the darkness that shadowed them. "That's why I worry about you."

"Pssh." She waved his comment away with a grin. "What's there to worry about?"

"Your bark is bigger than your bite, Blythe, let's be honest here," he told her candidly. "You're inclined to rush in and take on something more than you can actually handle. That's how people get themselves killed."

She felt her pride bruise at his words and her temper flared up to defend it. "You seriously underestimate me, Jax," she snapped, rising to her feet. "Remember I said that when I'm standing over Dante's dead body, gun smoking in my hand."

With that, she walked over, picked up her duffle bag from the floor by the front door, and headed toward the hallway that she assumed lead to the bedrooms.

"Which room should I sleep in?" she asked coldly.

"Second door on the left."

"Goodnight, then." She turned on her heel and left him alone, sitting on his enormous sofa, wondering what in the hell he was going to do about her when the time came for them both to face Dante.

Chapter Eleven

By the time morning came, she woke up knowing she'd overreacted. Not only had she gotten little sleep, but she also knew she was being touchy and bitchy to him when he didn't deserve it.

Yeah, he'd insulted her when he'd claimed she couldn't handle killing Dante on her own. But he was the demon hunter here, the professional who'd killed seventeen high-profile, extremely dangerous demons in the past. She couldn't compete with that record of accomplishment, and so she'd just gotten angry with him for pointing out what she knew was truth. She had the desire to kill Dante, but that didn't mean she had the ability. That was where Jax came in and why she needed him. He needed her to lure Dante and she needed him to execute the kill when the time came.

Knowing it—really knowing it—made her feel sorry for jumping down his throat. But she still had her pride, and she was never very good at apologies even when she knew she was wrong.

And yet she also knew she owed him an apology, and because it was him, and because things were different, she found herself slipping into her robe and going to find him.

She wandered out into the kitchen as the sun rose into the sky, hoping he was awake. Lucky for her, he was seated at his dining table, sipping coffee and reading the morning paper.

He looked up as she entered, his face carefully blank. She smiled warmly, hoping to ease the tension. When he didn't smile back, she sighed and sat beside him.

"I'm sorry, okay?" she blurted out, her eyes shadowed from lack of sleep. Underneath the table, her hands clenched with anxiety.

For a moment he didn't say anything, he just sipped his coffee. When he did speak, his voice was level and calm. "I'm not angry with you, Blythe. But I appreciate the apology."

She hadn't realized she'd been holding her breath, but she let it out with a shaky laugh. "Wow, that was easier than I'd expected." Her hands unclenched under the table and came up to run through her hair. "You're right about Dante, though. I don't know anything about killing demons, and I'm still new to shooting, and–"

"You don't have to explain yourself, it's okay." He reached out to cover her hand with his, the move natural and friendly. She felt much better when his lips curved into a slow smile. "You didn't call your family last night. Let me get them on the phone so you can talk to them."

He rose to get the phone and she sat there, stupefied that he wasn't even the slightest bit angry with her. In the brief time she'd known him, she hadn't thought him to be a very patient man. But maybe this was proof that things really were different between them now.

He wandered back over with his cell phone to his ear. She saw him smile as Thea answered, and listened as he asked for Lucian so she could speak to him. Her eyes filled as he handed the phone to her a minute later, her hand shaking slightly as she held it to her ear.

"Lucian?"

"*Good morning, honeypot.*" His serene voice came through the phone, and the simple pleasure of hearing it made her smile. She glanced at Jax and mouthed thank you, a single tear falling down her cheek.

He nodded, grabbed his coffee, and left her alone, his mind shifting gears to focus on Dante. He had to figure out their next move, and so far all he could think about was who the hell was meeting with Dante, and why. Until he figured that out, he was at a dead end. He had a couple other contacts he could speak to and he only hoped they would point him in the right direction.

About an hour later, Blythe hung up the phone. She laid it gently on the table, as though it might shatter. How precious it was to hear the voices of her family even though she was so far away from them. And while only speaking to them didn't quite dull the ache in her heart, it did help settle her mind that they were doing alright without her.

Rising to her feet, she wandered out to the front porch in search of Jax. When she opened the door and peered out, she saw him lounging in one of his wooden chairs, his feet propped up on the porch railing and Cooper curled up fast asleep beside him. She smiled instantly, the image so close to what she had imagined. The rugged Texas cowboy with his faithful dog, content with life just as it was. What was it about that concept that made the man so damn appealing?

He turned as she came out, the sunlight glowing brightly in her fiery hair, creating some kind of vivid red halo. In his eyes, the image suited her perfectly. She was neither a white angel nor the devil's daughter; she was the perfect mix of both.

"Thank you for letting me use your phone," she said, closing the door and walking forward to lean against the porch railing. "I've missed them so much."

"I know," he replied, sipping his coffee as he watched her, enjoying the view. She had slipped into a silk robe the color of honeyed gold, and the way it illuminated in the sunlight made her appear to glow. And her unpainted mouth, curved into that devious grin, always just slightly cocky and disobedient, suited her to the tee.

"Everyone's fine, I assume?"

"Yeah, they're good. They miss me and want me to ditch you and come home." She shook back her hair and laughed. "But they know me better than to expect that to happen."

"Mmm." He smirked as he sipped more of his coffee, his left foot reaching down to rub Cooper's back absently. Blythe watched Cooper stretch and yawn, tongue wagging at the attention. Maybe she could convince Thea to let her get a dog…she'd never really thought about having a pet before but it would be nice to have someone to accompany her on her morning runs. Which, she thought with a groan, she'd neglected to do for the entire week. But there were more important things to do now, she reminded herself. Much more important things.

"Did you get a chance to speak with your father, settle things?"

Blythe rolled her eyes, annoyed. "No, but I didn't really want to speak to him anyway. I'm still mad at him. Besides, he wasn't there. Lucian said he's left Euphora a few times this week, going God knows where. He probably found some other whore to sleep with."

She sulked, crossing her arms over her chest, wondering why it bothered her so much.

"No one knows where he's been going?" Jax asked, setting his coffee aside and sitting up in his chair.

Blythe frowned. "If he's told anyone, Lucian hasn't heard about it. Why do you care?"

"Was he gone two nights ago?"

"I don't know. I didn't think to ask for all the details. What are you getting at?" Her eyes narrowed suspiciously, while his flashed with understanding.

"Someone met with Dante at Ricky's bar two nights ago."

"You have got to be kidding me," she choked out an impatient laugh, even as her stomach churned uncomfortably. "Why would my dad be meeting with Dante? They hate each other."

"Maybe he's trying to convince Dante to leave you alone. Or maybe he's helping Dante stay one step ahead of us."

"No...there's just no way." Shaking her head fervently, she began to pace. "He wouldn't stoop that low, he couldn't. Not after everything that's happened. Besides, what could he possibly gain by helping Dante get away?"

"Maybe he feels bad for never being there for his little brother." He watched in amazement as she threw her head back and laughed.

"He doesn't think about anyone but himself," she told him, stopping mid-step to face him with her hands on her hips. "If he is meeting Dante, it's because he thinks Dante can give him something that he wants, and if he's sneaking around then his intentions are anything but noble."

"Fair enough." He stood up to lean against the rail beside her, resting his elbows on the smooth wood and staring out over the acres and acres of land. In the distance, he could see the city and the mountains that bordered it. He was working over the details when she suddenly spoke.

"You know, this wouldn't be the first time he's been blamed for something he didn't do," she mused, leaning against the rail with a hefty sigh. She tilted her head to watch him, uncertainty warring with the guilt she felt. "He's not perfect, but he's not necessarily a bad person, either."

Jax glanced at her, his lips curving at the edges. "Then we'll hold our judgments for now."

He stood up slowly, turning his body to face hers and lifting his hand to gently cup at the back of her neck. He smelled of soap and coffee mixed with a hint of leather from the boots on his feet.

"Is this the moment where we stop putting this out of our minds, cowboy?" she asked, fighting for calm while her heart leapt to racing speed in a near instant at his touch. Her breath caught when his hand tightened ever so slightly in her hair, the storm in his eyes raging.

"I'm not sure yet," he murmured, his other hand coming up to slide against her back, smooth against the silk of her robe. "I just know you look mighty pretty here in the sunlight this morning."

She smiled, tilting her head up in welcome, her eyes challenging him. "Then what are you waiting for?"

Nothing, and everything, he thought as he kissed her slowly, not wanting to rush. There was something about the lazy morning sunlight and the way she sighed against him that comforted and soothed. It was like melting into a warm pot of honey, golden and rich. Just like her eyes.

The tenderness surprised her, especially since she'd been fully prepared for an assault. But instead what he gave her was calm and gentle, a kiss that had her bones melting and her mind going blissfully blank. With an indulgent sigh, she wrapped her arms around his neck and felt herself sliding even further down that slippery slope into what she knew was dangerous territory. But at that moment, she wasn't worried about a damn thing.

In the distance, he watched them.

He stared through his binoculars from his hiding place in the branches of the ancient oak tree, jealousy a blinding hot fist to his gut. Why hadn't he anticipated this? Blythe and the bounty hunter…together? The very idea of it infuriated him.

At first it had humored him they were working with each other, and it had only made the chase more interesting. But the last thing he'd expected was for them to become anything more than casual friends. And now that it was blatantly obvious they *were* something more, he realized he needed to step up the game—and fast. He needed to touch her again, to make her see that he was the only one for her. She needed him by her side, not the goddamn bounty hunter. She would see, in time.

Fighting to push aside his rage, he slipped out of the tree and walked briskly down the road where he'd discreetly parked the stolen Mercedes behind an old barn.

Yes. It was time to step up the game and remind them that he was watching their every move and that he was more than ready for them.

When the cell phone began to ring from inside the house, Cooper immediately let out an excited bark, jumping to his feet and wagging his tailless behind joyfully. It took a second, more forceful bark for Jax to break from Blythe and glare down at his dog.

Before he could tell Cooper to be quiet, he heard Waylon singing about old Hank and realized his phone was ringing.

Cursing under his breath, he turned back to Blythe.

"I'll be right back, the damn phone is ringing."

He stalked back into the house, leaving her leaning against the porch railing, feeling empty without him.

Scowling, she glanced down at the dog, who was grinning happily up at her. Unable to help smiling back at him, she bent down to rub his fur.

"It's not your fault that some jerk had to call and ruin me and your daddy's moment, is it?" she crooned, pleased when he toppled over to let her rub his belly.

She was still basking in unbridled puppy love when Jax came out a few minutes later. He froze and watched her, surprised by the instant shock of pleasure he felt seeing her bathed in sunlight on his front porch, playing with his dog. His pulse quickened as she glanced up at him and smiled, the happiness on her face intoxicating. Why was it she looked so natural...*so right*...on his porch?

"What's the word, cowboy?" she asked, pushing back a curled strand of hair that had fallen over her face.

His eyes followed the movement, even as he tried to push all thoughts of her not related to their mission out of his head.

"That was Rian. He was able to find out the name of the elementary school Dante attended while living here in El Paso. He wants us to go undercover and see if we can get access to the records, see if there are any clues in there as to where he might be hiding out."

"Okay." All seriousness now, she stood up and nodded. "Let's do this."

The school was a few blocks from where Dante and Bristol had lived, and was also within a short drive of the strip club. Conveniently close, Blythe figured as they pulled into the parking lot, her eyes scanning the faded brick building aged by weather and time.

In a fenced playground off to the left side of the school, several children played on jungle gyms and swings, their cries and laughter carrying through the already steadily warming summer heat. Within days school would be out for the season and the children were already gearing up for the break.

She wondered if Dante had ever felt at home here, just as Jax always had. Just as she nearly did.

As she climbed out of the car she glanced at Jax, who was busy adjusting his tie. She had to bite back a laugh at how professional he looked, clad in black slacks, a long sleeved button up shirt in sage green paired with a diamond print tie in richer greens. He'd stressed the importance of making a good impression on these people, since they had to somehow convince them to release the record. And so he'd dressed up in business casual and insisted she do the same.

The only outfit she'd packed that was even remotely professional was a formal dress Capri had slipped into her duffle without her realizing it. It was a trim knee length dress in a rich, navy blue, with short sleeves that barely curved over her shoulders and a rather conservative V neckline. She'd paired it with simple black pumps and basic diamond stud earrings.

She wanted to look affluent, trustworthy, and capable. None of which she was certain she could portray without slipping up. She wasn't a very good actress; she was too in tune with who she was and always had a hard time pretending to be anything different. But this was important, and she knew she had to give it her best.

She'd also slipped on a ring Lucian had given her a few years before as a birthday present, a three carat rectangular cut ruby set in a brilliant gold band. She put it over the ring finger of her left hand, as Jax had somewhat awkwardly informed her he would be pretending to be her husband. He'd dug up his class ring from high school, a simple gold band with the name of the school inscribed in the metal. From just a glance, it didn't appear to be anything other than a plain gold wedding band.

"You ready?" Jax asked as she rounded the car toward him. With a bright smile, she held out her hand to take his.

"I'm always ready, cowboy."

Hand-in-hand, they walked toward the administrative building. Any onlooker would have simply seen a young, married couple possibly researching the area's schools as they planned for their family. No one would assume that the man hunted demons for a living and that the girl was the embodiment of the element of fire.

When they entered the school's administrative office, there was a pert blonde sitting at the reception desk reading a book. She glanced up as they entered, her eyes behind her glasses flicking immediately to scan Jax up and down. She dismissed the red head as short and boyish, and paid no mind to the rings on their fingers. She knew such things were never permanent; she had an ex-husband herself.

"Can I help you?" she greeted cheerfully, smiling her best smile at the man and swiftly stowing away her romance novel.

She leaned forward just enough to strategically show off her cleavage, which, to her extreme pleasure, was much more robust than what the skinny red head had.

Jax gently laid his hand on Blythe's lower back, and leaned in to whisper in her ear.

"Go sit by the door and pretend to cry. Trust me."

She sent him an annoyed glare, but knowing she had to play the part of the distressed and hopeful relative grieving the loss of her mother, she pretending to burst into sobs and let him lead her to one of the plastic chairs by the door. She buried her face in her hands and silently wished him dead for making her do this. It was incredibly embarrassing to act like such a sissy in public, even if it wasn't real.

Jax left Blythe and sauntered over to the receptionist, his smile apologetic. He had a distinct hunch he'd have better luck swaying the blonde on his own.

"Good morning, darlin'." He sent what looked like an irritated and embarrassed look over his shoulder toward Blythe, who was making whimpering noises as her whole body trembled. It took all he had not to laugh. When he turned back to look at the receptionist, his flirtatious smile had the blonde's heart fluttering. "I apologize, Kim," he said as he glanced at her name tag. "My wife is very upset."

"Aw, what's wrong with her?" Kim crooned, though she could care less. She was more focused on whatever delicious cologne Adonis here was wearing.

"Her mother just passed, and well, we're in quite the predicament. I sure could use your help."

"What is it you need?"

"Well, you see, my mother-in-law's dying wish was for my wife to reunite with her only living relative, her uncle. The only problem is, we don't know hardly anything about him, other than that he went to this school thirty years ago. If we could just take a quick peek at his records, maybe we'd find something in there to give us a clue as to where we can find him."

"That's so sweet." Looking at Blythe now, the blonde smiled pityingly. "Unfortunately though, I can't release the records to just any ol' body. You have to be the next of kin."

"Darlin', as far as we're aware, my wife is his next of kin." Jax leaned up against the desk, resting his hip there as he prepared to lay it on thick. "I'd be much obliged if you could run on into the back there and pull the record for me. It ain't gonna hurt none." His lips curved into a charismatic grin, his green eyes focused intently on the blonde's baby blues.

"I don't know…" Chewing her bottom lip, she pondered how she could somehow slip him her number discreetly so his wife wouldn't notice. Though she was still sobbing like a toddler in the corner, so who cared about her. He looked like he was sick of her, anyway. Her mind made up, Kim smiled warmly at him. "What's the name, honey?"

"Dante Williams." Using the alias Rian had told him, Jax watched the blonde wink at him and saunter off, making sure her generous hips swayed in his line of vision. Instead of watching her, however, he'd already turned around to stare at Blythe.

When she noticed the blonde had left the room, Blythe lifted her head and glared at Jax. "This is so degrading. I'm going to make you pay for this."

Enjoying the heat in her eyes, he simply grinned. "But you play the part so well. I was convinced."

"Oh and you play the part of the sleazy scumbag husband so well, too," she shot back, her lips curving. "And what is that bitch thinking, hitting on a married man? God, some people are low."

"That *bitch* is getting us the information we need, so be nice."

She stuck her tongue out at him, then suddenly shoved her face back into her hands as Kim returned. She resumed crying, upping the noise level in the hopes of embarrassing him.

Jax turned back to Kim, who handed him a file folder with a suggestive smile. "You can have a seat right here at my desk and peruse over the file if you'd like."

He looked back at Blythe, then faced Kim again, making sure to look embarrassed and grateful. "Thanks, darlin'."

He sat down at the chair beside her desk and opened the file. Inside, Kim's number was paper clipped to the top page. Glancing up at her, he smiled and slipped the number into his shirt pocket without a word, knowing she would keep quiet about this whole thing if he just played along. Then he got down to business reading the file.

His eyes narrowed as he searched through Dante's grades, his school medical records, his teacher's comments about his performance. He found Dante's basic information near the back, with his name, his mother's name, and their address in El Paso. When he came to the line for the name and address of his previous school, his breath caught in his throat at seeing an address in Phoenix listed. Well, well, he thought curiously. Looks like the detour in Phoenix had meant something to Dante as well. Which would also mean, logically speaking, that his next destination would match where he had lived after leaving El Paso.

He turned the page and found the student exit information. Only instead of the name and address of a school, there was simply a P.O. Box. To his dismay it was listed as being in Chicago, Illinois.

Cursing inwardly, he shut the file and got to his feet, startling the receptionist who had been covertly watching him from behind her book. He thrust the file back at her, too annoyed to worry about playing the part any longer.

"Got what I needed, thanks." He nodded before turning around and stalking toward Blythe, grabbing her by the arm and lifting her to her feet.

"Hey!" She scowled as he pulled her out of the office and out into the midday sunlight, leaving the bewildered Kim behind. They didn't slow down until they'd reached the car, and even then he was all thrumming frustration and nerves.

"What's gotten into you? What did you find in the file?" Blythe demanded, rubbing her arm bitterly as he reversed the car and shot out of the parking lot.

"I think Dante's taking us to the same places he and his mother lived when he was a kid." He ran a hand through his hair, still trying to work it all out himself.

"How do you know?"

"The file said he'd come from a school in Phoenix before attending the El Paso school, and then the forwarding address was to a P.O. Box in Chicago. I can't think of any other explanation."

He saw a flash of silver in his rearview mirror, but didn't think much of it.

"Well, good, now we should go to Chicago. How far is it?"

He laughed, shaking his head. "A day's drive or more. We'd have to fly. But I don't know. I just don't think he's left El Paso yet."

"Even if he hasn't, he's going to eventually. We can still head him off," she reasoned.

"I don't know," he mumbled, seeing the flash of silver again. Glancing in his rearview mirror, he spotted the silver Mercedes following close behind them. "Jesus."

He turned the wheel suddenly and whipped around a street corner, nearly clipping a pedestrian.

"Holy hell cowboy, where's the fire?" Blythe shouted, grabbing hold of the dashboard for dear life as he shifted into gear and shot past sixty mph.

"He's following us, get down." Jax kept his eyes on the mirror as he turned down another street, leading to what he knew was a dead end.

"Who's following us?" Blythe whirled around in her seat and when she spotted the silver Mercedes, her mouth dropped open. "Oh, shit. Where's my gun? Shit...shit...shit...did I leave it at home? Goddamn this stupid dress, why couldn't I have worn jeans like a normal person?"

"Shut up and get down, Blythe. And hold on." He gritted his teeth together as he swung the wheel again, taking them down a narrow street lined on both sides by tall buildings. About a half mile ahead was a dead end.

"Oh my God." Blythe's eyes widened as she glanced one last time behind them and saw the Mercedes pursuing them at full speed down the alley. "We're gonna hit."

He simply grunted as he suddenly pumped the emergency brake and spun the wheel, whirling the car around and bringing it to a screeching halt just feet from the end of the alley. Without missing a beat, he reached behind him and pulled out a pistol grip sawed off shotgun and proceeded to point it out the window directly toward the oncoming car.

The Mercedes slammed on its brakes and came to a skidding stop, smoke streaming up from the tires. Blythe's heart was pounding viciously in her chest as she stared wide eyed at Jax.

"That's a big gun you got there, cowboy." She gulped, needing some kind of moisture to coat her dry throat as she turned back to face the Mercedes. A young man came out, his hands raised.

"P-please, don't shoot. I'm not Dante, I'm just delivering a package from him," he stuttered, his eyes frantically glued to the shot gun. He looked like he was no more than seventeen, with sandy hair and dirty clothes.

Jax exited the car slowly, gun still pointed, not willing to take any chances.

"Let me verify for myself that you aren't him." He reached into his pocket for his phone with his free hand and tossed it to Blythe. "Take a picture of him."

"Okay." Fumbling a bit, her hands shaking, she opened the same program she'd seen him use, and selected Dante's name. Aiming the phone at the kid, she snapped a picture, then waited anxiously for the result. When NEGATIVE popped up, she let her breath, both in relief and in disappointment. "It's not him."

"Okay, I want you to tell me where he is, and how you found us," Jax ordered.

The man gulped and hesitated, trembling. "Look, I don't know where he is now, he said he had to go. He just asked me yesterday to find you and to give the girl this package." He reached in his back pocket and hastily pulled out a small white package. "He told me where you live and I followed you to the school and waited till you left. I just need to give the package to the girl."

"How do you know Dante?"

"We're old friends. I don't want any trouble. I haven't seen him in years, and he shows up and asks me to do this favor for him. Then he disappears. I don't know where he went."

"And he gave you his car?"

The young man glanced back nervously at the Mercedes. "He said he didn't need it anymore, that he couldn't take it with him."

"Because he was taking a plane?"

"I don't know. I didn't ask." Trembling, the man looked toward Blythe. "Just let me give her the package and I'll go."

"Fine, but hurry up." Jax followed the man with the shot gun as he approached Blythe and handed the package to her through the passenger side window. She clutched it numbly in her hands as she watched him scramble back into the Mercedes and whip the car around, speeding out of sight.

Chapter Twelve

It had all happened so fast, so abruptly, that her mind was still racing to catch up with all the details. The Mercedes was nothing more than a memory now and there was a new package from Dante sitting in her lap. She looked down at it, almost as if she had no idea how it had gotten there. When Jax climbed into the car beside her and stowed his shot gun behind the seat, she felt as if she were waking from a dream.

Without saying a word she reached over, grabbed his face in her hands, and kissed him roughly on the mouth. When she pulled away, her face was lit with a bright and devious grin.

"God, that was exhilarating!" She slapped her hand to her chest, trying to calm her fluttering heart. "You are quite the badass, cowboy. I haven't had that much fun since I went skydiving last year."

He stared at her blankly for a moment, completely taken off guard. "Fun?" he managed, confused by the thrill he saw in her eyes.

"Yeah, fun. The high speed pursuit, you pulling a 180 with the car and whipping out that enormous gun. Which, by the way, you never told me you had back there."

"It's for emergencies." He scowled, shifting the car into gear and flipping on the radio.

"We definitely need to do that more often." She was still smiling as she sat back in her seat, thrumming her fingertips on her knee caps as the adrenaline continued to pump through her veins.

He pulled out onto the street and glanced over at her, amusement in his eyes. "You sure are a strange girl."

She waved his comment away with a laugh. "You like me this way, I know you do. I keep you on your toes."

"Lord knows you do something to me," he said, more to himself than to her as he reached over to flip the station on the radio. Garth Brooks roared out about the game called rodeo as Jax gunned the engine and took them onto the highway toward his home.

Blythe watched him for a few moments, chewing her bottom lip in thought. The sun was beginning its late afternoon descent in the sky, the heat sweltering. The combination of the desert landscape out the window, the blistering heat, and the twangy southern rock on the radio had become so natural to her, so normal, that she wasn't even thinking of home anymore. This, and the born and bred Texan beside her, were something like home to her now.

"You should open that package," he said quietly, keeping his eyes on the road.

She glanced down at her lap, having nearly forgotten it was there. She tore it open, pulling out the letter first and then tilting the package upside down so her new gift fell into her open palm.

It was a ring, the same gilded bronze as the necklace had been, with a similar large amber stone set in the center. Along the band was the inscription: *Fire destroys fear, Fire lights darkness, Fire wields courage, Fire breeds glory.*

Pursing her lips, she tossed it back into the package, annoyed that she felt a connection to it. It was just a stupid ring that had been her stupid grandmother's…just an inanimate object that meant nothing. But she knew the bond was there, she could feel her blood call out to the ring. It was another heirloom, as ancient as the Earth itself, passed down the Fire Dryad line for centuries.

She forced her mind clear as she shoved the package away and opened the letter.

Blythe,

You're getting closer, but not quite there yet darling. Tsk, tsk on getting distracted with the bounty hunter. I hope you see the folly in your ways soon, as I intend to show you what you really deserve.

Dante

Her eyebrows drew together in confusion as she reread the letter over again, wondering what the hell he was talking about. Distracted? Show her what she really deserves? God, he was getting crazier by the day. Disturbed, she turned to Jax, wondering how he would take it.

He hadn't mentioned it yet, but she knew he must be thinking of it. The kid who'd delivered the package had said that Dante had told him where Jax lived. Had Dante been watching them? Had he seen her and Jax together?

"What does it say, darlin'?"

She read it to him then sat back to gauge his reaction. At first he said nothing as he processed the words, combing through them, deciphering the meaning as best he could. When one full minute had passed, Blythe chose to speak first.

"We've made him angry, Jax." And she wasn't the least bit ashamed of it.

"He was watching us." He gritted his teeth and slammed his palm against the steering wheel in frustration. "Damnit, the sick bastard was right there."

"Good, I'm glad he saw you kiss me. Pissing him off is going to make him screw up, Jax. He's jealous or something I guess, and now he's going to try even harder to get to me."

He glared at her, his eyes filled with fury. "He was on my land. He could have gotten to you while I was sleeping, or in the shower, or God knows when."

"Yeah and he could have done the same thing at the hotels we stayed at in L.A. and Phoenix. He found us there too, didn't he? He's still playing his game, and he's going to play it out until he's ready to face me head on. I can only hope that it goes down in Chicago, because I'm sure as hell ready for him." Her chin cocked up as she sneered, purely defiant. He had to force himself to calm down.

"He didn't say where he was going in that letter," he muttered, taking a deep breath and slowing the car as they pulled up to his house. "There's no way he knows we went to the school, because he was supposedly out of town yesterday."

"Maybe he's going to send us another letter." Blythe shrugged. "Either way, we know where he's going. I say we fly out there as soon as possible and try and head him off."

Jax parked the car and turned to look at her.

"I have to call Rian and Thea, give them the update. I'll book our flight after that." His lips twitched just slightly as he heard her stomach grumble unhappily. He reached out and patted her knee. "Why don't you try and make us some dinner?"

"Like, cook something?" One eyebrow cocked indignantly as she stared at him. "You know we have fairies who do that on Euphora. I've never had to cook a single thing in my life."

"I'm sure you can figure it out," he replied absently as he got out of the car, already imagining the nice, hot shower he intended on taking the moment he got off the phone.

"Okay, but I can't promise that whatever I make will be edible," she grumbled as she followed him inside. He disappeared into the back part of the house, so she wandered into the kitchen and glanced around, feeling lost.

It was a fairly large kitchen, decked out with rich oak cabinets and forest green granite countertops. Stainless steel appliances that she couldn't name seemed randomly placed throughout, and it took a few tries before she found one with food in it.

She felt a blast of cold air as she opened it and peered around at the jars and boxes, unsure what anything was. She spotted some peanut butter and strawberry jelly, one of the few things she recognized, and pulled them out. Setting them on the counter, she wandered around until she found the bread, stowed away in some kind of wooden box. It took her another few minutes to locate plates and a knife.

By the time she'd found everything she stared at it all, wondering if the jelly was supposed to go on first, or the peanut butter. With an irritated shrug, she decided to go with peanut butter first and began slathering gobs of it onto pieces of white bread.

She jolted when the phone rang, still unused to the sound. She called out to Jax, getting no response. When she wandered toward his room, she could hear the shower running. Annoyed, she raced back into the kitchen and grabbed the phone herself.

She hit a few of the buttons before one of them finally answered it. "Yeah?" she answered like she had seen Jax do as she licked peanut butter off her fingertips.

"I was hoping you would answer," a voice she didn't recognize said. A chill raced up her spine even as her hackles rose.

"Who is this?" she demanded, resting her hip against the counter, her eyes narrowing.

"Have you been enjoying your presents? I always liked the ring myself, but I wanted you to have it. Are you wearing it?"

"Dante," she nearly growled the name as she felt her knees weaken. Determined to stand her ground, she pushed aside her initial shock and geared up to play ball. "I'm not wearing the ring and I won't ever wear it. In fact, if you like it so much, why don't I give it back to you? Tell me where you are and I'll come visit."

"Hah, Blythe…you have so much to learn. When this is done you will know the truth and then you will see. Tell me, have you ever been to the windy city?"

"Is that what they call Chicago?" she asked as Cooper came into the kitchen and sat beside her, whimpering. She reached down to pet him absently.

"My, my. I'm impressed. I just flew in about an hour ago. I'm having a cocktail called a Red Headed Slut in your honor."

The coldness in his tone had the fury bubbling inside of her. "Listen real good, asshole. I'm coming for you and so is Jax. We'll find you and when we do, you won't stand a chance. You'll be dead in the ground with your vile mother."

He chuckled and the cruel, cold sound of it shuddered down to her very bones. There was that evil again…that pure, unadulterated evil…

"So fiery…that's what I love about you. You'll be eating your words soon enough, darling. Ta ta for now."

She heard a click on the other end and then silence. Cursing, she almost threw the phone against the floor, but held herself back. Breaking the phone wouldn't make her anger go away, it would only make things worse. Setting it aside on the countertop, she covered her face with her hands and screamed into them instead. At her feet, Cooper howled.

"Jesus Christ, what the hell!" Jax rushed in, his hair still wet from his shower. He had just been shrugging into a clean t-shirt and jeans when he'd heard his dog begin to howl. He approached her, pulling her hands away from her face. The angry tears in her eyes alarmed him.

"I'm going to kill him," she snarled, her face flushed with rage. "He makes me sick."

"What happened?" he demanded.

"The phone rang and you were in the shower, so I picked it up and it was him. He said he was drinking some cocktail called a Red Headed Slut in my honor," she spat, sneering as her hands clenched into fists.

"Wait…Dante called? Just now?"

"A few minutes ago." She saw the color drain from his face as he pushed away from her, curling his hands into his hair in frustration.

"Why didn't you come get me? We could have traced the call, found out his exact location." He whirled around, glaring at her. "Damnit, Blythe, we could've had him."

"Hey, it's not like I know phone calls can be traced, okay?" she snapped, fisting her hands on her hips angrily. "So don't get all pissy at me, hotshot, I dealt with it as best I could. He told me he's in Chicago, so that's something. You're just gonna have to deal with the fact that what's done is done."

He hefted a heavy sigh and rubbed his face in his hands. Cooper whined from all the hostile anger sparking in the air. Glancing down at his dog, he realized she was right. How could she have known that a phone call can be traced? Of course she wouldn't.

"Alright, so it's done." He looked at her, pleased to see her eyes were dry. "So what'd you make us for dinner?"

She let out a choked laugh and smiled, glad he wasn't still angry with her.

"I started making peanut butter and jelly sandwiches before I was rudely interrupted." She pointed toward the half finished sandwiches on the counter, amused at the look on his face.

"That was the best you could do?" He shook his head and chuckled. "I guess it works."

"Just have a seat while I finish your goddamn sandwich and be grateful." She smirked and shooed him away toward the dining table as she began to slather jelly on top of the peanut butter. A minute later she set the sandwich down in front of him, and dug into her own.

He glanced at his skeptically just to irritate her, then bit in and chewed happily. "Delicious," he said as he swallowed. She smiled brightly at the compliment.

"Why, thank you cowboy." She took another bite, then broke off a small piece to hand to Cooper, who was sitting beside her with eager eyes.

Jax chuckled as Cooper happily ate the scrap in one greedy gulp, then glanced up at her hoping for more.

"That's all for you, buddy. The rest is mine."

"He's gonna miss you when we leave tomorrow." Jax leaned back in his chair, studying her.

"Well, I'll miss him too," Blythe chimed, reaching down to rub her hands over Cooper's fur excitedly. "Yes, I will!"

He rolled over onto his back for a belly rub, and she obliged him, laughing when he sneezed a few times and then rushed up to chase his stubby tail.

She sat back down, her eyes lit with humor and her smile bright. His gut clenched uncomfortably just watching her, knowing this would be her last night in his home. Tomorrow they'd be in Chicago and from there…who knew? And then when the mission was over she'd go back to Euphora, and he'd come back here, without her.

"What is it, Jax?" she asked, seeing the troubled look in his eyes.

He shook his head, damning himself to Hell for feeling anything more than a casual attraction to her. When had it all changed? "It's nothing, Blythe. Absolutely nothing."

The truth was, despite how fervently he tried to deny it, he knew that everything had changed in El Paso, on his front porch, when he had seen her bathed in morning sunlight.

Chicago was a bustling metropolis the likes of which Blythe had never experienced. Sure, Los Angeles had hoards of people and tall buildings that glittered in the sun, but there was something much different about this city that set it far apart from other places she'd been.

As they cruised around in a dingy yellow cab on their way to the hotel, Blythe simply pressed her nose to the window and gaped. One thing was for sure: Chicago was worlds away from the dry deserts of El Paso. So what had brought Bristol here of all places?

Many of the buildings were a hundred years old or more, preserved in their most original state, built of limestone and granite. Paired with them were towering steel and glass structures that reflected the dense summer clouds that hung heavy in the late afternoon sky.

The streets were bustling with people from all walks of life, from the neat and trim businessman in a crisp suit just starting to wilt from the heat to the grungy homeless man begging for change on the street corner. She found herself fascinated by the ebb and flow of life that pulsated through the humid air, both out of necessity and need. Chicagoans, she decided, seemed hardnosed and tenacious, pushing through with what they had to keep the city moving. She couldn't help but admire that.

"This place is great," she proclaimed, sitting back in her seat and grinning at Jax.

He shrugged, his distaste for the city obvious as he stared irreverently out the window. "I've never been one for big cities."

Because she understood him better now, she reached over and playfully punched his shoulder. "Cowboys don't belong in big cities."

With one eyebrow raised he turned to look at her, unable to help the grin that curved his lips. "Neither do Fire Dryads, darlin'."

Suddenly his phone rang. He lifted it out of his pocket and stared down at the Caller ID before answering it.

"Hey, we just landed about thirty minutes ago. We're taking a cab to the hotel."

"That's good. We're already here," Rian's voice said.

Jax paused, unsure if he had heard his friend correctly. "You're where?"

"At the hotel. Capri and I just got here. We decided to drop in on you two, see if we can help."

Blythe watched as he grinned ear-to-ear, something that still took her by surprise when she saw it. "Well shit, son, I guess we'll see you in a few minutes."

With that, he hung up the phone and chuckled to himself, shaking his head. Blythe stared at him, eyebrows raised.

"Rian's here?"

"He and Capri are at the hotel waiting for us." He looked back out of the window, sincerely looking forward to some male company.

"Capri's here, too?" Blythe smiled, her eyes lit with pleasure as she clapped her hands together excitedly. She suddenly leaned forward toward the cab driver, tapping on the plexi-glass partition that separated them. "How much longer?"

"Five minutes," the man replied gruffly.

"Five minutes," Blythe repeated to Jax as she sat back in her seat, tapping her hands on her knees, unable to sit still.

"I heard him just fine," Jax told her, amused at her excitement.

"Whatever cowboy, don't ruin this for me." She sent him a wink and a devious grin before turning to stare out the window once more, her heart soaring as they continued to the hotel.

Five minutes later they pulled up, and Rian and Capri were standing outside hand-in-hand, patiently waiting. Blythe leapt out of the cab and rushed to Capri, pulling her into a tight hug.

"Oh, honey, I've missed you." She sighed, breaking away to look at her friend. She scanned Capri up and down with a grin. "Don't you just look adorable?"

Capri blushed, glancing down at the pale green skirt of her lace lined cotton dress. She had paired it with white strappy sandals and long strands of soft water pearls that hung around her slender neck.

"Rian bought it for me." She smiled over at her boyfriend, who had begun to help Jax unload the taxi.

"That's sweet." Charmed, Blythe hugged her again for good measure. "How's everyone? You guys bored without me?"

Capri shrugged, tucking a loose strand of her light blonde hair behind her ear. "It feels weird at home not having you there, but everything is alright I guess…Liam's worried about you. I don't think he trusts Jax enough yet. I keep telling him that Jax can take care of you, and that you can take care of yourself, but he worries anyway. I haven't really seen your dad too much lately, if he comes to dinner he eats without speaking to anyone and then leaves, so I assume he's worried about you, too. Rohan and Serendipity are speaking again, I guess they're trying to work things out. Nyxa's been reclusive, so I haven't seen much of her either." She sighed, sadness in her eyes. "Things are just different without you there. Everyone seems so gloomy now…it's like a dark cloud is hanging over all of us."

"I'm sorry, honey." Blythe hated seeing Capri upset, but there were bigger things at stake. "It won't be long now. I think we'll catch him here and then I'll come home, and everything will be right again."

Capri smiled, looking sweet as spring. "I hope so."

Rian and Jax approached then, carrying the bags and grinning. Rian nodded to Blythe, and she nodded back, knowing he was usually more comfortable not speaking.

Jax led the way into the hotel and checked them all into their rooms. For convenience and safety, he booked a double queen room for he and Blythe to share. It made perfect sense to her, but when Capri sent her a knowing look, she had to bite back a scowl. It wasn't like that between them, she told herself as they rose in the elevator toward the fifth floor. She and Jax had a physical attraction thing going on, but that didn't mean they were pursuing anything more than that. They weren't a couple, and as far as she knew he had no feelings for her, at least none that he'd shown. And any feelings she had for him would just have to be squashed as soon as possible. She wasn't going to let herself fall for him, especially since she knew she was dangerously close to doing so. El Paso had brought out something between them and she knew it, but all of that was over now. Now they were in Chicago and they needed to focus on finding Dante. End of story.

They refrained from touching each other anymore than necessary as they joined Rian and Capri for dinner at the hotel restaurant. Blythe wasn't sure but she had a feeling that Jax felt as awkward as she did at having their friends there, watching them like hawks, looking for any sign that they had a romance going on.

It was like they had to suddenly prove to themselves that what happened between them in El Paso was nothing more than a slip up—a mistake that had nothing to do with actual feelings. It irritated her because she never lied to herself or denied her true emotions, but for some reason she found herself doing so now. She supposed she was acting out of self preservation.

It took all she had to push it out of her mind as they settled in at their table and ordered drinks.

"So Dante called my home last night, spoke with Blythe for a few minutes," Jax jumped in, ready to get down to business. Rian's eyes sharpened and Capri made a small, startled noise in her throat. Blythe couldn't hide her irritation.

"What did he say?" Rian asked, his eyes on Blythe.

She rolled her shoulders, trying to keep her temper in check. "He asked me if I was wearing the stupid heirloom ring and I not so politely told him no. Then he said something about how when this whole thing is over, I'll know the truth. Whatever that means." She thanked the waitress as her margarita arrived. "Anyway, so then he asks me if I know where the windy city is, and I asked him if that's what they call Chicago since we had just found out that he was most likely heading there. He sounded surprised that I knew already, so I know I caught him off guard. Then he said that he was drinking something called a Red Headed Slut in my honor. The bastard, I could kill him for that insinuation alone." She clenched her teeth and met eyes with Rian, forcing herself to calm down. "I told him he'd be dead once I found him and he laughed at me. The scumbag just laughed and then he said that he loved my fiery side, and that I'd be eating my words soon enough."

She took a hefty sip of her drink, needing something to settle the rage pulsing through her. When Capri reached over and held her hand, she felt most of it drain away.

"Don't let him get to you, Blythe. That's why he says hurtful things, he wants to upset you," Capri reasoned, her soft gray eyes melancholy as they watched her.

"I know." Squeezing her friend's hand in her own, she faced Rian and Jax again. "So we know he's here in Chicago, but the only other thing we have is a P.O. Box, whatever that is. What's our next course of action?"

"Actually, maybe we have something else." Jax turned to Rian, his expression grave. "I told you about how my contact in El Paso saw Dante meeting with someone?" Rian nodded silently. "We think it may have been Brock."

Capri gasped, cupping a hand over her mouth. Rian's hand rubbed her knee under the table, comforting.

"Why do you think it was Brock?" he asked, keeping his voice level.

"Lucian said he's been leaving Euphora a few times for the past week and he didn't know where he was going," Blythe put in, sipping more of her drink to soothe her throat that had gone dry at the mention of her father. She hadn't forgotten that little possibility, which had been nagging at the back of her mind ever since Jax had brought it up.

"It's not him." Rian sat back in his seat, keeping his eyes on Blythe. He knew she needed to hear the truth. "I've had the Enforcers monitoring him every time he leaves Euphora, for his safety and ours. He's been going to Las Vegas and gambling. He hasn't gone anywhere else."

"That's what he's been doing?" Her heart ached a little that she had doubted him. "Of course that's what he's been doing. It makes sense. He would never purposely seek out Dante, he wants nothing to do with him."

Jax watched her closely as she dealt with the guilt and the shame. He felt sorry he had been the one to put it in her mind to begin with.

"So if it wasn't Brock, then who was it?" Jax asked Rian.

"Maybe it was that demon you came across yesterday who gave you the package," Rian said, taking a swig of beer.

"No, I don't think so." Jax frowned, running a hand through his hair. "Why would he need to hide his appearance? Demons can change bodies so no one would recognize him regardless, so why the disguise?"

"So you think he was meeting with someone, or something else? A human, maybe?" Blythe asked.

"Or someone else from Euphora. Or a crooked Enforcer." At Rian's impatient huff, Jax chuckled. "You know they exist, Rian, and have for centuries. Few and far between, but it happens. So where does this leave us?"

"Maybe we should start by figuring out exactly why Dante brought you to this city in particular," Capri put in suddenly, blushing when everyone turned their attention to her.

"We've already decided that he's taking us to the same places he and Bristol lived when he was growing up. Most likely because he knows these places and feels comfortable," Blythe told her.

"Yes, but...well, maybe it's not it at all, but..." Capri began, feeling a bit embarrassed.

"Go on, baby," Rian reassured her. She looked him in the eye and felt a bit more confident. "It's just don't you find it odd that he and Bristol lived in so many different cities? Maybe you two wouldn't know, but Jax and I do. Human's don't tend to move around that much unless…well, unless they're running from something."

"Or someone," Jax added, nodding at her. "No, you're exactly right, Capri. What other reason did Bristol have for moving from place to place, only leaving a P.O. Box as a forwarding address for her son's school records? She must have been on the run."

"But why?" One eyebrow arched, Blythe stared at the three of them. "Who would she be running from? No one from Euphora was after her and my dad never cared to look for her. I just don't understand it."

"I guess there's something we're missing, some piece to the puzzle that we haven't found yet." Capri rested her elbow on the table, her chin in her hand as she sighed. Suddenly her eyes lit up and she gaped at Blythe. "What about the gifts he's been giving you? Don't you think it's strange that he's so focused on giving you Bristol's most treasured possessions, and giving you a picture to show you how much you look like her? I think in his mind you are Bristol, and he's trying to make you understand that."

Her first reaction was to brush the thought away, but the sinking feeling in her gut convinced her otherwise. Capri was definitely onto something, and Dante's adoring letters and gifts were certainly proof of his affection. But could it be that he wanted her to take the place of his dead mother?

"Well, he's going to be disappointed because I'm not going to play this game with him. I'm not her and I never will be her," she spat, shifting to glare at Jax. "Let me guess, you think she's right."

He leaned back, sipping his beer as he watched her. He saw the heat in her eyes, that flare of temper. But beneath it he saw the devastation. She knew it was true regardless of what he thought.

"I think she's on to something," he offered, keeping his eyes level with hers. "Dante is obsessed with you, that much we know. He's given you priceless Fire Dryad heirlooms that one would imagine he'd want to keep for himself, but instead he passes them on to you. He gives you a picture of his mother wearing the necklace, only a year younger than you are now. I think it's quite possible that he does want to make you into Bristol."

"But I'm not her!" Blythe shouted, causing people to stare. Jax put his hand on her arm, as much to calm her as to control her before she spun off on a wild tirade. She was staring at him, her eyes wide and desperate and furious all at once.

"None of us are questioning that, Blythe," he said evenly, his other hand reaching out to cup her face, keeping his eyes on hers in an effort to steady her.

"I'm not her," she repeated quietly, more to herself than to him. She needed to believe it, needed to push herself away from everything she'd felt when she had held the heirlooms in her hands and stared at the woman in the photo who looked identical to herself. She wasn't Bristol, she was Blythe, and nothing Dante said or did or gave her would change that.

Without even realizing it, her hand had come up to join his at her cheek. She felt better having him there, knowing he understood her. It amazed her, frightened her, and humbled her all at once.

Her cheek was smooth beneath his hand, the flush anguish and rage had given her skin fading as she calmed. Her lips were slightly parted and he damned himself for looking at them and wanting nothing more than to kiss her, to lose himself in the flames until nothing was left. He nearly gave in until reality caught up.

Rian cleared his throat, shocking them both out of the moment. They jolted apart guiltily, with Jax sitting back and lifting his beer for a generous swig and Blythe taking a deep, shuddering breath.

"Blythe, let's run to the ladies room," Capri said suddenly, rising to pull Blythe to her feet.

"Alright," Blythe said numbly, not even glancing back at the table as Capri led her toward the back of the restaurant where the restrooms were. She pushed open the door and held it open for Blythe. Capri checked the stalls to be sure they were alone before rounding on her friend, excitement in her eyes.

"There *is* something going on between you two, isn't there?" she said giddily, gripping Blythe's shoulders in her hands.

"What?" Blythe managed, shaking her head automatically. "No...no there's nothing between us, Capri, just let it go." She scowled down at the ground, worried she'd betray herself if she gave in to Capri's persistence.

"Don't lie to me, Blythe, I can tell." And because she could also tell her friend was troubled, she reached out to gently tip Blythe's chin up until their eyes met. Capri's were soft with understanding. "I'm sorry this hurts you...I'm sorry that Dante gets under your skin like this and that I can't do anything to help you. But you're strong, Blythe, the strongest person I know. If anyone can get through all the emotional trauma you're going through right now, it's you. And as for Jax..." She paused, unable to hide her smile as Blythe's eyes sharpened dangerously. "There's sparks between the two of you. I noticed it from the very first moment I saw you looking at each other on Euphora. Can't you feel it?"

"Damnit, of course I do," Blythe sulked, shrugging away from Capri to pace, pain in her eyes. "But just because they're there and just because I'm getting all emotionally sappy over him doesn't mean it's gonna go anywhere. We're just too different. I should have never let him kiss me."

"Oh, Blythe." Pressing her hands to her chest, Capri sighed blissfully. "Was it romantic? The first time Rian and I kissed was so lovely..."

Blythe bit back a grin and eyed Capri. "He kissed me at a gas station in New Mexico. It wasn't what you would deem *roman-tic*." But the memory of it left her wanting and she knew it had definitely meant something. Then there was El Paso...

"Well, still...I think you should pursue this. It'll be good for you, I just know it." Mind made up, Capri crossed to Blythe and hugged her. "Now c'mon, let's go back out there and have a good time. We'll worry about everything else tomorrow, okay?"

Pulling away, Blythe managed a grin. "Okay."

Chapter Thirteen

She awoke the next morning to the smell of freshly made coffee. Sniffing the air with her eyes closed, she rolled over onto her back and felt her lips curve into a smile. Stretching her arms over her head she groaned and slowly opened her eyes, the sunlight just starting to glow through the window shades.

Turning her head she spotted Jax sitting in the armchair by the television, wearing nothing but faded Levi's. In his hands was a cup of coffee and the morning's edition of the New York Times.

"So what's going on in the world today, cowboy?" she asked sleepily, rubbing her eyes and sitting up. He glanced up at her as he sipped his coffee.

"Not much that would interest you." Setting the paper aside, he focused his attention on her. "How did you sleep?"

"Like a rock." She grinned and rose to her feet to get coffee. As she padded across the room wearing nothing but an oversized t-shirt, Jax made sure to keep his gaze from traveling down to her slender legs. He watched as she loaded her coffee with sugar and creamer and noted the satisfied smile that crossed her face as she took the first sip.

"We're meeting Rian and Capri downstairs for breakfast in an hour." He rose to his feet, tossing the empty Styrofoam cup that had held his coffee in the trash can beside the chair. "I'm gonna take a quick shower, run on down there to make some phone calls. I'll see you at breakfast, okay?"

"Alright." She watched him warily as he stepped toward her on his way to the bathroom, pausing in front of her. Her eyes held his, both aware and uncertain. Before she could speak, he patted her on the shoulder and walked past, shutting the bathroom door swiftly behind him. The smooth dismissal had her head reeling with confused emotions. Let it go, Blythe, she told herself. Let it go.

After Jax left to go make his phone calls, Blythe watched television for awhile, trying not to think. She took a shower, dabbed on a little bit of makeup and tried to do something with her hair. She still had ten minutes till she had to be downstairs for breakfast so she took the time to look once again at Bristol's picture.

She didn't know why she felt like looking at it again, but something was drawing her to it. Maybe it was simply curiosity over who Bristol had been running from and why. It seemed like this great mystery hanging over them and she wondered if this was the truth Dante said he'd make her see in the end.

The end...God, she could only pray it was coming soon. Being on the road was wearing on her. It was probably in her best interest to get home and break from Jax as soon as possible, before her feelings finally got the best of her.

She heard a soft knock on the door and rose to answer it, thinking maybe Jax had left his key card behind or something. Instead behind the door was a maid, her tidy black hair in plastered curls on her head and her dark eyes beady as they blinked at her.

"Housekeeping. I clean your room?" the woman said in a thick accent. Blythe smiled.

"Sure, whatever." She stood aside to let the maid in, wondering if she should leave. She supposed it wouldn't hurt to get to breakfast a little early, that way she could raid the buffet first before the rest of the weekend crowd got there.

The photograph was still in her hands, and she noticed the woman stare down at it and smile.

Assuming the maid was only being polite, Blythe turned around to shove the photograph back into her duffle bag. She glanced over and saw the maid setting fresh towels carefully on the desk, which struck her as an odd place to put towels. She was about to make a comment when the woman looked up at her, lips curved in a strange grin.

"Was that a picture of your grandmother?" she asked, pausing in her cleaning to stare at Blythe.

"Uh, yeah, it was." Blythe eyed the woman skeptically. "Why?"

"You look like her."

"I guess." Annoyed, Blythe began to step around the beds to leave the room and the nosy maid. But the maid suddenly reached out with her hand and stopped her. Alarm bells went off in Blythe's brain as the woman's hand clamped on her arm and clenched down so tight it made Blythe wince. "What are you–"

She lost the words as the woman's dark eyes seemed to melt in their sockets, thick black smoke oozing out of them. She began to shudder and tremble, but her hand remained in a dead-lock on Blythe's arm.

Darkness began to seep out of her nostrils, ears, and mouth–until it trailed down the woman's body and pooled on the floor. As a desperate act of self defense, Blythe grabbed the woman's wrist and released fire, burning the skin instantly. The hand released her and the maid slumped to the floor, unconscious. Blythe stepped back, poised to run as she turned to face the demon now curled on the floor of her hotel room, red eyes blazing.

She didn't know why, or how, but she knew. There was something more sinister and even more evil about this demon that gave it away. And instead of fear she suddenly felt a rising rage boil up and consume her.

"Dante, you bastard." She shot a fireball at him, only to watch it dissipate into nothing in the smoke. The snake swirled around and suddenly stretched out, slithering sickeningly toward her on the carpeted floor. And the sound he made as he rushed at her, backing her into the corner, was like a laugh. A wicked, vicious, blood chilling chuckling that was both guttural and warped. Her heart froze in her chest, her mind momentarily dazed as she suddenly found herself cornered. Then her lips curled in a snarl as she leapt forward and stomped on the dark, shadowy snake with her foot, unsure whether it would even do anything to him. She didn't care, her rage was so consuming that she saw nothing but a haze of red, her mind intent on only destroying him.

The maid suddenly awoke and, startled by the commotion, desperately crawled out of the room, muttering rapid prayers in frantic Spanish. Blythe barely noticed her leave.

She heard a shriek and wasn't sure if it came from her or him. When she bolted for her duffle bag, knowing her gun was tucked inside, she knew she had mere seconds before he had her.

She stumbled over the bed, her breath ragged and her mind singularly focused. Get the gun...get the gun. She came over the side of the bed and saw he had simply slithered beneath it, meeting her on the other side. He snapped up and bit her lower leg with surprising solid force, shocking her system with pain. With a growl, she kicked hard to shake him off, satisfied when his jaws released and he landed a few feet away.

She dug into her bag, her hand finding purchase on the gun. She whirled around, gun pointed, murder and vengeance in her eyes.

"I don't know what's taking her so long." Jax tapped his fingers restlessly against the table in the hotel restaurant, not even touching his food. Rian looked up at him, amused to see how fidgety his friend was about Blythe. Who knew the Reaper Man, as the demons lovingly referred to him, would worry so much over the lateness of a woman.

"She's probably putting on makeup or something," he said, earning a headshake from Capri.

"No, Blythe doesn't really wear makeup. And she's usually very punctual." There was worry in Capri's voice which did nothing to help Jax's agitation. If Capri was worried then something had to be wrong.

"Blythe doesn't miss breakfast." Jax glanced around, hoping to see her bright smile and her shock of red hair strolling through the entrance of the restaurant. Instead he just saw an elderly couple and a few kids. "It's been fifteen minutes since the buffet opened. She'd want to get first dibs. I know her. Something's wrong."

"Maybe I should go check on her." Capri started to stand up, only to have both Rian and Jax motion for her to sit back down.

"No, I'll go." Jax got to his feet and rushed out of the restaurant, hoping he was just overreacting. It was foolish, really, but he had this sick feeling in his gut that he couldn't shake. Worry for her was driving him crazy.

She was probably just taking an extra long shower or maybe lazing in front of the television. Maybe she'd lost track of the time or had fallen back asleep...

No, that didn't sound like her and he knew it. He jumped in the elevator, cursing every second the doors took to close. He punched the button for the fifth floor several times before the elevator finally began its ascent.

Tapping his foot, arms crossed over his chest, he glared at his reflection in the mirrored doors. Lord, what the hell had come over him? She was just a girl, nothing more. She wasn't even that pretty or that interesting. Hell, she drove him crazy most of the time, and she had a vicious temper and rarely if ever acted like a lady. At least not like any ladies he had ever known.

But maybe that was just it. She wasn't like anyone else he had known. She teased him for the hell of it, and had a throaty laugh that bounced off walls and filled a room. She was daring, brave, and ridiculously stubborn, a combination that he couldn't help but admire.

And he was only lying to himself by pretending he didn't think she was attractive. She was like hellfire that came at you with a swift punch to the gut, knocking a man senseless with desire with one lift of an eyebrow and a curve of those arrogant lips.

God, who was he kidding? He was crazy about her. And for that reason alone he burst out of the elevator when it reached the fifth floor, aiming to throttle her if she was tormenting him with her lateness on purpose. He stalked down the hallway toward their room, his key card out, prepared to duel it out with her. Yeah, that was good. He had some things to say to her anyway and a fight was as good a place as any to start. She could say her peace, he'd say his, and then they'd decide where they stand.

He reached the door and paused, hearing noises inside that couldn't be coming from the television. He heard something heavy thud against the floor and a crash of glass paired with a scream. Fumbling to put the card in the slot, his breath quickened desperately as he fought his way into the room, shoving open the door, eyes wild.

He saw her on the floor, her leg torn and covered in blood, her hands clenched tightly around her pistol and pure, untamed wrath in her eyes. She was sitting up, her chest heaving, the mirror over the desk shattered to pieces on the floor. That was when he saw the dark shadow slither across the floor at an impossible speed before stopping and rearing up to face him. He knew, without even having to confirm it, who the demon was. There was just something infinitely more evil about him that resonated through the air. Dante glared up at him, eyes red and burning, before making his retreat.

Jax immediately reached down to pull his revolver from his boot. Before he could do more than aim, Blythe began firing at the snake as it escaped into the bathroom, her teeth bared like some warrior in the heat of battle. She didn't stop until her clip ran out of ammo and then she attempted to get to her feet to chase after Dante.

Jax raced ahead of her into the bathroom and watched Dante slither down the drain in the bathtub and out of sight.

"*Where is he!*" Blythe shrieked, stumbling into the room, her eyes huge and feral.

"Gone." Jax grabbed her as her leg gave out, holding her back even as she continued to try and get to the tub.

"No...no, he's not gone. He can't be. I got him, I know I did. Damnit, Jax, let me go." She smacked at his arm, desperate and angry and weak all at once. When he didn't let go, she struggled, only to have him pull her against him and shudder.

"Shut up." He had to get a hold of his breathing, had to fight against that feeling of helplessness he'd felt when he'd seen her on the floor–bleeding– her eyes on fire. "Christ, Blythe, you're covered in blood."

"Shit." She glared down at her leg, the pain returning as she focused on the wound. It was four neat puncture holes consistent with snake teeth, and in the struggle of the fight the blood had smeared up her entire leg and was trailed across the floor. At the moment, though, all she could think about was Dante. "God, Jax, he got away."

She lifted her eyes to stare at him, ashamed at the tears she had to suddenly blink away. Her chest ached and her throat tightened. "I'm pretty sure I hit him, but with these stupid lead bullets it just grazed whatever part of him was solid. Damnit, I should've grabbed your spare gun with the liquid nitrogen bullets instead of mine, I wasn't even thinking."

"Blythe." He forced her to look at him when she tried to turn away, all the anger and fear he'd felt multiplying to constrict painfully in his chest. She was trembling, more from pain and shock than terror, and he had to push aside his own fury over Dante hurting her so he could stay focused. "Lord knows I should be mad at you for trying to fight him but I know better than to think you'd do anything else." He tried to smile, but it didn't reach his eyes.

"Damn right," she said weakly, the pain consuming her now. She winced and exhaled a sharp breath. "God, this hurts."

"Okay, darlin', let's get you on the bed." He carefully lifted her into his arms, carrying her over to the bed that hadn't been pushed off its box spring. He laid her down with a gentleness he didn't even know he had, then reached for the towels the maid had left on the desk. As he grabbed the top one, something slipped out and fell to the floor with a soft thud. He didn't bother to look at what it was. "Here, wrap this around the bite and let me get some soap and water. Demons don't have venom, so it's just a bad bite." He pressed the towel to the wound and then swept into the bathroom for a wet towel and soap, and the first aid kit he kept in his bag. When he returned a few moments later, Blythe was on the floor, a faded, leather bound book in her hands. "What the hell is that?"

She shook her head numbly as she opened it, hands trembling. The words written on the inside cover said it all. "It's Bristol's diary. It fell out of the towel."

"Okay. It's just another gift. Get back on the bed and let me bandage your leg." Jax took the book from her and set it on the desk, then hefted her back up onto the bed. He went to work on her leg with patience and efficiency, distracting her from the pain as she watched him. His face was drained of color, his mouth set in a determined line and his eyes cold and hard. She had the sudden urge to reach out and touch his skin, to smooth away the worry lines creasing his forehead. She wanted nothing more than to see him smile, to hear him laugh.

"Tell me a joke, cowboy." She inhaled sharply as he applied disinfectant to the bite, but managed a shaky grin.

He looked up at her, disbelief in his eyes.

"A joke?"

"Yeah, make me laugh." She pushed away at a tear that fell down her cheek. "God, I need to laugh right now, please."

"Alright." He thought a moment and when he began to speak, he heard her sigh contentedly and saw her eyes close as she listened. "So there's a woman sitting in a small boat in the middle of a lake reading a book. Her husband had left all his fishing gear in the boat, but she didn't mind too much. A patrol boat pulls up and a man hollers down to her. He says 'Ma'am, I'm afraid you're in a restricted fishing zone, I'm going to have to bring you in and fine you.' The woman says 'But I'm not fishing, I'm just reading a book.' 'Don't matter,' says the patrolman, 'you have all the equipment in there, so I need to bring you in.' So the woman, being wise as women are, says 'Well then I'll have to charge you with sexual assault.' The patrolman, shocked, says 'But I haven't even touched you!' and the woman just smiles and says 'Doesn't matter, you have all the equipment.'"

Blythe burst into laughter, collapsing back against the bed as Jax finished tying her bandage. She continued to laugh as he sat on the bed beside her, then leaned down to lay with her, a somewhat relieved smile curving his lips.

She sighed and tilted her head to look at him, her eyes wet with amusement. "That was a good one." She smiled, and the sight of it had his gut clenching.

"Blythe," he murmured, his hand reaching out to brush a strand of hair out of her eyes. Her smile slowly faded and her eyes sharpened with awareness. She turned and curved toward him, her hands roaming over his face, his neck, his chest.

Unable to even find words, she simply pressed her mouth to his and let herself sink in, sliding deeper until she knew she was lost. His arms came around her, pulling her closer until they were pressed tight against each other. Her mouth cruised over his, taking what she wanted but giving so much more. She felt this deep, drugging emotion course through her as he murmured her name again, and she knew it was done. It was over for her; she was caught.

She was in love with him.

"Jax..." she groaned when his tongue trailed along her neck, shuddering out a breathy laugh as she clutched at his shirt. "I lo–"

"Oh my God, Blythe!"

Her eyes flew open and she saw Capri and Rian standing in the doorway, surprise on their faces. Behind them, the hotel manager held the master key in his hand, utterly shocked as he looked at the damage to the room. Clearly somebody had come across the maid stumbling around the hallways, disoriented after having been possessed.

They sat up as Rian and Capri rushed into the room, Jax eyeing the hotel manager hesitantly. There was only so much he could say in front of humans, so he'd have to fill Rian in with code for now.

"D was here, he attacked Blythe. The drain." He gestured with his head toward the bathroom, and from Rian's nod he knew he was understood. "She was bit, but I bandaged it up. She's going to be alright."

Rian nodded again and glanced over at Capri, who was hugging Blythe and crying.

"He left this." Jax reached over and grabbed the diary, handing it to Rian. "It's Bristol's diary."

Rian didn't open it, only stared at the cover for a moment before meeting eyes with Jax again. "I'm going to go straighten all this out with the hotel. Take Blythe and Capri and book us at another hotel, I don't want them anywhere near here." He handed the book back to Jax. "Make sure Blythe reads this as soon as possible. It may explain why Bristol was on the run and give us a clue as to where we can find him."

With that, Rian swept from the room, leading the hotel manager away. Jax sighed and turned to look at the women, who were sitting side by side on the bed, clutching hands tightly.

The lovely blonde and the bold redhead, he mused as he watched them. They were so different, but he supposed that was what made them such good friends. Their differences complimented each other. And it was now up to him to herd them both away to safer ground.

"Here." He handed Blythe the diary, his expression carefully blank. "Put this in your duffle bag and get all of your things. We're going to another hotel, far from here. Capri, once Blythe and I have our things we'll run to your room to get yours, and then we're out. Okay?"

"Whatever you say, cowboy." Blythe got to her feet, a bit shakily, but with fresh determination in her eyes.

They made it to a motel on the outskirts of Chicago, in a quaint suburb with tree lined streets. It wasn't as grandiose as the hotel in downtown Chicago, but it seemed safe. And that was Jax's number one requirement.

He paid for their taxi and the room and then carted both Blythe and Capri's bags up the stairs to the second level of the motel, because it didn't have an elevator. Capri helped Blythe walk, even though she felt foolish and weak for needing the help.

When they reached their room, Jax unlocked the door and stepped inside, dumping the bags on the floor by the beds.

"Rian should be here in a half hour or so. He has to be done with the manager at the hotel by now," he told Blythe and Capri as they followed him in and sat on one of the two queen beds.

"I hope they were able to straighten everything out." Capri frowned as she glanced up at Jax, worry in her eyes.

His smile was kind as he turned to look at her. "Rian knows how to handle situations like this pretty well."

"Yeah, you're right." She smiled back at him sweetly, then turned around to scold Blythe for itching at her bandages. The ensuing bickering had him shaking his head and chuckling.

He found Capri to be charming and considerate, and undeniably selfless. It made him happy that his friend had been able to find a girl like her, someone who believed in him wholeheartedly and would stand by his side no matter what.

Blythe would do that, too, he mused, taking a seat on the other bed to take off his shoes. Only she was more inclined to fight in the battlefield with the men versus being the support system on the home front. But that was just where the two women were so different. Capri was a lover, a comforter, a listener. Blythe was a fighter, an avenger, and a commander. He knew without even thinking twice which one he preferred.

"So the diary is your grandmother's?" Capri asked Blythe, tucking a strand of hair behind her ear.

"Supposedly." Blythe chewed her bottom lip worriedly. "I guess we'll see once I read it."

"If you don't feel comfortable, I'm sure Jax will read it, or I will, if you want," Capri offered. Because Blythe knew Capri meant well, she just patted her friend's knee lightly.

"Thanks, honey, but this is my burden to bear." She laid back against the bed and shut her eyes, exhaustion sweeping over her. It had been quite the day, that was certain, and all she wanted to do was take a nice hot shower and curl up in bed.

There was a swift knocking on the door, and they all rose to full alert mode as Jax got up to answer it. After peeking through the peep hole he pulled open the door and greeted Rian.

"Capri and I have to go," Rian said as he burst in, and for the first time Capri saw true worry in his eyes.

"What is it?" Panic tore through her as she jolted to her feet and rushed to him. Blythe and Jax hung back, watching tensely.

"Brogan just called me, he says something's wrong with Nyxa. She hasn't been eating, and she hasn't been working or speaking to anyone. He's worried about her. I have to go help him." He reached out for Capri's hand, just to touch her, to comfort her as well as himself. Then he glanced up at Jax apologetically. "I'm sorry, Jax."

"No problem, son." Jax nodded, crossing his arms over his chest. "Do what you have to do. We'll take care of things from here."

"You know where to reach me if anything changes."

Capri went to Blythe, hugging her closely before letting go. "Be careful."

"I know." Blythe bit back a wave of grief as she watched her friend leave, feeling suddenly empty without her. When the door closed behind them, Jax stepped forward and immediately wrapped her in his arms.

"Want me to tell another joke?" he asked, pleased when she let out a watery laugh and tilted her head up to look at him.

"No, that's okay." She let out a long breath, distracted as she pondered Rian's words. "I wonder what the hell is wrong with the bitch now."

With a snort, he turned her head so she was facing him again. "Nyxa is your mother?"

"Unfortunately." She was unable to hide the animosity in her voice, or the instinctual sneer. "Though we both wish we weren't related by blood. I swear, if she's just causing dramatics for the hell of it, pulling Rian and Capri away from the mission, I'm going to throttle her."

"I know him. He wouldn't have left if he hadn't thought it necessary to go." Thoughtful, he ran his hands through her hair, then brought them down to cup her face. "You aren't even a little bit worried about her?"

This time she snorted, one eyebrow arched crossly. "Hell no. If she's suffering because my father cheated on her, then I'd say it's just karma coming back to bite her in the ass. It doesn't concern me one bit, except that her antics are now affecting our efforts in getting Dante."

Absently, he traced his thumb over her arched brow, his eyes amused. "I love it when you get that look, darlin'. Don't worry yourself, though, we're almost to him. After you peruse that diary we'll have our bearings and we'll catch him."

Anger properly deflated, she huffed out an annoyed breath. He had a way of diffusing her temper without dampening her spirit, something only Lucian had ever been able to do.

She glanced down at the bandage on her leg, regretting she hadn't made as much of a mark on Dante. "The next time Dante and I meet, he won't get off as easy."

"But until then, you should sleep. You've had a long day." His eyes sharpened callously as he remembered her lying on the ground, blood smeared across her leg and on the floor. Dante would pay for that alone.

"No, not just yet." Feeling better, and not noticing the heat in his eyes, she bit back a grin as she retreated away from him, pulling his hands gently from her face.

"Give me a second." She winked and whirled around, stepping toward the alarm radio that sat on the nightstand between the two beds. She flipped it on and dialed the tuner until she found what she was looking for. Ronnie Dunn's crooning voice sang out a smooth and aching country ballad about what his woman gets for loving him. Blythe turned around and smiled, earning a dubious look from Jax.

"Since when do you like country music?"

Since I decided I love you, she thought, biting her lip to keep from saying it. Instead she just shrugged. "I suppose it's grown on me. Now c'mon and dance with me, cowboy."

She grabbed his hand in hers, pulling him toward her, happy he didn't resist. His arms came around her waist, hers wound around his neck. When she tilted her chin up this time he leaned in to kiss her.

For now, at least, she could let go and just exist. At that moment she was simply a girl, and he was simply a boy, with nothing more between them than mutual respect and attraction.

No confused feelings, no mission, no deadly half demon, and most of all, no dead grandmother's diary.

Chapter Fourteen

When morning came, he left her bright and early so she could read the diary in private. He said he was going to hit up his few contacts in Chicago who he had managed to get a hold of the day before to see if they had seen Dante. But she knew he was just trying to give her space. What he expected the diary to contain, she had no idea. She only knew he was purposely giving her distance in case she needed to grieve.

Which she certainly didn't plan to do, she assured herself as she settled into the comfy pillows on the hotel bed and laid the unopened diary in her lap. Whatever she found inside, she couldn't allow it to skew the facts.

Bristol had slept with a demon, given birth to Dante, was banished by Thea, and then was never heard from again. And now Dante, the evil creature she had created, was a plague on everyone living on Euphora and the reason Blythe had grown up without her real father. So unless pigs started flying in the sky, Blythe was certain she would feel no different after reading the diary then she did now.

With an impatient sigh, she opened the plain, leather bound cover and, fighting to ignore the clenching feeling in her gut, she settled in to read the first entry.

April 7th, 1966

Today was not only a great day because I finally turned eighteen, but also because the Enforcers arrived with news that they destroyed the demon that had been wreaking havoc in the Caribbean. Silas and Gerald came by to tell Thea and to join us for my birthday party, and I made my move. Father doesn't approve, but I don't care what he thinks. Silas is so handsome, so brave and intense...it's a good thing father wasn't around to hear the naughty things he whispered in my ear while we ate cake on the settee in the lounge. I always knew I'd fall in love with an older man, and really he's only thirty, just twelve years older than me. And he's an Enforcer, one of the most courageous men I've ever met. Hearing him speak of his demon hunting conquests makes my heart flutter like it never has before, especially not with any of the boys here on Euphora, who are all so dreadfully boring. Silas could never bore me, it's impossible. We've only known each other since I was sixteen, but now that I'm of age he says he's ready to marry me. Oh, it was the best birthday present I could have ever asked for. Even the grand party and finally getting the Fire Dryad heirlooms from my father couldn't compare to this. Silas Ashburn will be mine, forever and always. Thank God for it.

Blythe paused at the end of the entry, absorbing what she had read. So Silas must be her grandfather...why had she never heard of him before? Where was he now, if he was even still alive? He would be well into his seventies by now...

Hoping to find answers, she continued to read.

June 20th, 1966

Father has finally accepted Silas' proposal, even though Thea and Sebastian had accepted it almost immediately. I guess all my pestering finally wore him down. The wedding is in one short month, and I can't wait. It's going to be so grand, and held right here in the courtyard under the stars, just like I'd always imagined.

Silas took me to the beach today and to dinner on the pier. It was lovely, and he is such a gentleman. He quite simply adores me and would do anything I asked of him. Including live on Euphora as often as he can once we are married. Even though it would be nice, he knows I can't leave my work, just like I know he can't leave his, at least not permanently. His career is so important to him and he knows I support him one hundred percent.

In thirty short days, I will be Mrs. Silas Ashburn!

July 30th, 1966

Just got back from our honeymoon! The wedding was so beautiful and my dress like something out of a fairy tale, all frothy lace and shimmering silk. Silas looked so handsome, as always, and father behaved himself and shook Silas' hand. I still don't understand why he feels I shouldn't be with Silas, but then again, he and I have never understood each other, so why should we start now?

Our honeymoon was on this remote island in the Pacific and it was so romantic. We went snorkeling, hiking, cliff diving, rock climbing…and we made love every chance we got.

I have never been happier than this moment, coming home with my husband, ready to start our lives together.

I love him so much.

September 14th, 1966

> *I'm pregnant! Silas and I haven't really talked about children, but I can't see how he couldn't be happy about this. I'm thrilled and Thea is, too. I'm the first of the Dryads to be with child so our baby will be the oldest of the new heirs, which is such an honor. I hope it's a boy and I hope he has my Silas' smile.*

It would be a boy, Blythe thought grimly, slowly shaking her head. A boy who you would end up abandoning and who's life would be destroyed by your selfish actions…God, this was more difficult than she'd imagined. It was hard not to get emotionally involved, not when she felt so passionate about getting justice for her father and for Capri.

And it also made it harder to see how young and innocent Bristol had been, so optimistic and hopeful for the future. And so in love, as well.

I'm nothing like her, Blythe thought somewhat bitterly. Never once did she imagine falling in love or getting married in the courtyard, mostly because she assumed she never would and she knew she didn't need that to be happy. And she most certainly would never wear a lace wedding gown–yuck.

So Dante was wrong. She had nothing in common with her grandmother; they didn't even think alike. Bristol seemed much more lighthearted, more innocent and definitely more spoiled than Blythe had ever been.

Maybe if her life had been less difficult up until this point she would have been like Bristol. But the reality was that because of Bristol, Blythe's life hadn't stood a chance to be so carefree.

Irritated, she skimmed over the next few entries, which seemed to only document the pregnancy. Apparently Silas wasn't around nearly as often as Bristol had hoped, which she brushed off as being part of an Enforcer's duty. But from the sound of it, Bristol was defending him more to herself than to anyone else.

She was clearly irritated by his absence and the fact that she had to deal with being pregnant alone, which she described in great detail as not being any fun.

But when she found the entry detailing Brock's birth, it seemed that Bristol forgot all about being upset.

April 3rd, 1967

He's beautiful. Damn Dryad genes made him look just like me but I don't mind. He's the loveliest baby I've ever seen and he's mine. Brock Silas Ashburn, the newest Fire Dryad.

Silas couldn't make it out today, but he says he'll be here first thing in the morning to see our son. I know he's as excited as I am to welcome Brock into the world. He will be such a strong, handsome man, I just know it. I can't wait for the other Dryads to have babies so he has friends to play with. Maureen is pregnant with the newest Earth Dryad; his name will be Rohan. I know he and Brock will be the best of friends. Thea and Sebastian are so happy for me and even father smiled today when he held Brock. He sees my son's potential just as I do. Even right now, he's asleep in his bassinet by my window, his hands glowing red hot with barely contained fire. It warms my heart just to look at him.

Life has never been better than at this moment.

She skimmed through several more entries about Silas and her father as a baby, then as a toddler. Then she noticed that the entries became more and more spaced out, with longer and longer times between. She paused when she came to a page where the writing was scrawled and uneven, with what looked like tear stains on it. Her throat tightened as she read the entry.

March 10th, 1970

Silas came home today and informed us that his partner Gerald had been killed by a demon in the line of duty. We are all in shock, and I am so distraught I don't know what to do with myself. Silas has shut himself in the library and won't let me comfort him and it's driving me crazy with grief. I know he's hurting, but he should also know that I can make him feel better. He loved Gerald like a brother and losing him appears to have destroyed a part of his soul. I ache for him, even as I hold Brock in my arms and try to comfort myself in my room. Brock asked me why his daddy was so mad and I didn't have the heart to tell him his Uncle Gerald is dead. I've never lost someone close to me, and have never dealt with this deep, violent pain in the heart and gut. I suppose I'll have to tell Brock eventually, but right now I don't have the stomach for it. Instead I will simply pray for Silas and hope he lets me back in.

September 1st, 1970

I never thought I'd say this but I fear Silas has gone mad. It's been a slow process, but a process nonetheless that I regretfully have been unable to prevent. He's turned to drinking and has turned away from me, closing himself off emotionally. He blames himself for Gerald's death, even though he could have done nothing to save him. But he won't listen to me when I try and comfort him, and the few times he has come to me he has either been in a fit of rage or a deep, lulling depression. I've woken up in the middle of the night hearing him sobbing, a glass of whiskey in his hands. Other nights I have been the target of his aggression, and God, I never thought he could, but last night he hit me. Naturally, I fought back and set fire to his coat, frightening him enough to leave me alone. I haven't heard from him since, as he's gone back to the Enforcer's headquarters. I don't know what will happen now. All I know is that Brock needs me to be strong, and so strong is what I will be. I can't tell anyone of our arguments, of his depression or the drinking…it's both a matter of pride and a matter of protecting my son. He does not need the shame of a drunken father, and I can only hope that Silas succeeds in battling whatever demons rage inside his head before he comes back to me. He has to come back to me…

December 21st, 1970

Things have only gotten progressively worse, I fear. Silas has not hit me again, but he has resorted to emotionally abusing me. I never thought I'd succumb to it, thought I was tough enough to handle anything that came my way. But hearing the man I love accuse me of adultery, accuse me of neglecting our child, or of doing drugs and countless other horrific things has eaten away at me. I'm standing strong still, at least on the outside. Thea and the others can never know, can never see what Silas has slowly become. A monster, a frightening, terrifying monster. All I can do now is care for my son and keep Silas from destroying everything I have.

Why, after everything, do I still love him?

"God," Blythe muttered, setting down the diary and laying her head back against the pillows, her eyes shutting tight against the tears she felt burning in them. I can't get emotional over this, she thought with anguish, shaking her head to try and clear it. But nothing could have shaken her disgust, the torment of knowing how Bristol felt. How horrible it must have been to be helpless to save the man you loved from himself. She liked to think that she could have done something to force the bastard to shape up, but then again, how much was really within the woman's power when the man's mind was lost?

Shuddering, she wrapped her arms around herself and let a single tear escape to run down her cheek.

When Jax returned, Blythe had tucked the diary safely away in her duffle bag and had settled in to watch TV. He eyed her speculatively as he dropped takeout bags on the mattress beside her. "You get some reading done today?" He sat down opposite her to remove his hat and his shoes. She shrugged, then reached over to dig through the bags.

"Some. What'd you bring me?" Pulling out a Styrofoam box, she opened it and sniffed. "Mmm, smells good."

"It's called curry chicken, it's Indian." He got to his feet and went into the bathroom to wash up.

"Curry chicken, huh?" Curious, she dug out the other boxes, found jasmine rice and some steamed vegetables. And, thank the Lord, forks. Chop sticks had not served her well last time so thankfully this food did not appear to require such odd eating utensils.

Jax wandered back into the room and reached into the bags to pull out his own food as Blythe began to dig in.

"This is good," she mumbled, her mouth full. She tried to smile at him, but he just rolled his eyes.

"Glad you like it," he said as he took a bite himself, satisfied with his choice of restaurant. It had been a gamble to find something good in a city he hardly knew. "So, what did you find out from the diary? How far into it are you?"

"I read a little bit." She stuffed some vegetables into her mouth to give herself time to think about how she could get out of this conversation. She wasn't sure she was ready to explain what she had learned just yet. The gaping wound had barely healed.

But when he simply sat back and watched her patiently while eating his dinner, she found she couldn't escape the explanation for long.

"So it's like this," she began, setting aside the curry chicken box. He handed her a bottle of soda and she gratefully chugged down a few gulps before speaking again. "She met this guy, an Enforcer, and they got married–"

"What was the Enforcer's name?" Jax interrupted.

"Silas Ashburn." Waving it away as though it weren't important, she continued. "So they got married and she gets pregnant with my dad. Then a few years later, some guy named Gerald, Silas' partner, got killed by a demon, and I guess Silas blamed himself. So he subsequently became an alcoholic, beat up on my grandmother, and accused her of adultery and drugs. All the while she had to maintain some semblance of a normal life so that my father could grow up without the weight of his father's madness on his shoulders."

"And that's where you stopped?" Sipping on the soda, he watched her carefully.

"Yup." Turning away from him, she focused back to the TV. "I'll read some more before bed, then pick it up again tomorrow. I just needed a break, you know?"

"Alright." Knowing she was troubled by what she had read, he left it alone. And when she picked up the diary a couple hours later, he took a shower and went downstairs to call Rian and relay what they had learned, including what little he had found out from his contacts in downtown Chicago.

Blythe stared at the cover of the diary for a long, full minute before opening it, trying to mentally prepare herself. Sure, she was dying to know what happened next, that was just natural curiosity. But part of her dreaded it because she knew what she was reading was real, not just some plot in a mystery novel. This was her grandmother's life, her words and her emotions put down onto paper. It meant something, whether she wanted to admit it or not, to have this opportunity to know the truth behind the mysterious woman who had supposedly been the root of everything that was wrong in her life.

And so she opened it slowly, turned systematically to the page she'd left off on, and dove in head first.

To her surprise, the entry succeeding the last one she'd read took place six years later.

June 12th, 1976

It is amazing how fast time passes, how the years flash by like lightning, out of my grasp and out of my control. It hurts and it humbles to read this diary, to know how innocent I was, to remember how wonderful life had been at the tender age of eighteen. I am twenty eight years old now, and I feel no more youth in my bones. If it weren't for Brock, I swear I'd wither away like an old maid, cowering in bed, waiting for death. But he gives me life and he gives me purpose. He is nine now, and so clever and funny, he charms the socks off of everyone he meets. He's best friends with everyone here and such a sweet child. A bit too careless about breaking the rules, but I'm sure he'll grow out of that with age.

Silas still drinks, but he's become accustomed to it, almost as though the alcohol is what keeps him normal and in control. I only see him once a month when he comes to Euphora to visit us, and even then we rarely kiss or even make love as we used to. It astonishes me how the passion he once possessed has been so diminished now, like a flame extinguished by the wind. The man I fell in love with does not exist within Silas any longer, and I suppose I've come to terms with that. As long as he continues to be somewhat of a father for my son, then I will be content. Brock is my only priority right now.

I suppose I chose to return to writing in this diary because I am finally feeling at peace. The last six years have been the most difficult of my life, but I feel I have settled into a routine that can sustain me. With Brock getting older, I am finally able to teach him more about his powers, and instruct him so he will be able to take over for me when it is time. I thank

God now that Brock looks nothing like Silas. I don't think I could bear looking at him every day if that were the case.

In other news, our ten year wedding anniversary is almost here. I suppose when your marriage is in relative shambles, an anniversary doesn't mean much, but Thea is insisting on throwing us a party. As far as she knows, we are still happily in love. If only I could tell her the truth, but I know that the truth would only destroy the life I have built so carefully for my son. He's all I have.

July 21st, 1976

I suppose I shouldn't be surprised, but that does not prevent me from being infuriated. Silas and I are through for good now, and there's no turning back from this point. I'm done, flat out done, and I will never, ever fall for a man's charms again.

What kind of man shows up to his tenth wedding anniversary party, only to sneak off with one of the Muses and screw around on his wife? Much more, what kind of man is it that when his wife discovers him buried inside said Muse, simply laughs and tries to shake it off, like it means nothing? Oh, and there's no way this is the first time. No, he had cheated before, probably regularly, while I have been faithful to him from the beginning, despite our distant relationship. Well, he got what was coming to him, that was for sure. And hurling that fireball at his face, knowing it scorched his flesh and disfigured him gave me enough satisfaction for what has felt like a lifetime of living under his abuse. And hearing his screams of pain, seeing the girl run in fear, gave me back my sense of power that I thought had been lost all these years.

If it's the last thing I do, the bastard will never see our son again.

My heart will never again feel the ache of love for a man.

Go, Grandma, Blythe thought with a swelling of pride, knowing she would have done the exact same thing to the cheating bastard. Closing the book gently, she set it aside and laid back to stare up at the ceiling, her eyes unseeing as she lost herself in thought.

So Silas Ashburn had gotten burned. Her lips curved slowly as she imagined just how shocked he must have been to see his wife's fury and to feel the wrath of a woman scorned. She didn't know for sure, but she liked to imagine him slinking off somewhere to die a miserable death in a sewer. Grandfather or not, he had certainly been a rotten human being, definitely not someone she would have wanted to know.

Jax came back into the room, stowing his cell phone away in his pocket. They met eyes and he frowned when he saw her triumphant look.

"What is it?"

"Apparently Grandpa Silas cheated on Grandma, and Grandma wasn't too happy about it and burned the shit out of his face." Sounding probably way too cheery considering the context of the conversation, Blythe grinned.

He couldn't help but laugh at the look on her face. "Sounds just like you, darlin'." He crossed his arms over his chest as he stared at her.

"It does, doesn't it?" With a sigh, she rubbed her hands over her face and groaned. "God, it does."

"Give it a rest for tonight." He started to head into the bathroom to wash up for the evening, when she called him back.

"Jax?" When he turned, she smiled as sweetly as she could muster. "Can I borrow your cell phone for awhile? I really want to talk to Liam."

"Alright." Lifting it out of his pocket, he tossed it to her and disappeared into the bathroom.

She studied the phone in her hands for a moment, realizing she hadn't the slightest idea how to call home.

"How do I use this thing?" she called out, turning it on and hitting random buttons. By the time Jax came out of the bathroom and yanked the phone out of her hands, she had opened his calendar, the weather report for the day, his text messages, and had managed to make a call to the local pizza parlor back in El Paso.

"You couldn't wait to mess with it until I came over, could you?" he scolded her, his face stern as he dialed Thea and handed the ringing phone back to her.

Blythe grinned up at him. "You know I'm impatient."

Snorting out a sarcastic laugh, he spread out on the queen bed beside hers and picked up the murder mystery novel he'd brought along.

When the phone picked up, Blythe couldn't help the smile that spread over her face. "Hi, Thea."

"Blythe. Is everything alright? Where's Jax?"

"He's right here, reading a book." Blythe glanced over her shoulder at him, laughter in her eyes. "Say hi, cowboy."

When he only scowled at her and continued reading, she laughed and laid back against the pillows of the bed. "Thea, I'm calling because I want to talk to Liam…is he there?"

"I'll send for him."

There was a brief pause as Thea asked Sebastian to bring Liam.

"He's coming. Jax told us what happened yesterday morning with Dante. I am proud of you for fighting back but you need to be careful. We could have lost you."

"Yeah, yeah." Blythe shrugged, pushing aside any guilt she felt. She fought back, that's what any rational person should have done. And if she'd let her temper get in the way and the rage take over, then so be it. If she'd just selected the right gun, Dante might not have gotten away.

"Please promise me you will be more careful from now on."

Blythe sighed and rolled her eyes. And even though Thea could not see her, the expression was evident in the tone of her voice. "Okay, I promise."

"Good. Here's Liam. Good luck, Blythe."

"Thank you, Thea." She heard some shuffling on the other end, and then Liam's voice came over the line.

"Hey goofball, what's the word?"

She grinned and closed her eyes, reveling in the sound of his voice. "Just reading my dead grandmother's diary. You know, the usual."

His laugh echoed over the line, calming her. *"Well, I hope it helps you more than hurts you. I can't imagine it's a cake walk."*

"When has my life ever been a cake walk, Liam? I do everything the hard way."

"How's the bounty hunter treating you?"

She bit her lip, knowing he was more likely than not going to react negatively to the notion of her being madly in love with the bounty hunter. Not to mention Jax was still sitting nearby, probably listening even though he was pretending to read. "Well he's feeding me so I guess it's a start."

"And yesterday morning? Thea told us Dante attacked you. Where was Mr. Bounty Hunter then?" The irritated sarcasm in his voice annoyed her.

"He's not here to fight my battles for me, Liam. I took care of myself just fine." She pouted even though she knew it was petty. "I handled it, okay?"

"I know." She heard him exhale slowly, as though trying to calm himself. *"It's just I worry about you, you know that. And he's supposed to be protecting you even though your stubborn ass acts like you don't need it."*

"Look, it wouldn't have made much of a difference regardless if I was alone or not. Dante had possessed a maid and came into the room pretending to clean. It was just unexpected and I did my best. Besides, I have a handgun now."

"*You're kidding me, right?*" His voice lightened as he laughed. "*God save us all now that you're armed.*"

"Hey, I happen to be a pretty good shot!" she snapped, though there was humor in her voice. "We'll target shoot when I get home and I'll kick your ass."

"*Hey I never said I knew how to shoot,*" Liam defended, chuckling again.

"So how are things back home?"

"*Not so good.*" He paused as he considered how to explain everything. "*Your dad has been going on binge drinking and gambling trips to Vegas, but Thea has basically put a stop to that now. He says he needs to relieve the stress of having his only daughter out risking her life, but most of us think he's just trying to distance himself from Nyxa. She's been horrible lately, Blythe. Being humiliated like that by Brock switched on something crazy in her head. The few times I have seen her she's been mumbling to herself, pulling at her hair, sobbing uncontrollably. No one knows what to do with her. Some days I don't see her at all, so I think she's been going somewhere. She barely eats, looks like she hasn't slept, and refuses to speak to anyone, not even Brogan and Nova.*"

"So all of that is the reason Brogan called Rian to go back to Euphora?"

"*Basically. Brogan doesn't know what to do. I feel sorry for him, really, as he's just trying to help her. She's all he has left other than Nova.*"

"But doesn't he get that there are more important things going on than Nyxa's antics?" Blythe spat as her temper flared. "We are, after all, trying to catch a deadly half demon here."

"*Don't ask me to explain why Rian decided to come home. Apparently he thought you guys were doing alright on your own without him and figured Brogan needed him more.*"

"Yeah, well until I finish this damn diary, we're at a dead end." Feeling frustrated, she took a deep breath and sighed, attempting to fight it back. Liam didn't deserve to be lashed out at. "So they still haven't figured out what's wrong with her?"

"No. Rhiannon's been talking to Brogan and filling me in some. She says that he's blaming Brock for everything, that Nyxa is going through this mourning period over him and that until Brock either apologizes or leaves for good, she may not recover. But Rhiannon thinks something else is up."

Huffing indignantly, Blythe sneered. "Not like I care what little Miss Princess thinks, but what did she say?"

"She thinks Nyxa is involved with something that's draining her both physically and emotionally. She thinks she might be planning something, maybe revenge or who knows. I think she's right."

She felt something cold slither down her spine at his words. "You think she's planning some kind of revenge against my dad?"

"It's all speculation, but it's possible."

"But what could she possibly do? I mean, sure he cheated on her in a way, but they were never officially back together I don't think, and really if anyone should be thirsting for revenge it's Rohan…"

Liam was quiet for a moment and the silence hung heavy between them. When he spoke, his voice had taken on a darkness she wasn't used to hearing from her happy go lucky brother. "Dad's managed to talk with Rohan a little bit these past couple weeks. He's in a bad state, kind of a numb, concealed depression, but he's controlling himself enough to maintain his dignity. And, despite what you may think, he and Nyxa have not banded together to get revenge. Rohan has too much class to do anything more than accept and move on."

"Rohan, class?" She laughed even though nothing about the comment was funny. "Because it was real classy a couple months ago when he pulled my hair and dragged me across the floor like a crazy person. Or when he immediately blamed me for letting Dante onto Euphora when Capri was possessed."

"I never said he was a saint, I'm just saying that revenge is not on his mind. He just wants Serendipity to stay the hell away from your dad. And so far, she has. She seems to be repentant, so we will see if he ultimately forgives her."

"If I were him I wouldn't," she replied fiercely, remembering how her grandmother had reacted to being cheated on. "I would teach the bitch a lesson."

"Ah, but we all aren't as hot headed as you, love." Because it was said with adoration, she smiled, softening.

"I miss you."

"I miss you, too. Between dad and Capri the carpet in the parlor is getting worn thin by them pacing with worry over you. You better come home soon or there won't be anything left but stone on the floor."

She laughed at the visual even though guilt crept into her gut. "Tell them not to worry and you shouldn't worry either. We're almost there, I can feel it. I'll finish the diary tomorrow and then we'll have our answers. Tell everyone important I said hi."

"I will. I love you, clownface."

"I love you, too."

She hung up the phone and glanced over at Jax, who was still reading. He didn't bother to look up until she got up to sit beside him, handing him back his cell phone.

"Thanks for letting me use the phone again, cowboy," she murmured, feeling sentimental after the call to Liam. He took the phone from her and set it on the nightstand, his eyes on hers.

"Any time." He watched her carefully, noting the pain she was feeling. Setting the book aside he sat up and pulled her into his arms. "Why the long face, darlin'?"

She clung to him, fighting back the tears she suddenly felt aching behind her eyes. "I don't know, I guess I'm just exhausted, mentally and physically, you know?"

"I do know," he said quietly, his hand stroking her back lazily. When he pulled away, he cupped his hands around her face and pressed his lips to hers in a soft kiss, intended to comfort. On instinct, she deepened the kiss, her arms wrapping around his neck to pull herself closer.

"God, why does it seem like love does nothing but ruin those who succumb to it?" she murmured, saying what was in her heart.

She felt him stiffen, then heard him exhale slowly as she pressed her face into his neck.

"Love is an imperfect thing."

"My grandmother loved Silas and he ruined her. My mother loved my father and he used her. He loved another man's wife and by taking her he destroyed them both. Lucian loves his wife, but not in the deep, passionate way we all hope for. He respects her, and she trusts him, and so they had children together, but there's no real love there. I don't want to end up like that, Jax. I'm terrified to end up like any of them."

"Rian and Capri seem happy," he murmured, trailing his hands up her back. His face was turned into her hair and because he couldn't help himself, he relished in the woodsy scent of embers that seemed to be as inherent a part of her as her smile.

"They're perfect and lucky." She trailed her lips along his neck, enjoying the way his pulse jumped. Her breath quickened as her heart began to pound in her chest, and she hoped he could feel it. "And what are we, Jax?"

"Lord, Blythe, I think we're fools," he managed, fisting his hand in her hair and yanking her head back to look at her, his eyes haunted.

"Then let's be fools." She crushed her mouth against his and lost herself in him. Maybe she wasn't ready to tell him she loved him, but she was damn ready to show him.

And when they tumbled back against the bed, neither of them noticed the dark figure hovering just outside the window weeping with enraged misery.

Chapter Fifteen

July 30th, 1976

Thea has accepted that Silas will not be returning to Euphora. Unbeknownst to her, I threatened to flay him alive if he even tried and so he won't. He's too much of a coward. She's accepted my explanation that his adultery was the only reason, and in doing so I have saved face for both myself and my son. We can live in relative peace now.

March 31st, 1977

Something both horrific and wonderful happened today. I met someone and my hardened heart is torn between those first, soft feelings of attraction and between cold, safe distance. My mind has abandoned me, as none of my thoughts seem logical now. Damn my mind for having always been strictly governed by my heart.

It happened at the beach. I'd taken Brock to Santa Monica for the day so he could play in the ocean and as I was sitting on my towel enjoying the sun, a man approached me. He had a dog with him, this big chocolate Lab that bounded right up to me and started licking my face. The man apologized and had such a kind smile. We got to talking and I found out that he lives right there in Santa Monica, and works at the local farmer's market. He was incredibly nice and courteous, and a bit shy. I suppose at first my frostiness intimidated him, but when I saw the kindness in his eyes I couldn't help but warm to him.

His name is Peter. God help me, but I'm seeing him again in a couple of weeks. He was so good with Brock too, such a natural with children. Brock gets along with everyone, but he seemed to like Peter especially.

I wonder if I'm ready for this, but maybe there's no harm in having an innocent friendship with a nice, human man. And if it progresses to something more, then I'll deal with it when it comes.

Until then, he will be my little secret.

April 17th, 1977

I saw Peter again today at the beach. We got lunch on the Pier, and sat and talked for hours and hours…until the sun set in the sky. Then we walked the shoreline with his dog, Max, and talked some more. He's so considerate and so sensitive…it makes me wonder how any man could be so nice. He makes me feel so at ease when I'm with him, like there's nothing to worry about in this peaceful little bubble we're in. He was brave enough to reach for my hand today, and even though I told myself no, I still let him. My heart beat faster when he looked at me, a soothing confidence in his eyes. He's nothing like Silas, not arrogant or intense or even handsome. He's just…kind. Perhaps that's all I've ever wanted, without even knowing it. Someone to be kind to me.

May 27th, 1977

Today was our fourth date and he kissed me. It was so sweet to see him so nervous, fumbling with the key to his apartment so I could see where he lives. And after he'd given me the tour, we were standing on his balcony, the sun setting over the horizon, and he kissed me. It was gentle and sweet, and heartwarming. God, against my better judgment, I think I may be falling for him.

Brock just adores him, and he adores Brock, something that makes me enormously happy. But one critical fact has been lingering on my mind for awhile now, and I just can't shake it. How would Peter react to me telling him what I really am? Could he be the kind of human who could accept that? I'm not sure and I'm almost too scared to find out. I don't want to ruin this, whatever we have. It's become so precious to me...

"God, this couldn't be important." Blythe murmured, shutting the diary and setting it aside.

"What is it?" Jax asked, busy shaving in the bathroom.

"Bristol fell in love with some human guy. I should probably skip ahead."

"Wait." Stepping out of the bathroom, shaving cream still half on his face, Jax pointed his razor at her. "Just how do you think a demon gets a woman pregnant, Blythe?"

She snorted out a laugh. "I don't know and I don't really care. Ain't my business."

He rolled his eyes. "They have to possess a human in order to, you know...do it." He made a few hand gestures, earning another hoot of laughter from her. "So maybe this guy was the human the demon possessed."

"You mean kind hearted Peter is the demon?" Disbelieving, Blythe shook her head. "I just don't see it."

"Just keep reading." With that, he returned to his shaving, leaving her alone with the diary once more.

"Sure thing, boss," she grumbled sarcastically, lifting the diary and opening it again, convinced that she was wasting her time.

July 5th, 1977

Peter and I have been seeing each other for a few months now, and it's been wonderful. I never thought my heart could love again, but I think it has. I still haven't told Thea or any of the others. He is still my little secret. Thea's been asking me where I've been going all this time and I keep making excuses. I don't want her to have any influence over this. I know she would say that this is not in Brock's best interest, but I don't see how it's causing him any harm. He spends so much time with his friends anyway, I don't see how me seeing Peter once in awhile is hurting him.

I have made my decision not to tell Peter what I am. It's too risky, and I feel I can keep what we have in tact long enough for Brock to be old enough to take over for me on Euphora, and then I can live down here with Peter. He's already talking about marrying me and I know I should be afraid, but I'm not. I feel exhilarated.

July 26th, 1977

God, I'm pregnant…I almost don't want to believe it, but part of me is so overjoyed about it. I haven't told anyone yet and I don't think I will. Only Peter knows and he's so happy. He wants me to move in with him and marry him once the baby is born.

I guess my long term plan to leave Euphora is going to have to happen immediately, before I begin to show. Thea won't understand, but she'll have to accept it. And Brock…my first baby, my constant love…I can't take him away from his home and his legacy. But he's such a happy child, and he'll be eleven in less than a year. He doesn't need me much anymore; he's so headstrong and confident. The other boys all look up to him. I know he will be okay without me and I will try and see him whenever I can.

July 30th, 1977

I broke things with Thea the best way I knew how. I fought with her and I threatened to leave, even though that was my full intent all along. She fell for it, and tried to bait me by saying she would raise Brock herself, hoping that would sway me. But of course it didn't. I want her to help Brock along as best she can when I'm gone.

And so it is done. Within months I will have another baby, Peter's baby. I can only hope this is the right decision…but, then again, life has always been a gamble for me…

There was a suspicious break in the entries with a few blank pages between, as though Bristol had skipped them on purpose for symbolism. Blythe flipped through them, her brow furrowing when she found the next entry scrawled in hurried and desperate writing, alone in the center of the page. Her heart fell as she read the short sentence, dated some nine months from the previous entry.

April 1st, 1978

What's done can't be undone. —William Shakespeare

A shiver ran through her that had nothing to do with being cold. Rubbing her arms, she fought against the urge to burn the book to ashes—anything to stop reading it. She wasn't sure she could handle it. She was beginning to fear what she knew was coming…and it terrified her like nothing had before.

Her chest aching miserably, she set the book down and curled into herself, and let the tears fall.

August 1st, 1978

What can be said, except that I am a fool? I should have seen it coming, should have known that nothing so beautiful could have been real. But the betrayal…oh, God, it hurts almost worse than the outcome itself.

I was too trusting and will damn myself for the rest of my life. I abandoned my son, my home, my life, all for a lie. Peter was nothing but a disgusting lie…

I gave birth to my son on April Fool's Day…how fitting, because nothing describes how I feel better than that. Peter and Silas both played me for a fool.

You see, my only friend Peter was not what he seemed. And it took the birth of my son for me to finally realize the elaborate con Silas had conducted against me.

I knew something was wrong the moment I held my son in my arms, my little Dante, and his eyes flashed red. Oh, the horror that clenched my heart, the disbelief over what I had seen with my own eyes. He has demon blood was all I could think…how in the world does he have demon blood? And then Peter came into the room, and Silas was with him, and they both looked at me and smiled so hideously…I knew it then. I knew they had both betrayed me. Peter had been a demon all along, pretending to be human, and I was the fool who fell for it. And Silas had contracted him to do this to me, to ensure I was shamed and destroyed. And he succeeded. I am ashamed and my life as a Fire Dryad is over, I can never return to Euphora now…

I went to Thea and I tried to explain, but she wouldn't believe me. When I showed her Dante and told her the truth, she became so cold, so unfeeling, so unlike I had ever known her to be. And she did what she said she had to do…she banished me and my new son for good. She wouldn't even let me see Brock one last time, such was her disgust with me over something I had no control over.

And so now it is done. I will live the remainder of my days amongst humans, caring for the only son I have left. Despite the demon blood in him, he is still my son, and I cannot abandon him. I will not make the same mistakes I made with Brock, will not let my own selfish needs get in the way ever again. Dante will have as good a home as I can provide, and I can only pray that my influence will keep the demon inside of him at bay...

Blythe set the diary aside and stared ahead, stunned and unseeing. Nearly an hour later Jax found her, almost comatose. It took a swift shake to awaken the soul within her—the soul that had shuddered and burrowed out of sight in revolt to what it had witnessed. And when her eyes met his, glassy against her ghostly pale skin, he feared she would never be herself again.

"Jesus, Blythe, what is it?" he demanded, anger charging ahead to combat his fear at seeing the hollowed, haunted look in her eyes.

"It was a trap...she'd been fooled. She hadn't done anything wrong except love a man she thought was kind...I think I'm gonna be sick." She vaulted forward, charging into the bathroom and emptying her stomach horribly, shaking with grief as tears fell down her face. Jax silently came up behind her and pressed a damp cloth to the back of her neck, soothing away the worst of the queasiness.

She shuddered and laid back against his chest, welcoming the arms that enfolded her. He didn't use words to soothe, didn't try and baby her or excuse her pain away. Instead he just held her and let her grieve. It was exactly what she needed.

Minutes passed and then she finally spoke. "All this time I was so wrong. I was so horribly wrong about her."

"You can't change that but you can change what you do now," he reminded her, rocking her gently. She closed her eyes against another onslaught of tears, knowing they were useless now.

"It was Silas. He told the demon to use her...to make her love him and get her pregnant, all so she would be disgraced. All because they hated each other. Nothing I could have imagined compares to how revolting the truth is."

She felt him slowly exhale as he processed what she'd told him, imagined his eyes hardened with aversion and his mouth set in a firm, unwavering line. He would want vengeance just as she did, only there was quite possibly no one to get vengeance against.

"Thea banished her even though she told the truth. She refused to accept her back, knowing she had created a child with a demon, willingly or not. How could Thea have been so cold?" Shivering, not just with sorrow but with a rising fury that was swiftly coursing through her system, Blythe gripped the nearby sink and pulled herself to her feet, cursing her weak knees. She turned when Jax got to his feet, and her eyes were dry and hard as gilded steel. "Thea will have to answer to me now," she snarled, her voice low and feral. Jax was once again reminded of a fiery warrior, primed for battle, thirsty for bloodshed.

"We don't have time for that." He knew he was treading on dangerous waters, but she had to control her temper. They were wasting crucial time by not finishing the diary, which he was certain held the key to where Dante was going next. Where he most likely already was. "Finish the diary, we'll get Dante, and then you can have it out with Thea."

Her fists clenched together and she whirled around to stalk into the bedroom, letting out a strangled growl to release her frustration and some of her anger. The fact that she knew deep down that he was right only pissed her off more.

"I don't think you get it, Jax," she spat, needing to take all of her emotions out on whoever was handy. She turned to face him, watching as he left the bathroom and leaned casually against the doorjamb, crossing his arms over his chest in that irritatingly superior way he had. Seeing it only fueled the fire that was rapidly exploding in her system. "My entire life, the very memory of this woman has been a thorn in my side. I've blamed her for nearly everything that's gone wrong for me, and tossed some of the blame my father's way too. Then, in a few short months, I discover that not only was I wrong about my father all these years, but I was also wrong about my grandmother. So, what it boils down to, Jax, is that I have let other people convince me to hate my own family for shit they didn't even do. I let myself be taken for a goddamn fool, and Thea of all people, let me. Thea, who knew the truth about what happened with my grandmother, whether she believed it or not, and yet never shared it with me. Sure, she told us all about how Bristol had given birth to a half demon baby, but let us continue believing that she had welcomed it, that she had purposely tried to create this monster. But she didn't, Jax. She was just a woman who'd fallen for the worst kind of con from the worst kind of man. God, I'm mortified and I hate myself right now. I hate myself for every time I called her a whore. Every time I let myself hate her, or blame her, or shit on her memory. She didn't deserve any of that. She didn't deserve it..." Her voice choked as her anger smoldered into ashes, the result of expelling everything that was inside of her. An odd sense of relief filtered through the hollowed, destroyed cavities in her heart. "But I know the truth now. I know the truth and I'm going to make damn sure that everyone else knows it, too. No one will ever speak ill of Bristol again, not while I'm still kicking and breathing."

She sat down on the bed, taking a deep breath to soothe the ache in her chest. Glancing up at Jax, she tried a smile.

"I'm sorry I yelled at you." She wasn't that sorry, just a little since he'd been the recipient of her angst. But it had to be someone and he had the misfortune of being present.

He nodded slightly, one eyebrow raised. "You going to take a bite out of me if I come any closer?"

She laughed even though it hurt her throat that was sore from both crying and screaming, She patted the comforter beside her. "If I do, I promise it isn't lethal."

"Oh, well, that makes it so much better," he chuckled, approaching to sit beside her. He hunched over and stared at his hands, wondering what to say. He could only imagine the pain she felt, but could appreciate the forcefulness of her resolve to clear her grandmother's name. That was something he could faithfully stand behind.

"When this is all over, I want you to sit down with Thea and read the diary with her. If anything will make her understand, it's that." He tilted his head to look at her, his eyes calm and steady.

Blythe nodded, knowing he was right. "I guess I should finish reading it myself. We still don't know the next place he's going."

He patted her knee before rising to his feet. "My demon contacts haven't seen him so I'm willing to bet he's hightailed it out of here already. We're wasting time."

"Okay." With a groan, she reached for the diary and settled back onto her pillows. She cracked it open and hoped to God it didn't get worse.

August 3rd, 1978

I've taken Dante to Phoenix, Arizona. I've really only ever been to a few places in the human world, and all of them Silas knew of. I can't go anyplace where he may find me. I don't know if he's hunting me or not, but it wouldn't surprise me. His madness knows no bounds, I understood that when I saw him and Peter side by side. Silas has this evil inside of him now that is all consuming, and if he gets it in his head that my disgrace is not enough payback, he may come after me and Dante. Dante is all I have left. I have to protect him.

Phoenix isn't all bad…it's a bit hot, but that doesn't bother me. I've found a room to rent in a house with a nice older couple, and they've given me a job cleaning their house for them. I don't know the first thing about cleaning, but I'm going to wing it. I'm doing what I have to do to get by. That's really all I can do. Dante cries all the time…I think he senses my stress and my grief. I have to push them aside and be strong.

January 5th, 1982

I don't know why, but it feels like someone is watching me at all hours of the day. I hardly ever leave the house, except to run errands for Margaret, but I feel as though there are eyes on me everywhere I go. It's been like this for weeks and I just can't shake it. Could Silas have found me after all this time? I've become so fearful for my life and that of my son…I must be going crazy. But I don't think I can risk it. If Silas found us, if I let my guard down for even one moment, he may hurt Dante. I could never forgive myself if that happened.

It's time to move on to somewhere else. I can't stay here.

January 20th, 1982

I was able to purchase a car with some money I saved, and Dante and I hit the road. We drove and drove for days, leaving the past behind us. Running away from the demons that haunt my every waking moment. We've arrived finally in a place called El Paso. It feels good here and the people are nice without being too nosy. Maybe it wouldn't hurt to just stay here awhile.

There's a dance club called the Devil's Gate. The name makes me shudder but the women are nice and they've offered me a job waiting tables. If I can, they've said maybe I could dance there too, make some real money. Money is what makes the human world go round, as I've discovered in my years here, and my thirst for it is hardly ever quenched. Dante will be starting preschool soon and he needs new clothes.

I'll stay here for now, but who knows for how long.

January 7th, 1984

It's back, that old feeling again of being watched. God, could he have found me this time? I want to stand up and fight, but I fear I no longer can. It's been years since I've used the fire within me. I don't know if such things can die out but I think it may have left me for good. Either way, it's probably time to move on. Life has been decent here in El Paso, I've made some friends and have lived in a nice home...but I'm craving something more. I hear Chicago is a booming city with lots of jobs and decent schools for Dante. And it might just be crowded enough to lose myself in. How could Silas find me in a city that size? We're going to leave tomorrow. I'll miss this place, but I do not feel at home. It's time to move on, once more.

June 1st, 1992

It feels like I only write when something drastic happens in my life...but maybe those are the times when I feel the need to expel the worries in my heart onto paper. It's been eight years since I've been in Chicago and Dante is grown up now. He's in high school and gets fairly good grades. Never having gone to school myself, I can't really be the judge of his learning ability, but he seems to be a bright and clever boy, if not a bit distant with me sometimes. A few years ago I finally told him the whole story of where he came from and who he really is. It was hard for him to understand at first, but he came around. I think it hurts him to know he's so different from his classmates at school, but that will pass. He asked me why his brother gets to live on Euphora while we have to live with the humans. It hurt me to tell him that they don't want us. I realize now that maybe I should have sugar coated the truth, but he needed to know that he can never go there. Because of what he is, he doesn't truly belong anywhere, except with me. I will always be there for him.

The city is cold. I never realized how cold until I came here, and by then I had run through most of my savings just to get us an apartment and food. We have been virtually stuck here ever since. But I finally have enough saved for us to move again. I've resigned myself to the fact that Silas was never after me, and that he will never come looking for me. I don't even know if he's still alive, or where he is now. I suppose it doesn't matter any longer.

I think we should go someplace quieter, with milder weather and calmer people. One of the ladies at the hotel I work at is from a place called Richmond...she says it's lovely. It's far away, but driving has always soothed me. Perhaps a change of scene will be good for Dante, too. He's been so cold lately, detached. I think the city has hardened him.

Please, God, let me find peace in Richmond.

June 4th, 1995

Who is this young man that is my son? He has committed an unthinkable act. Something abhorrent and vile, and yet somehow convinced me of the justice of it. Without my even realizing it, he slipped through the cracks and contacted Balgaire, one of the Furies, and managed to use both his own jealousy of my son Brock paired with Balgaire's hatred and the two of them schemed to destroy him. Dante tells me that it's justice for Brock never attempting to find me or contact me in all these years, but I just don't see it. I never expected him to...I wanted Brock to live his life as best he could, even if it was without me. But now they have executed some kind of dirty plan involving killing an innocent woman and abducting a child...God, the child was so beautiful and innocent, and even my cold, aged heart broke at the sight of her. She's the Air Dryad, such a tiny thing with big gray eyes and light hair. In a fit of remorseful passion I managed to convince Dante not to kill her, but to leave her in the alley. No one on Euphora will ever find her, I told him. But let her live, even if it is just amongst the humans. Thank God he listened and we left her there. I hope she survives…she's almost the same age as my own granddaughter, Brock's baby girl, Blythe… I've never known her, and probably never will, but by saving the Air Dryad child I felt somehow connected to Blythe.

God, what monster have I created that would do such horrid things? And yet, I love him…my heart is full of love for him because he is all I have. He is still half a part of me despite his demon blood. But the demon was who I saw tonight after he returned from the raid. The demon inside of him is full of rage and thirsts for revenge that I fear will never be sated…he confessed to me tonight that a week ago he killed both Silas and Peter…is this justice? Or is it madness?

December 2nd, 2005

I'm dying and while I'm doing it I'm laughing at how absurd it all is. The human doctors call it cancer…I asked them if it was some kind of virus I contracted from being around other people, but they informed me that it has been growing inside my body for some time, something that happened naturally. I have never heard of such a thing, so I do not believe them. But I do believe them when they say I have little time left. My body is withering away, and I am only fifty seven! Maybe my life was never meant to be long. It certainly hasn't been easy, but I have done my best with what I was given.

I hear Brock is living in Las Vegas. Thea banished him after Dante framed him. I wish that my two sons could have known each other as friends and not as enemies. But there's no time for regrets. I can only hope he's getting by as I did, one day at a time.

Dante is agitated and I hate to leave him this way. He says I can't die, that if I do he will be all alone. But how can I change this? It is beyond my control.

Blythe would be fourteen years old by now, with no father or grandmother to guide her. God, was it really my mistakes that led to that? I can only hope she is strong, resilient, and bold enough to take charge of her own life. I've certainly learned that life throws you many curveballs, and that the only way to survive is to plant your feet firmly on the ground and swing with everything you've got. I hope she is wiser than I was, and I hope she has a questioning and skeptical mind. I hope she learns to love herself long before ever loving someone else.

She may never know my story, but I hope she forgives me.

December 31st, 2005

At least in my sleep, the world loses its painfully sharp edge. At last, I can rest.

Chapter Sixteen

She closed the diary and set it aside for the last time. Jax looked up at her expectantly and she noticed the apprehension in his eyes, as though he was worried she would fall apart again. God, since when had she become *that* girl? The one that can't hold herself together? Well, this time her eyes were dry and her resolve in place.

Knowing the truth, the whole truth, brought her great comfort. No longer would she judge blindly what she didn't know or understand. And once this was over, she would educate everyone who would listen who her grandmother had been, and how they had all wronged her.

Until then, they had a mission to complete.

"Dante's in Richmond," she told him, brushing back her hair and stretching her arms over her head. "It was the place he and Bristol went after Chicago."

"Any specific place in Richmond?"

"I don't think so, it doesn't say where they lived or anything." She stood up and stretched out her legs, groaning at her unused, strained muscles. "God, I haven't run in forever."

"You can run all the marathons you want once this is done," Jax informed her, setting his own book aside. "Let's get some sleep, catch the first flight to Richmond in the morning."

Yawning, Blythe nodded. She climbed into bed and curled beside him, comforted when his arms came around to hold her.

As she tumbled into sleep she dreamt of her home, and to her horror she watched it become rapidly consumed by flames.

It didn't occur to her until they had landed in Richmond and were standing in front of the baggage carousel, staring at the conveyer belt.

"Oh!" She smacked his arm excitedly, earning a scowl from him as she grinned. "Do you think Dante is going to the alley where he left Capri? That would be a good place for a show-down, don't you think?"

Rubbing his arm, Jax glared down at her. "That's precisely what I was thinking. Now what the hell did you hit me for?"

"Sorry, I was excited." She beamed and suddenly reached down to haul his duffle bag off the carousel for him, tossing it down beside his feet. "There, now we're even."

"No, even would be me punching you in the arm in retaliation," he grumbled, even as his lips twitched at the edges.

"Normally I'd say give it your best shot, but seeing as we're in a public place, I don't think hitting a woman would be very wise, cowboy." She flashed a grin at him and winked. "But I promise to give you ample opportunity later, in private."

Inspired, he grabbed her and pulled her in until her mouth was inches from his. "Anything else go along with that promise, darlin'?"

"Mmm..." She leaned toward his ear and whispered something that had his blood heating and his pulse quickening. Pulling away, she patted him on the cheek and then reached out for her own duffle.

Amused and irritated at the same time, Jax led the way out of the airport and to the rental car he'd booked for them.

When they hit the road, Blythe turned to him. "So how do I know you really were thinking that Dante would go to the alley, and you weren't just stealing my idea?"

"The hotel I booked for us while we waited for our flight is one block away from the alley. Ain't no coincidence." He flipped on the radio and cruised the channels until he found something he liked.

On impulse, Blythe reached into the backseat and dug into his duffle bag, unearthing his Stetson. "Don't forget your hat, cowboy. Can't listen to country music and drive without it."

Patting it down on top of his head, she sat back and marveled at him. God, he was cute when he wore that damn hat, and the way his forehead creased in both humor and frustration only made him more appealing.

"You know, we should just go to the alley right now, skip the hotel. He might be hanging out, waiting for us to show up," Blythe encouraged, hardly able to contain her excitement.

"If this is indeed the showdown we're expecting, I don't want to go in blind. We've got to survey the surrounding area, make sure he's not gearing up to ambush us. This is his home turf, Blythe, and he's got resources here that we don't."

"Yeah but we've waited this long and we're so close. Let's just do it."

"No." His voice was stern as he continued to the hotel. "We're going to do this the right way, Blythe."

"And maybe miss our chance? For all you know he might wander off while we're twiddling our thumbs and *planning*." She made exaggerated and sarcastic quotations with her fingers, emphasizing her point.

"He's not going to wander off. He's going to wait for us because this is where he wants us to be. But I'm not going to charge in there unprepared before I know the lay of the land."

Huffing out an annoyed breath, she sat back in her seat and stared out the window. Arguing with him over this was like beating against a brick wall. He was never going to cave. She would just have to take matters into her own hands if necessary.

Hours later, after surveying the area, scoping out local demons, talking with a few of them, and putting together what Jax termed a 'location study', they settled into their hotel to organize and plan.

It was late in the evening, nearly eight o'clock, and Blythe's stomach grumbled as they waited for the pizza delivery. Sitting together on the floor, they spread out a map of the area, and began locating where Dante lived according to the local demons, and where that was in conjunction with the alleyway that Capri had been discovered in, along with the tree he had supposedly used to transport himself from Euphora to Richmond all those years ago.

They reviewed their notes from conversations with the local humans who knew Dante, along with what they had gathered from the few demons they'd found.

It always took Blythe by surprise how fearful demons were of Jax, and how easily they could be convinced to divulge information to him. His reputation preceded him everywhere he went, and though she admired that fact, she also found it infuriating. While the demons slavishly showered Jax with information, they took one look at her and were revolted. Her Dryad blood made it hard to convince them to talk, so Jax left talking to the humans up to her.

So she'd walked around, asked about him, and managed to get some responses. Mostly they said he kept to himself, that he was rather shy and reclusive. The women she talked to said he was handsome, but kind of creepy. He never flirted with anyone, or dated anyone as far as they knew.

There was a brisk knocking on the hotel door and Jax rose to answer it. Blythe groaned thankfully when he came back with two boxes of pizza.

"I could never get tired of pizza," she told him as she ripped open the box and greedily grabbed a slice, biting into it and moaning. "So much greasy cheese and crispy pepperoni…it's heaven."

Jax shook his head and smirked as he opened his own pizza and took out a slice. "It's the food of champions."

"Mmm hmm." Grinning, she polished off the slice and grabbed another. "Anyway, so we know the ins and outs of the alley, including any doors and what shops they go to. We know the names of the shops in the area, and we managed to locate where Dante lives, a mere five blocks from the alley, and we spoke to both humans and a few demons nearby who know him. What else is there to do?"

"Tomorrow we drive by the area with the sensor, see if we find any activity happening down the alley. He should be expecting us there any time, so if he's lying in wait we will see him before he sees us."

"And then what?"

He swallowed a bite of pizza, then leaned over the map to make another notation. "Then we move in, but carefully. He can sense you because of what you are, so it might be best for you to wait in the car a block away so I can try and get to him before he realizes we're there."

"I don't want to wait in the car," she scoffed, insulted. "That's stupid. If we rush in there and take him by surprise, it won't matter if he senses me. I will have already shot him."

"Why do you think it'll be so easy? Dante is smarter than most demons and he's prepared for this. He's expecting us to rush in because he knows how you are, and he only thinks he knows me. We've got to sneak up on him and I can only do that alone. You can attack him all you want once I have him tied up, okay?"

"That's not good enough." Rising to her feet to pace, Blythe felt her hands shaking with temper. "We're in this together, cowboy, and I won't be pushed aside to wait while you go in and save the day."

"You're missing the point, Blythe," he fired back, equally as heated. "We won't catch him at all if you're right there. He can sense you, damnit, you know that!"

"So I'll wear perfume." she combated haughtily, cocking her chin at him. He huffed out an incredulous laugh and began gathering up the materials they'd spread out over the floor.

Standing up, his arms full of papers, he sent her a cold glare. "I know you're not that stupid, Blythe," he muttered, his voice low and his eyes dangerous. "Now get some sleep and this will be done tomorrow."

Tossing the map and papers aside onto the desk, he stormed into the bathroom and shut the door. She heard the shower hiss and had to bite back the urge to set fire to all his stupid papers and maps.

Hours later, he lay sleeping beside her. She hadn't been able to fall asleep as her mind had been on warp speed since their disagreement.

She understood his point, of course she did. He was right, she wasn't stupid enough to believe that Dante couldn't sense her. But this was about confronting Dante herself. It was a matter of pride and necessity. For herself, for her father, for Capri…even for Bristol. She had this feeling in her gut that if they went to the alley, even if Dante sensed her, he would want to speak to her. He wouldn't just try and kill them, or try and run away. No, all of his letters and gifts over the past weeks had been leading up to this finale.

And if Jax didn't understand that, then perhaps it was best that she acted alone. He could thank her later, when she had Dante and the job was done.

Slipping soundlessly out of bed, she dressed in the dark, shrugging into jeans and a black shirt. She tucked Jax's revolver filled with liquid nitrogen bullets into the back of her jeans. On impulse, she put on the Fire Dryad heirlooms, the ring and the necklace, as talismans in honor of her grandmother. She didn't know why, but wearing them made her feel safer and stronger.

She sent one last glance at Jax before she left, blowing him a noiseless kiss.

Even if you won't forgive me, cowboy, this is how it was probably always going to go down.

She let the door click softly behind her, and, like smoke rising out of a smoldering fire that dissipates into the air, she was gone.

It didn't take her long to reach the alley; it was only a block from their hotel. Even though she was aware of the various access points through different shops and housing complexes, she knew in her heart that it had to be the main entrance. She wanted him to see her coming for him, wanted him to see that she wasn't afraid. No, she had determination and vindication in her heart now, perpetuated by the heirlooms of her forefathers.

She walked the short distance to the alley, her footsteps muffled on the sidewalk. It was nearly midnight and the full moon glowed eerily overhead, highlighting the near empty street.

It wasn't the best neighborhood, and even though she spotted a few shady people drifting here and there, she kept her mind focused. No one and nothing could hurt her now, not when she was this close to her goal. The thirst for it resonated inside of her, beating itself into her very bones.

Perhaps in a way she should be thanking Dante for giving her this renewed strength of purpose. Without him, she would have never had the heirlooms, and she would have never known the truth about her grandmother. But despite her gratitude, none of it made up for the horrific misdeeds he'd committed to her family and to her.

She approached the mouth of the alley, nerves and anticipation thrumming through her veins. The alley was lit only by the moonlight and a few dim streetlights that cast a vague yellowish glow over the brick of the buildings. She stopped and stared down the lane, noting the clotheslines that hung overhead, shirts and pants hanging motionless in the still night air. The lack of breeze and sound had the hair rising on the back of her neck.

Biting her tongue to center herself, she stepped into the alley, her hand itching to reach for her weapon. But she didn't want to scare him away, didn't want him to know she was armed. She wanted him to think that she had come to him to surrender, to give him what he wanted.

She stepped forward a few feet, her eyes scanning. It bothered her that she couldn't see the end, that it was too shadowed by the dark of night for her to make out more than vague outlines. And as she was staring at those outlines, wondering if she was looking at trashcans or something much more sinister, she caught movement off to her right.

Her head jolted to the side, eyes locking on a figure that moved toward her, sliding over the ground. Her heart lodged in her throat as she stood her ground, determined not to scream. He wouldn't see her afraid, she wouldn't allow it.

But when moments later the slithering dark shadow on the ground began to morph into the shape of a human, still guarded by the shadows, she couldn't help the shiver that raced through her body. And when that figure stepped out into the yellow light of the streetlamp, the sight of his grinning face stopped her heart.

"Blythe." His voice was a whisper, deep but hushed, as though he didn't want to startle her or felt no need to speak louder. And the truth was, she heard him loud and clear in the silence of the alley.

He looked different from what she remembered from the night club in Los Angeles weeks before. Then he had simply been another guy on the dance floor, with dark hair and no distinguishable features. But now that she really took a good look at him, it startled her to see just how unique looking he was. How she had missed it was beyond her.

His long hair was jet black and pulled into a ponytail at the nape of his neck. His raw boned face was tanned and sharpened, with high cheekbones and a narrow, crooked nose that ended in a point. His mouth was curled back over perfectly straight teeth, in a grin that was more evil than any she had ever seen. And his eyes, Lord, his eyes were the same amber as hers, but harsher, and impossibly more vivid. They seemed to glow under the shadow of his dark brows, staring at her with both lust and loathing.

"You have come to me, alone? I was beginning to think you wouldn't come at all...oh, but you've shown up at just the perfect time. I have a surprise that I know you'll enjoy." He kept walking toward her, slow and deliberate, each step like a carefully planned waltz, gliding without pause.

She fought back the urge to attack him tooth and nail, knowing she needed to get him right where she wanted him. Just distracted enough for him not to notice the bullet she'd plug right into his gut.

"I came alone because I wanted to thank you for giving me the truth," she told him, relieved her voice didn't betray the emotions rushing through her. Lifting the necklace, she smiled coyly at him. "And to thank you for these. I'm wearing them after all."

"I knew you would." He chuckled as he reached out to her, his hand trailing down her cheek. He was several inches taller than her and thin as a rail with rangy muscles visible beneath his shirt. She flinched when he touched her, and the fact that she did so made him laugh even more. "Ah, but you won't let me touch you?"

Gritting her teeth, she cocked her chin up at him. "What do you want from me, Dante? You've shown me the truth about my grandmother, what else do you want?"

His eyes flashed wickedly as his grin spread wider. In a swift and dangerous move, he reached out to grip her neck just under her jaw with one hand while the other pressed into her back, pulling her violently against him. He leaned down until his mouth brushed against her ear, and what he whispered to her made bile rise in her throat.

"I wanted to make you my wife...we would make such a great team, you and me...but you're spoiled now."

He whipped her back and grabbed her hands just as she was about to burn him, shaking his head, cool madness in his eyes. "Tsk, tsk, Blythe. You've tried that already, remember? The revolver you carry would be much more effective, but as you can see," he reached behind her smoothly and removed the gun, tossing it to the side carelessly, "you no longer have that defense."

"You bastard. I'll kill you with my teeth if I have to," she snarled, bucking against him to try and free herself. He merely grabbed hold of her with surprising strength, pulling her to the ground and pinning her.

"If only I'd realized before what a rotten whore you are, Blythe, I would have never pursued you. Don't think that you would have found me otherwise; I'd be on a beach somewhere far, far away from here. You and the idiot bounty hunter only found me because I wanted you to. But now that I know you've let him have you, you're ruined."

"I would have never been with you, Dante," she said through clenched teeth, still fighting against the hands that held her down. "Haven't you ever heard of goddamn incest?"

The red glow that flashed through his eyes made her fight even harder, until her skin was raw and bruised from both his hands and the sidewalk.

"I thought because you looked like her and acted like her that you would be like her, but you are nothing close." Infuriated, he lifted her and slammed her against the ground, causing her to smack her head hard on the concrete. Stars sprung behind her eyes as she gasped for air, the pain tearing through her viciously.

"Damnit, you are such a disappointment. All of my efforts, for what? For a worthless, selfish slut. None of that matters now. The second part of my plan is about to begin. You see, I had hoped to take you with me to Euphora as my new companion, and then you could tell them what you've learned and I would be welcomed back to my true home. I would have still killed them all for their sins, the goddamn hypocrites, but at least they'd die knowing they were fools."

She groaned as he shifted, pulling something out of his pocket. "But, as it so happens, you won't be at my side. You'll be here, helpless to do anything, as I destroy everything you love. That's justice, darling."

He uncapped the syringe with his teeth and before she could react he'd slipped it into a vein in her arm.

"Relax now, let this kick in. You should be awake again in about half an hour or so. Then you will be in for a splendid surprise."

He lifted her and stowed her nearby, hidden in the shadows. The world was spinning beneath her as she tried to fight back, but her arms felt like useless air and the dizziness consumed her as she drifted into blackness.

She awoke to the sound of voices. But though her eyes were open, her vision was blurred and her body felt paralyzed. She managed to glance down and see that he had tied her up with rope, and had gagged her. Tears sprung in her eyes as she choked against the gag. But the effort it took to move made her stomach turn, so she stopped, closing her eyes and fighting to breathe it away. She wasn't going to vomit against this gag; she would choke and die.

She heard the voices again as her system began to come fully back, and managed to open her eyes again. She spotted Dante beneath a streetlamp, someone else at his side speaking in hushed tones. Blythe thought it sounded like a woman, though her mind was still foggy from the drug. Was it her grandmother?

No, Bristol was dead. Then who was it?

Forcing her vision to clear she stared hard at the figure, and when the woman tilted her face to look at Dante, her blood froze.

Mother. What in the hell was Nyxa doing in Richmond talking to Dante?

The answer came to her with one swift, vicious punch. This was the surprise. Dante was using Nyxa to get onto Euphora. That was why she'd been acting strangely and why she'd been disappearing. She was meeting with Dante, plotting against her own family, most likely Brock, and now she was ready to assist Dante in getting revenge for the two of them.

Feeling sick again, Blythe tried to free herself from the ropes, knowing she had to get home, had to warn everyone.

"This can't fall back onto me." Nyxa's voice rose in a shrieking pitch that shocked Blythe back to reality. "You get to that bitch and destroy her. Take whoever else with you, I don't care. Just leave Brock. Once Serendipity is gone, he'll finally be free of her spell and he will love only me."

You goddamn selfish bitch, Blythe thought violently as she felt her blood boil in her veins. I always knew you were rotten.

"Anyone else, but Brock?" Dante crooned, confident and slick as he stroked his hand down Nyxa's arm. She was too self involved in her own hatred to notice the glint of evil in his eyes.

"Yes, yes...Capri, Thea, I don't care. Just leave me Brock."

"Very well." Dante chuckled as he shifted away, his thin frame casting a long, narrow shadow across the ground. He suddenly began to speak in the language of demons, the sound guttural and throaty, and out of the shadows appeared men, bulky and dangerous, equipped with demon weapons like she'd seen back in Phoenix. There were at least ten of them, and Blythe sat helpless in the shadows against the brick wall, fearing for her family.

Good God, he's going to raid Euphora again, she thought wildly. She tried to shoot fire from her palms, only to realize he'd covered her hands with aluminum foil and bags, eliminating the oxygen. Without the oxygen, her fire couldn't form.

Tears spilled down her cheeks as she watched one of the brutes drag a potted tree into the alleyway, setting it in front of Dante. He gestured gallantly to the tree, his eyes on Nyxa.

"Madam, if you would be so kind." He smiled, watching her as she stepped toward the tree and gripped it tight with her right hand.

"All of you, grab onto the tree," Dante instructed, doing so himself. Just before Nyxa transported the group to Euphora, Dante glanced over to where Blythe was hidden and grinned wickedly. In a flash of golden light they were gone.

Chapter Seventeen

The instant the golden light faded, Blythe saw Jax burst into the alleyway, pistol grip shotgun in his hands, aimed at what was no longer there. He glanced wildly around, his heart racing as he stared at the empty alley. Damnit, he just saw the flash of light, it had to have came from somewhere…

Blythe mustered her strength and shifted her body against the ropes, attempting to crawl on the ground toward Jax. She made it about three feet before she collapsed and her chest heaved for air, but it was just close enough.

He spotted her and raced over, whipping out a sharp knife from his boot and slicing at the ropes.

"Goddamnit, Blythe," he hissed, yanking the ropes off her, then pulling the bags from her hands and the gag out from her mouth. She gasped for air, her body heaving with nausea from the drug. He held her upright, fighting for control as he examined her body, terrified he'd find her bleeding. "What the hell happened? Are you hurt?"

She gripped his arm with near violent strength, her eyes wild and frenzied. "He's going to Euphora. He's going to kill them—all of them."

"Jesus." Cursing under his breath, Jax pulled her to her feet. "Can you walk?"

"Damnit, I'm fine. We have to go!" Blythe barely glanced at him as she stumbled to the tree still sitting in the center of the alley, looking as misplaced as a palm tree in the snow. Without hesitation, he followed her and gripped the tree as she did, and listened as she chanted the words she'd used all her life. Golden light flashed around them as the alley faded and the meadow appeared in its place. Only it felt as though they had landed not in the middle of a peaceful, nighttime field, but on the precarious outskirts of a war zone.

Beyond the wall of the courtyard, balls of fire shot through the air, exploding in trees and onto the ground. Cries and screams and eerie laughter resonated through the air, echoing off the stone walls. Fear gripped her heart as she sprinted through the meadow and opened the gate, her eyes watching demons wreaking havoc inside her home.

"God, they're everywhere." She started to race forward, only to have Jax pull her back.

"Where's my gun, the one you took when you left me sleeping?" She could tell by the look in his eyes that he was irritated with her, but that hardly mattered now.

"Dante threw it somewhere. I don't know," she managed, straining away from him. "I'm sorry, okay? I made a mistake, a big mistake. I'll pay for a new gun."

"Damnit, it's not that," he growled, reaching into his boot for a second, smaller revolver. "This is loaded with the liquid nitrogen bullets. I don't want you unarmed."

She numbly took the gun, her eyes meeting his as she blinked away grateful tears. "Thank you, cowboy."

With that, she raced away from him and plunged into the turmoil. Around her, the demons were darting through the trees, lighting fires and maniacally firing gunshots into the air. One of them had a demon fire whip, which he was snapping in the air as he approached the castle. Dante and Nyxa were nowhere to be seen.

To her relief, she spotted the adult members of her family standing at the entrance to the castle, preparing to fight. The younger ones were likely holed up inside where it was safer. How they had woken up and assembled so quickly was beyond her. Hell, Dante and his crew had only arrived minutes ago...

Pushing the thought aside, she ran full speed down the cobblestone pathway, dodging fire and bullets as she went. Her body was still weakened, but her resolve was iron strong. Determination alone kept her mind sharp and her body moving. She shoved away all traces of pain from the wounds on her head and arms, and focused entirely on her goal of reaching the castle. Her family needed her.

It all seemed like some garish nightmare, she thought, chaotic and unreal. But then she realized that she'd had this nightmare before, and now to her horror, it was coming true. Whether it had been a premonition or a culmination of her greatest fears, she couldn't know. But the fact remained that this was real and she was primed to fight.

"Blythe!" Liam grabbed her as she reached the entrance, pulling her close and hugging her. He held her briefly then pushed her back so he could look at her. "What are you doing here? Did Rian call you?"

"No...no." She fought to control her adrenaline, her hands trembling with sheer lust to fight. "I confronted Dante in the same alley he left Capri in fifteen years ago. He told me a lot of creepy things, most of which aren't important now. But he managed to tie me up and drug me, and made me watch as he and his demon buddies left for Euphora. Liam, it was Nyxa who helped them. Nyxa wants Dante to kill Serendipity and anyone else he wants as well. We have to stop her."

"We knew all that already," Liam told her with a grin. Beyond them in the courtyard, an explosion rocked the entire grounds, followed by insane laughter and cheers from the demons.

"How the hell did you know?" Blythe sputtered, her eyebrows raised.

"I told you before that Rhiannon's been keeping an eye on Nyxa lately, and she figured it out," Liam said proudly, and the look on his face had Blythe rolling her eyes. "And when she saw Nyxa sneak away tonight, she followed her and heard her mumbling about Richmond and Serendipity. So she waited until Nyxa left Euphora, and then she ran and told Thea and the rest of us. We prepared ourselves and waited, and low and behold, barely twenty minutes later Dante and his cronies were here."

Blythe couldn't hold back her resentment at Rhiannon for having beaten her to it first, but at the same time she was grateful. Because Rhiannon had been perceptive enough to notice Nyxa's behavior, her family had been warned that this was coming. And she would bet the breath out of her own lungs that Dante was pissed. She couldn't wait to confront him again. She just had to find him first.

Thinking of him made her remember Jax. She whirled around, looking at those who were crowded around the entrance with her. It was less than she had thought, only the Muses, the two remaining Fates, Thea and Sebastian.

"Where are the others? Capri?" Blythe asked Liam, her eyes searching the courtyard in desperation. And, damnit, where the hell had Jax gone?

Liam smiled and pointed upwards. Her eyes followed as she tilted her head back, and she saw Capri and Clynn in one of the top windows, creating a massive storm system over the courtyard that was already pulsating and shivering with lightning. A loud rumbling thunder echoed out and shook the ground, causing a few of the demons to gaze up at the storm in alarm.

"Oh, shit." Blythe choked out a manic laugh as she grinned back at Liam. "I like what I'm seeing. What about Lucian, Rian, and Brogan?"

"At the back end of the castle. Rian had a sneaking suspicion that Nyxa would lead Dante there, that the other demons were here to distract us. Rohan and Brock are with them, too. Your dad figured maybe he could talk some sense into Nyxa."

"Unlikely. She's crazy," Blythe said pointedly as she glanced back at the courtyard. Thea and Sebastian were confronting the demon with the fiery whip, and seeing the sheer power they held mystified her. She had rarely seen the two of them in action; they were simply magnificent.

Thea sent thick vines of ivy sprouting from the ground around the demon, wrapping themselves around his bulky human body. Razor sharp thorns emerged from the vines to puncture his skin as he buckled against the bonds, trying to thrust himself free.

Sebastian was busy pulling lightning bolts down from the storm system that Capri and Clynn were creating, each one landing to jolt the demon. He hadn't even stood a chance, Blythe thought as the whip fell and he crumbled to the ground. The demon spurted out of the human's mouth and weakly tried to slither away, but Sebastian was there with a crossbow he'd unsheathed from a holder on his back. The tip of the arrow glowed bright, hot silver, just like the contents of the liquid nitrogen rounds she had in her own pistol. He aimed and shot the arrow straight into the serpent. Blythe watched with wide eyes as the demon shuddered once and then froze, its body now solid as though encased in ice. All practical efficiency, Thea stepped forward and swiftly pulled a gleaming sword out of a hilt on her side and rammed it through the frozen demon's body, shattering it into a million, glittering pieces. As she did, her long mane of dark curls seemed to float around her, surrounding her gypsy face of golden skin and gloriously dark eyes. Then she sheathed her sword and turned to smile at Sebastian, who pulled her in for a quick kiss.

"We've always made such a good team, my love," she told him, her eyes glowing with power.

"The best," Sebastian replied, enjoying her for a moment before stepping away. The Muses rushed forward and pulled the unconscious human left behind to safety inside the atrium, where they could hold him until the others could be rescued as well. Later, they would have to erase their memories and send them back to Richmond, wounded but alive.

Sebastian nodded in Blythe's direction, his smile and eyes vivid as his long blonde hair, free from bonds, shifted and flowed with the movement. He looked more like a Nordic warrior with his bow and arrow than the soft, ethereal man she'd known her whole life. "Our Fire Dryad has returned, my sweet, in case you didn't notice."

"Indeed I did," Thea replied, looking over her shoulder to smile at Blythe. "I do hope you're ready to battle, my dear. We are, as they say, in the fray."

"I'm always ready for a fight, Thea." Blythe grinned as she approached, Liam at her side. The two Fates beside them were armed with swords, looking apprehensive as they awaited Thea's orders. The Muses held back, ready to rescue the next human.

"Good, because there are more approaching, and I'm getting tired of them destroying my gardens." Unbridled power flashed over Thea's face as she turned away and faced the three demons who had now dared to come closer. She and Sebastian faced the demon in the center, while the Fates took the demon to the right.

Blythe stood her ground and raised her arms, focusing on the first demon on the far left. He was a big, brawling Italian guy with hairy arms and a mean scowl on his face. In his hands was a giant steel mallet that glowed bright orange. His eyes flashed red as they met hers, reminding her of the evil she was about to destroy.

She turned her head and nodded to Liam, who acknowledged her with a grin. It was time to prove that they made just as good a team as Thea and Sebastian.

Hands held out, she shot a stream of fire directly at the demon's eyes. He growled and swung out with the mallet blindly, only to drop it and cover his face, stopping mid-step. Liam shot a stream of water that rushed toward the demon, freezing it as it swirled around him, forming an icy tomb that reached up to his chest, pinning his arms. Blythe stopped spewing fire as Liam polished off the ice, and then both of them stood and watched as the demon struggled to free itself. Realizing its host body was trapped, the demon released itself and tried to flee, only to have Blythe whip out Jax's revolver and aim it gleefully.

"Oh, no you don't, you bastard," she announced as she cocked it and fired off a shot. She could see the blast from the bullet and could almost see it coursing through the air before it made contact with the dark, shadowy demon. The liquid nitrogen bullet froze the demon's body from the inside out, encasing it in ice. With a wicked grin, Blythe glanced over at Liam. "Go ahead, give it a good kick."

Though he looked puzzled at first, Liam followed her order and stepped toward the ice-covered serpent. With a primal yell, he swung his foot forward, smashing it into the demon, which burst into sparkling glass pieces as they exploded into the air. Triumphant, he whirled around to smile at her, but she wasn't looking. Instead, she was staring in horror at the opposite side of the castle.

Lucian and Brock appeared, both looking worse for wear, battling back the same demon who was armed with a flame thrower that was emitting bluish flames. The demon was backing his way toward the front of the castle, with Lucian and Brock keeping back just out of reach of the flames.

Seeing her chance, Blythe flew towards them and jumped onto the back of the demon, clawing at his eyes with her fingers. He howled with pain and tried to buck her off, the flame thrower shooting fire in every direction—scorching the grass and just missing the Fates who were fighting their own demon.

Brock and Lucian watched in terror and shock as the demon threw Blythe over his head and onto the ground, where she landed on her back. He shifted to aim the flamethrower at her, but she spun around and kicked hard with her right foot and knocked it out of his hands. Agile as a cat, she leapt to her feet and punched his shocked face square in the jaw. It stunned him more than hurt him, but he was confused long enough for Lucian to step forward and incase his head in a bubble filled with water. The sudden lack of oxygen made the demon pull frantically at the bubble, only to find it had hardened to ice. In an act of desperation, he started smacking his head against the ground, but it only rattled the human's brain and did nothing to break the ice. With the human body now unconscious, the demon had no choice but to vacate the body and pass through the ice. The moment he did Blythe pulled out her gun, only to be stopped short as her father pulled out his own and maliciously fired at the demon, freezing it. Her eyes met his as they both stood, weapons aimed, identical grins on their faces.

"Nice work, dad," Blythe told him, tilting her head up in a nod. He simply nodded in return, then stalked over to smash the demon to pieces with his foot.

Lucian turned to Blythe, his hands on her shoulders, and released a sigh of relief. "What in the world were you thinking, Blythe?" he asked, his eyes wet with unshed tears. "Jumping on his back like that?"

She grinned shakily, hating the fact that her actions had put that terror in his eyes. But she was alright now, wasn't she? "It was a split second decision," she decided, shrugging her shoulders. "Besides, it worked, didn't it?"

"Maybe you should go inside, help the Muses or help Rhiannon bring out extra weapons and ammo from the Furies storage."

Disappointment and anger blazed through her in one brutal swipe. "Lucian, I'm not going to go inside like a child. I'm going to fight."

"Let her go, Lucian. She's a tough girl. Hasn't she just proved that?" Brock cut in, placing a hand on Blythe's shoulder. She stared down at his hand, her heart torn viciously in two as she warred between siding with the father who shared her blood, and the father who had always been there for her.

"Brock, I don't think you understand just how dangerous this is. How will you feel when she gets hurt, or worse, killed? She has no training in fighting demons and should not be doing so." Lucian rounded on Brock, poking an indignant finger in the larger man's chest. Even though they were the same height, Brock's build was much heftier to Lucian's lean and lanky frame.

"I don't think you have any say, Lucian. This is my daughter," Brock countered, temper sparking as his fists clenched at his sides.

"And what a great father you've been," Lucian snapped, his anger beginning to boil. He rarely got angry and it was even rarer for his temper to get in the way of common sense. But right now he could care less if it came to blows. He loved Blythe like a daughter and he would do what he thought was best.

Brock's eyes narrowed to angry slits as he reached up to grab Lucian's shirt, pulling him close until the two were eye-to-eye. When he spoke, his voice was low and dangerous.

"I couldn't control what happened all those years ago and I lost fifteen years of being her father because of it. And yeah, I made a mistake recently that may have cost me more time with her, but goddamnit I'm going to make it up to her if it's the last thing I do."

"Then you can start by ensuring she survives this raid," Lucian muttered, frowning as Brock released him.

In any other circumstance, it might have amused her to see them square off with each other, simply because they were polar opposites. It doesn't get much different than fire and ice. But in this case they were fighting over her and seeing it only gave her pain. She didn't want them to be at odds because of her; she had never wanted that. What she wanted was to have both of them equally in her heart.

She stepped between them, pushing them apart with her hands as she glared back and forth, meeting each man's eyes.

"Are you done?" she asked, one eyebrow arched skeptically. When they both nodded she stepped back and faced them together. "While I respect both of you wanting to do what is in my best interest, I'm afraid I have to remind you that I am no longer a child and therefore I am capable of deciding for myself. And because of that convenient fact, I'm going to go ahead and kill some more demons because that is what I do. I fight; I do not cower in the background like a child. I would encourage you both to respect that."

She stalked away, intent on finding Jax, leaving both of her fathers gaping like fools. She wondered if he had found Dante yet, and more importantly, if he had managed to destroy him.

Her thoughts evaporated when she heard a scream. Panic tore through her as she rounded the side of the castle toward the sound and found Nyxa cornering Serendipity, one of the demons at her side with an axe. Serendipity, defenseless without a weapon, was staring wide eyed at Nyxa, shaking her head in disbelief.

"Please, Nyxa, it's over with Brock. You have to believe me. It was a mistake, I promise it's over," Serendipity pleaded, stumbling as she backed against the stone wall of the castle, fear in her eyes.

"Couldn't just be happy with the man you married, could you, you little minx?" Nyxa's hands reached out, eager to grab Serendipity's throat.

Incensed, Blythe raced forward and rammed her fist into Nyxa's cheek, sending her flying onto the ground. Without missing a beat, Blythe whirled around and hurled a ball of fire at the demon, his axe held high. The fireball singed the flesh on his hand, sending the axe to the ground. Seeing her chance, she grabbed the axe and tossed it to Serendipity.

"Run and get help, I can't take this bastard on my own," she ordered, fire in her eyes. Serendipity nodded and raced off, her trembling legs almost giving out on her.

Now that the demon was unarmed, Blythe faced him with her fists up and chin cocked. "Come on asshole, I ain't afraid of you."

The demon growled, baring his teeth as his eyes flashed. He lifted his hands to grab her, but before he could charge he suddenly jolted as a lightning bolt shot out of the sky and hit him. He crumbled to the ground, quivering and twitching uncontrollably. Blythe glanced up and saw Capri staring out at her from one of the windows, a big smile on her face.

"Saved you," she called down, waving. Blythe grinned and waved back.

"Thanks, honey." Pleased, she reached for her pistol to destroy the demon when it vacated the human, only to see Nyxa rising to her feet. A vicious anger flashed through her as she turned to face her mother. "I can't believe you did this. Actually, maybe I can believe it because you always were a rotten bitch."

Nyxa sneered with equal dislike as she fought to stand on her feet, her cheek pulsating with a throbbing pain from where Blythe had struck her.

"How dare you hit me," Nyxa spat, walking toward Blythe. The two women were suddenly eye to eye, glaring bitterly at each other. "I gave birth to you, twenty hours of horrific labor and this is the thanks I get?"

Snorting out an indignant laugh, Blythe smirked. "It's always about you, isn't it, mother? You only think of yourself and how shit affects you."

"I'm only trying to keep my husband," Nyxa snarled, her dark eyes searing. "He betrayed me but it was only because that woman has always had her claws in him. She deserves to die."

"Damnit, no she doesn't." Blythe rolled her eyes, the urge to throttle her own mother overwhelming. "Yeah, she's a terrible wife who cheated on her husband and I can understand why that hurts you because your ex-husband was the one she cheated with. But that's not a crime that deserves death. Of course you've killed before, so I suppose it doesn't even occur to you to consider these things before pulling the damn trigger."

"Balgaire deceived me, lead me to believe that the man I truly loved was a murderer. He deserved to die for that." Nyxa tossed back her dark and wild frizzy hair with an air of righteousness.

"Fine, that I'll agree with. Balgaire was scum. But, damnit, mother, Serendipity is just a weak, pathetic excuse for a woman. If she has any sense at all, she'll beg Rohan for forgiveness and this will all be over. Letting Dante onto Euphora to kill her was not only idiotic but it's put all of us in danger. What about Brogan? Or Nova? Do you even care what happens to them? Or have you given up on them the way you gave up on me all those years ago?"

"You were too much like him for me to bear. I had no choice. Facing you every day was killing me," Nyxa retorted, her voice suddenly hollow and empty as the painful memories swam through her.

Blythe just shook her head, not ready to forgive. "Yet again proof of you only caring for yourself."

"Lucian took you in, didn't he?" Nyxa shot back, a tinge of bitterness in her tone now. "You didn't need me and I needed nothing more than to move on."

"And you did such a good job at it, didn't you? Moving on was easy for you." Shaking with more than anger, Blythe turned away, not wanting to face her mother any longer. After a few moments she spoke again, her voice heavy with grief. "How come you could be a mother to Balgaire's children but you could never be one to me...the daughter of the man you claim to love so damn much?"

When Nyxa said nothing, Blythe turned around and faced her once more. "What, you don't have an answer to that?" she snapped, throwing her hands up in the air. "God, I don't know why I even bothered asking."

Before Blythe could turn away, Nyxa reached out to grab her daughter's arm, pulling her back. The look in the older woman's eyes took Blythe by surprise. It was almost as if…as if she was sorry.

"It was easier to hate you than it was to love you," Nyxa said quietly, her face void of emotion. She was nothing but a hollow shell, her dark eyes stark against her pale face. Knowing that was as good an answer as Nyxa would ever give, Blythe simply nodded.

"Alright, then." With that, Blythe turned, prepared to finish destroying the demon, when she suddenly saw her father charging at them, a mixture of fear and purpose in his eyes. In what seemed like slow motion, he tore past her and tackled the demon that had risen to his feet, apparently not hurt enough from the lightning bolt. The demon fell under Brock's weight and within seconds Brock was pounding his fists into the demon's face. Alarmed, Blythe watched as her father pummeled the demon to a bloody pulp, forcing it to slither out of the host body and try and escape. But Blythe was ready. She pulled her gun and fired, then pulled at her father to stop him from continuing to punch the unconscious human.

"Stop it!" she snapped, trying to hold back his arms. "It's done, he's not in there anymore. You need to stop."

Stopping, he tilted his head to look at her, his eyes glassy with rage. His hands were shaking and his chest heaved with labored breathing as he tried to come back to reality. Assured he was finished, Blythe left him and shattered the demon to pieces, pleased to add another to her current count of three.

When she turned around, she saw her parents wrapped around each other, kissing frantically. She shook her head, thinking she was imagining things, but the image wouldn't go away. A hysterical laugh escaped her throat as she gaped stupidly at them.

"What the hell is going on?" she asked, dumbfounded. Brock pulled away from Nyxa and smiled sheepishly at Blythe.

"I came to save my two best girls," he announced, earning an appreciative smile from Nyxa. "Mission accomplished."

"She set this whole thing up to kill Serendipity, you do know that don't you?" Blythe managed, her head still shaking in disbelief.

"I guess I've always loved her vindictive side," he laughed and resumed kissing Nyxa.

"You're both crazy." Blythe rolled her eyes and turned away, annoyed that part of her was happy to see her parents together. Why in the hell should that make her happy now, when it never had before?

Knowing this wasn't the time to sit and contemplate such things, she raced off in search of Jax and hopefully Dante as well.

Chapter Eighteen

All was quiet on the backside of the castle. What had been an explosive gunfight was now silence as no one moved or spoke. The smoke from the simmering fires that surrounded them hung heavy and hot, making it impossible to see more than a few yards ahead. Somewhere beyond in the courtyard, thunder boomed.

Jax turned to Rian, his hand steady as he held up the demon sensor. They both glanced down, noting the three red dots that hovered in the trees just ahead. Beside them, Brogan held his weapon so tight his knuckles were white, intensity in his eyes.

Rohan had gone to get more ammunition with Rhiannon, so all that remained were the two Furies and Jax.

He was partially annoyed because this wasn't his fight and this wasn't his home to protect. His only business was to get Dante and getting involved in some massive battle had not been in his plans. But now that he was here he figured he should help out. Rian needed him and he would do anything for the man. However, the instant Dante tried to escape, because he had a gut feeling that eventually the bastard would, he would be on him like white on rice. He wasn't letting him get away this time.

They could hear muffled and distant screams coupled with booming explosions from the courtyard, but that seemed worlds away. Blythe was out there, he thought anxiously. But she could take care of herself, that much he knew. Worrying about her would only hinder his ability to do his job and that had to be his priority. Focusing again, he made a few quick hand signals to Rian, suggesting they try and move out by using the smoke cover to their advantage and ambush the demons.

Jax had an instinctual feeling that the demon on the far left was Dante so he wanted to take that one. Rian nodded and motioned for Brogan to stay put to protect the door to the castle. He shifted silently past their cover and into the smoke shrouded grass.

Jax mirrored his movements on the other side, keeping low and stepping lightly to avoid making noise. He kept the device on so he would notice immediately if the demons tried to move. So far they remained stationary.

Sawed off shotgun in hand, he scanned the back gardens, left mostly wild in comparison to the trimmed gardens out front. Here the grass was left to grow tall and untamed, surrounded by charming wildflowers and shady trees. It was perfect cover for both man and demon. Glancing down at his device, he noted the tree he thought Dante must be hiding behind. Carefully he made his way over, only to curse himself as the dot he'd been monitoring blinked off. Swiftly he changed the setting to Dryad and with adrenaline pumping he saw a red dot suddenly running away from him toward the side of the castle. Though the smoke was still so thick he could barely see, he jumped up and raced after the dot, knowing he had his man.

He hated leaving Rian behind but he knew that Rian would notice on his new device that the demon had fled and that Jax had followed him. He only hoped the Furies could handle the other two demons without him.

Boots pounding the ground, he burst through the worst of the smoke when he reached the side of the castle and spotted Dante running ahead of him. Picking up speed he kept moving, never letting Dante out of his sight.

Suddenly, he spotted a flash of red hair and his heart clenched viciously in his chest as he realized Dante had just run into Blythe. He watched Dante falter and then swerve and keep going. Blythe whirled around and gave chase almost immediately.

They emerged into the courtyard where madness was still ensuing. Jax caught a glimpse of Thea slashing a demon with a gleaming silver sword and the Water Dryads capturing another with a mountain of ice. Overhead the storm still raged, lightning bolts raining down and striking the ground.

He pushed ahead as they skirted along the side of the courtyard, keeping to the shadows and smoking remnants of trees. He had to duck under fallen branches scorched by flame and dodge an ash filled pond. He watched Dante reach the entrance to Euphora and then swiftly change into demon form and disappear.

Immediately he changed the setting on the device back to demon as he kept running, coming only to a stop just outside the gates where Blythe was waiting.

She was breathing heavily but her eyes were hard as stone. "He's here somewhere, the coward."

"I know," he responded, scanning the area. He began walking forward into the clearing with Blythe following him.

All was quiet beyond the gates of the courtyard. The night sky above them was filled with stars and a cool breeze whistled through the air. Ahead of them, the large oak tree was nothing but a dark shadow, highlighted only by the soft, pale moonlight. As his eyes adjusted he scanned the area, wondering if Dante had managed to get away after all. But no, they would have seen the flash from the tree…

Blythe was silent beside him and he assumed she was being vigilant, scanning the grass around them as he did. But when the dot popped up on the scanner it appeared right next to him.

"Shit, I must have left it on Dryad," he muttered, switching back to the home screen to select demon. Only as he did, he saw it was already set to demon. At first he thought the device was broken or stuck on the wrong setting. But when he turned to stare at Blythe, who stood placidly beside him, he realized the device was fine. However, there was something very wrong with Blythe.

Her eyes were different. They were staring at him cold and harsh and they had lost their usual fire. And she was standing different—straight as an arrow with her arms at her sides and her feet planted firmly together. Blythe had a cocky stance and hardly ever stood straight. And when she grinned, he knew it wasn't her grin either. This wasn't Blythe. This was evil.

"Dante." Backing away, Jax pointed his shotgun at the woman he loved, and the war raging inside him nearly took him to his knees. How could he look at her face and pull the trigger?

"What are you talking about Jax? It's me, Blythe." She stepped toward him, a quick faltering step that was as unnatural as the demon inside her. And paired with the wicked, echoing sound vibrating within her voice, she sounded, quite simply, demonic.

Jax moved further away, knowing he had to get Dante out of her. If only he was a Fury, damnit, he could summon him out of her. But he was just a human with a gun that would kill her before it would kill Dante. His hand that held his gun trembled once.

"Come on, kiss me." Blythe's arms reached out to touch him as she came closer and with revulsion he watched her blank stare as her face tilted up for a kiss. Then the eyes he'd stared into so many times flashed with blood red light and he could do no more than shove her away.

"I'll kill you for this," Jax snarled, only to watch her laugh jauntily and skip away toward the tree. Without hesitation he raced after her, grabbing her arm and yanking her around to face him just before she could reach it.

In a flash, she whipped around, a demon blade suddenly in her hand that sliced at his face. He cried out in anguish as the skin on the left side of his face bled and burned at the same time. Despite the blazing pain, he reached out just as she grabbed the tree, managing to touch her hand just as Dante transported them away from Euphora.

The next thing Blythe knew, she was gasping for air and fighting for consciousness in the alleyway in Richmond. Her head felt heavy and groggy, and her body felt weak and useless. Frightened, she fought to open her eyes, blinking to clear them. She heard a groan beside her and suddenly realized she was slumped on the ground with Jax beside her.

"Jax." Her voice was hardly more than a whisper, and seemed to echo in her head. Rolling over, she tried to prop herself up to look at him. "Jax, where did he go? What happened?"

But when she managed to get a good look at him her heart plummeted in her chest and her eyes bulged. "Dear God!"

There was a long, thin gash down the left side of his face, running right past his left eye and down to his chin. It looked as though it had been cut with a razor and then burned shut. Her eyes filled as she reached out to gently touch the wound, her body shuddering as he flinched away.

"Your face, Jax," she cried, tears spilling down her cheeks as she pressed her own face into his chest, gripping his shirt tightly. Sobs wracked her body as she cried, knowing this was all her fault. She should have gone to Euphora alone, then he wouldn't have been hurt.

He reached out to touch her, his hands in her hair. The pain was unbearable but at least he was alive. It felt like a million tiny needles were burning into his skin. But it was only pain. Pain disappeared with time.

"Blythe." He sat up and pulled her into his arms, cradling her against his chest. "Don't cry, darlin'."

She lifted her head and looked at him, her red rimmed eyes full of hate. "He possessed me, didn't he? And then he used me to attack you?"

He said nothing, only nodded. She bit back a furious wave of madness as she pushed away from him, her eyes frantic as they scanned the dark alley.

"Did you see where he went?" she demanded, ready to rise to her feet and fight despite how fragile her body felt.

"He's gone," Jax grunted, rising to his feet. He held out his hand for her. "We need to get back to Euphora and tell Thea."

"How do you know he's gone? Did you check your device?"

Jax simply shook his head. "Trust me, he was running away. He's long gone by now."

"So now what? We just let him go and try again another day?" Frustration mixed with guilt and grief in her gut, and she had to clutch her torso to keep from falling apart.

"There might not be another day for me, Blythe," Jax began, knowing how much this would hurt her. Hell, it was destroying him to even consider the possibility, but she had to know before it became a reality. "Thea may very likely take me off the case after this. I let him get away."

"Bullshit. He hurt you and he possessed me. What could you have done differently?" Blythe demanded.

"Not let my feelings for you get in the way of my job," he said flatly. Even though he was itching to touch her, he crossed his arms over his chest, not wanting to make this harder than it had to be. "If I hadn't hesitated, I might have had the chance to hold you down or keep you away from the tree until Rian could come and force him out of you. But because I couldn't hurt you, I let him get the better of me. It's unforgivable in my line of work."

Blythe couldn't believe what she was hearing. "Thea will listen to you, she has to."

"Like she listened to your grandmother?" He knew it was a cheap shot, but he had to make her see just how serious this was.

"Damnit." She cursed with no feeling, hanging her head. He was right. Thea did not have a history of being reasonable when it came to complicated situations. But there was hope. "I'll convince her. I'll explain everything to her, that way your story is backed up."

"I don't want you getting involved in this, Blythe." He stepped toward her, gripping her shoulders tightly and shaking her. "If she takes me off the case it's very likely she'll erase my memory. I won't remember Euphora…or you."

Shock flashed across her face as she stared at him with wide eyes. "No…no she can't do that," she faltered, desperation in her heart. "I won't let her. I'll tell her the truth and she won't do this. And if she insists then I'll threaten to leave Euphora. I'll move to El Paso, live near you, get to know you again."

"I won't let you give up your life for me, Blythe."

"It's my life to do with as I please." She suddenly gripped his shirt tightly in her fists, her temper flaring. "Damnit, Jax, don't you see that I would risk everything I have, everything I am, for you?"

He stared at her, finding no words to say. His throat felt tight and the pain from the gash on his face seemed insignificant to what raged in his heart. She was, as he had always known, the type of girl to stick by a man through the bloodiest battle. And now she wanted to stick by him through this. Impossibly moved, he pulled her against him and kissed her, finding no other way to show her what her words had meant.

He turned his face into her hair, his hands pressed into her back to hold her close.

"We should head back now, darlin'," he whispered, shifting away to look at her. Her eyes were still red from crying but it relieved him to see them dry.

"I will fight for you. It's what I do." Blythe reached up and tenderly touched the scarring cut on his face. He watched her carefully as she traced her finger down the line he knew he would have the rest of his life. Demon blades caused permanent, irreparable damage.

Taking her hand in his, he nodded toward the tree that still sat in the alleyway. Above them the sky was beginning to lighten, the sun starting its daily ascent.

Together they placed their joined hands on the tree and left the alleyway in Richmond for the last time.

When they walked through the gates on Euphora, Blythe paused to take it all in. She bit back a fresh wave of tears at seeing her home tarnished and destroyed. Though the castle was untouched the gardens were in ruins; the trees and plants burned, and fire still simmered throughout. Thea had brought on the morning sun early so they could assess the damage and begin the tedious process of restoring what had been.

She spotted Thea, Rohan and Rhiannon repairing the destroyed trees and plants, growing fresh leaves and branches to replace what had been burned. Lucian and Liam were busy putting out the remaining fires. Sebastian, Clynn and Capri were blowing the ashes and remnants of plant material into piles on the cobblestone pathway, while the Fates were clearing debris out of the ponds. Just outside the entrance doors, ten humans slumped together, blissfully asleep after having their memories altered, ready to be transported back to Richmond. The Muses were bustling around them tending to what wounds they could.

Jax squeezed her hand, bringing her back. She glanced at him and tried to smile, though she knew he would see through it. They continued into the courtyard walking hand in hand down the cobblestone path. Lucian glanced up first and when he called out the others all turned. He and Liam raced forward, along with Capri and Clynn, rushing Blythe and barraging her with questions. She answered them dully, never releasing Jax's hand, and waited for Thea to approach. When she did, the others backed away, making room for Mother Earth.

Thea said nothing and looked at Jax and Blythe, noting their joined hands. Her dark eyes were rich with power, yet reserved with emotion. What she saw before her were two people, as different as can be, standing united. It made her wonder what they were united about.

"We wondered where the two of you had gone," Thea said softly, her eyes on Jax. "What happened to your face?"

Before he could respond, Blythe jumped in, all spitfire and furious devotion. "Jax and I chased Dante out into the field. He possessed me and used me to taunt Jax, to hurt him. He bought a demon blade in Phoenix and he must have had it on him because that was what he used to lash out at Jax. Then he tried to get away, and Jax grabbed him just as he transported us to the alleyway in Richmond, where he fled, leaving us both lying in the alley. I was disoriented, obviously, and Jax had a giant cut on his face that was causing him a lot of pain. I'm sorry, Thea, but Dante got away from us this time. But the second we can, we're gonna go back out there and find him. I promise you."

"I see," Thea said, keeping her expression carefully blank. The others around her watched in stunned silence.

"Look, I know what you're probably thinking. You're thinking that Jax and I failed you and that you'll have to send someone else to find Dante. But that's not fair, Thea. We got closer to Dante than anyone else could have and we shouldn't be taken off the case just because of this one misstep." She paused, fighting to keep her voice level despite the urge to shout and scream in violent anger. Thea's calm expression was driving her mad. Had she already made her decision?

Taking a deep breath, she continued. "Dante gave me my grandmother's diary and when I read it, I realized just how mistaken all of us, especially you, were about her. Damnit, you made a huge mistake banishing her, she was a good person who got taken advantage of. But you didn't listen to her explanation, did you? In fact, you probably looked at her just the way you're looking at me now, with goddamn superiority. Well, I'm not having it, Thea. My grandmother was innocent but she bore the brunt of your harsh judgment. I will not stand by and let you do the same thing to Jax."

Something flashed in Thea's eyes as her face tightened and Blythe knew she'd hit some deep, buried regret. "Standard protocol with an Enforcer or other agent who has failed in his duties would be to erase his memory and disbar him."

"If you do that then I go with him," Blythe said between clenched teeth.

Thea's eyebrows raised in surprise. "You would leave Euphora? Why?"

"Because I love him!" she shouted, her emotions boiling over, her heart damn near bursting. The admission she'd wanted so badly to say aloud, was finally said. Everyone around them gaped and Thea pressed a hand to her heart in shock. Jax just watched her with storms in his eyes.

When Thea felt she could speak again, she approached Blythe, laying a hand on the girl's shoulder.

"I'm not perfect, Blythe, and I have made mistakes, especially in regards to your father and apparently to your grandmother. But trust me when I say that I will not make the same mistake with you."

A single tear fell down Blythe's cheek as her wild emotions sizzled into dust, replaced swiftly by soothing relief. "So you won't erase his memory?"

Thea tilted her head to peer up at Jax, humor in her eyes. "Not unless he wants me to."

He shook his head, his eyes sober and his expression humble. His eyes left Thea's to glance down at Blythe, who turned to smile at him.

She let out a shaky laugh, then on impulse jumped into his arms, cupping his face and kissing him deeply. He spun her around once before planting her back on the ground and releasing her, grinning. Lord, that girl made him smile.

Blythe slept like the dead for almost twelve hours. The entire ordeal had taken everything out of her, draining her both physically and emotionally. But at least it was temporarily over. She could rest until it was time to continue the search for Dante, which they had no leads for now. The Furies would have to use all the Intel they had to get a heading on his location and then they would make their move.

One day she hoped to destroy Dante once and for all. He was the single most destructive force in her life. And in one way or another, he had touched every single person she loved. Even though she could respect him for showing her the truth about her grandmother, she still saw him for what he truly was: evil.

The first thing she did when she woke up was go for a run. The old, familiar feeling centered her as she raced through the woods and cruised alongside the cliff's edge, the ocean breeze soothing as her muscles warmed and strained after the hiatus. The only thing that had changed was the music in her iPod. Instead of sprinting along to the manic guitar of Zeppelin she listened to outlaw country and thought of Jax.

He was resting comfortably in one of the guest rooms in the castle. The Muses had tended to the cut on his face, and had soothed away the worst of the pain and physical damage to his skin. It would heal eventually, but he would have a thin, white scar for the rest of his life. Blythe had joked that it made him look even more like a badass than he had before, which he supposed was her version of a compliment.

After her run, Blythe showered and dressed, then went immediately to see Jax. Along the way she was stopped by Brogan and Nova in the hallway.

To her surprise, they wanted to end the feud that had been silently raging between them for years. They said that because Brock had defended their mother so valiantly after her transgression and that he had managed to convince Thea to not banish Nyxa, they saw how much he loved her, and what he was willing to do to protect her. And when they'd heard how Blythe had done the same with the bounty hunter, they knew she had the same caliber of good in her as well.

At first Blythe wanted to push them away and ignore their request, but she knew it was the wrong thing to do. She'd waited a lifetime to have them accept her, and now they were, so who was she to back away? After awkward hugs and forgiveness all around, Blythe continued to Jax's room, feeling lighter and more carefree than she had in days.

She poked her head in, pleased to see he was awake, reading a book in bed.

"Hey." She stepped in and closed the door, biting back a grin as he lifted his head to look at her.

"Hey, back." He smiled and set his book aside, motioning for her to sit beside him on the bed. She instinctively curled against him, wrapping her arm over his chest.

"How did you sleep?" She brushed her cheek over his shirt and sighed, enjoying listening to his heart beat strong beneath her ear.

"Just fine. I had all these pretty ladies tending to my battle wounds."

She smacked him on the arm halfheartedly, looking up to grin at him. "You better not have liked it."

He chuckled, holding her closer. "They ain't got nothing on you, darlin'."

"Damn right."

They lay together in silence for a few moments, content. After everything they had been through, it was a blessing to the both of them to know they were safe.

"Thea came to see me a little while ago," Jax began, stroking his hand through her hair softly. "She read the diary while you were sleeping. I'm sure she'll get around to talking with you about it but she feels bad. Make sure you forgive her, Blythe, like she forgave me. She's tough because she has to be, because all of you depend on her to be the leader. But even leaders screw up."

Blythe sighed. "I know. I'll forgive her. But I'm going to make sure she helps me get Bristol's story out to everyone. I don't want another bad word said about my grandmother ever again."

"She also said she's sending Brogan to look for Dante."

"What?" Blythe sat up now, staring down at him dubiously. "Why?"

"He's just going to check around Richmond, see if Dante left town or not. She thinks I need bed rest." He grimaced, annoyed already at being fussed over. He was fine enough to do his job.

"Okay, well as long as she's going to let us pick back up again once the Furies get another lead."

"You still want to tag along?" His lips curved slightly as he reached out to tug playfully on her hair.

"Of course I do." She batted his hand away, looking imperiously at him. "No one knows him better than we do, Jax. And now that he not only failed at making me his wife, but–"

"Hold up, make you his wife?" Jax growled, his eyes flashing angrily.

Blythe huffed out a breath, waving the thought away. "Yeah, he had it in his head that if he got me to see the truth behind what happened to Bristol, that I would see him as worthy of living on Euphora and being a Fire Dryad. He figured I would be his ticket in and then he would exact his revenge after he'd duped me. But he was pissed because he knew you and I were together, sort of, and he said I was tainted and a slut and therefore no longer worthy of his love. As if I wanted his love to begin with, the incestuous creep."

"And he told you all of this last night when you went by yourself to confront him in the alley?" He hadn't yet asked for an explanation on why she had left him sleeping to charge right into the mouth of the treacherous snake, but now was as good a time as any.

To her credit, she managed to look innocent even though guilt swam in her gut. "I had a hunch he'd want me to go alone, that he would be taken off guard if I did and that I could get the upper hand. So I went with my gut. I'm sorry I didn't include you, but if we had waited till the morning like you wanted, he would have gone to Euphora with my mother and all those demons without us knowing, and the battle would have waged without us. So, ultimately, I made the right decision."

He glanced down at her arms, where bruises bloomed brown and blue upon her skin. "He hurt you."

She rolled her eyes, though the pain in his voice upset her. "I'm fine, Jax. He hurt you a lot worse than he hurt me and you're insisting that you're fine."

She started to stand, but his hand jolted out and held her back, the green in his eyes sharp enough to cut glass.

"Do you know what I went through when I woke up and realized you were gone? It took me about three seconds to know exactly where you went, especially since you'd taken my gun."

Now she really had to bite back the shame, even as her pride reared to take over. "Look, I know you're angry with me, but it's all over now, so—"

"I wasn't just angry, Blythe," He said evenly, his mouth set in a grim line. "I was scared. Scared that I was going to be too late, that I'd find you dead in that damn alley. And I would only have myself to blame."

She shivered at the look in his eyes. "If I had let him kill me, it would've been my fault and my fault alone, cowboy."

"No, it wouldn't, because Thea told me to protect you. I knew you wanted to go there that night and I should have known you'd try something drastic. But I didn't. I was so sure I was right that I didn't even think."

"Well, it's all over now," she managed, trying to smile. "Can we call a truce?"

"Can I say one more thing?" He let out a long breath, fighting to calm himself. When she nodded slowly, he reached out to cup her face in his hand. "I love you."

She let out a husky laugh as her eyes filled, her face split in a wide grin. "Do you, now?"

He grinned back at her, leaning in to kiss her hard and fast on the lips. "Lord knows you're crazy, stubborn, temperamental, arrogant and blunt, but, damnit, it works for me."

"You're a stubborn ass too, ya know." She giggled as he pulled her in for another kiss, her arms circling around his neck. "Does this mean I can come visit you in El Paso? See Cooper and your mom?"

He paused, tilting his head back to look her in the eye. "You're always welcome there…"

"But?" she finished, seeing the doubt in his eyes. "What is it?"

"Thea mentioned it to me earlier and at first I didn't even consider it, thinking it was crazy," he began, shaking his head as he spoke. "I have a life down in Texas, my home, my family…but I have you, up here."

"Thea told you that you could live here, didn't she?"

When he nodded, she had to bite back a grin. "Well, then maybe once things are officially back to normal, we can trade off. A couple weeks there, a couple weeks here…whaddya think?"

"I'm thinking I'm gonna love seeing you on my front porch with my dog, watching the sunset…"

She smiled and kissed him again, the image as clear as day in her mind. "Just promise me you'll wear that damn hat, cowboy. It suits you almost as well as I do."

THE DRYAD QUARTET CONTINUES

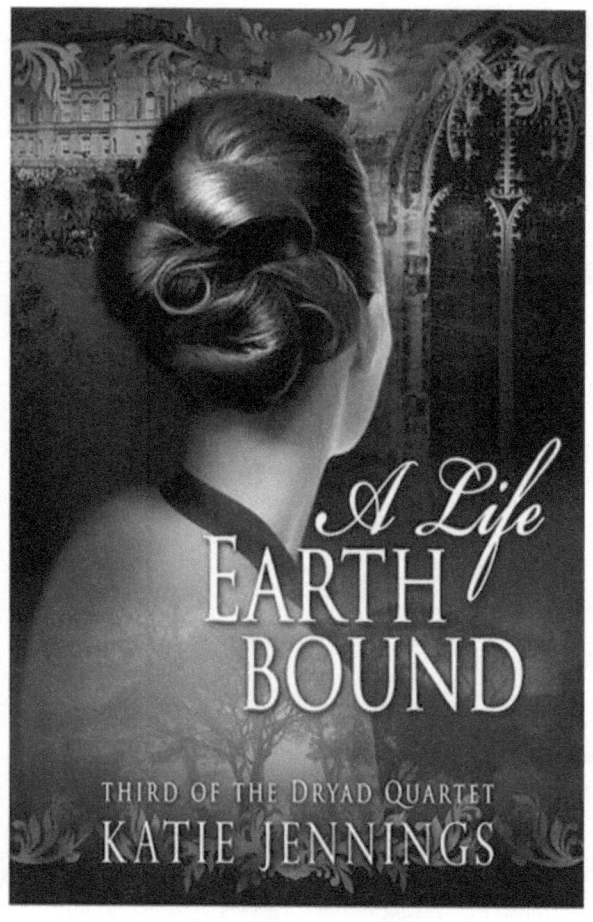

ALSO LOOK FOR BOOK FOUR

Nothing can compare to the exhilaration of discovering, at last, a mode of release for the imagination. Mine came, after years of struggling to visualize my creativity, in the form of the written word. I found myself with my nose constantly in a book, absorbing the life of the characters and the beauty of the setting. It was intoxicating, to say the least, and the only thing I knew was that I wanted to give writing a shot, and take the thousands of characters and storylines in my head and put them down on paper and form them into something real and compelling.

In truth, I'm just a girl from a small town north of Los Angeles with an imagination for days and thank goodness a keyboard at my fingertips. And even though my husband thinks I'm a nerd and my mom is undoubtedly my biggest fan, at the end of the day I'm loving life and enjoying giving breath to the characters living in my heart and sharing with others all of the creativity I can harness.

I believe in true love and I've always believed in happy endings. And that is just the beginning of the story.

K.